BUCKSKIN BORDER

OTHER FIVE STAR WESTERN TITLES BY LES SAVAGE, JR.:

BUCKSKIN BORDER

A WESTERN QUINTET

LES SAVAGE, JR.

FIVE STAR

A part of Gale, Cengage Learning

GALE
CENGAGE Learning®

Detroit • New York • San Francisco • New Haven, Conn • Waterville, Maine • London

GALE
CENGAGE Learning®

LIBRARY OF CONGRESS CATALOGING-IN-PUBLICATION DATA

Savage, Les.
    Buckskin border : a western quintet / by Les Savage, Jr. —
First Edition.
    pages cm.
    ISBN 978-1-4328-2764-9 (hardcover) — ISBN 1-4328-2764-2
(hardcover)
    1. Western stories. I. Title.
PS3569.A826B83 2014
813'.54—dc23   2013040872

First Edition. First Printing: March 2014.
Published in conjunction with Golden West Literary Agency.
Find us on Facebook– https://www.facebook.com/FiveStarCengage
Visit our website– http://www.gale.cengage.com/fivestar/
Contact Five Star™ Publishing at FiveStar@cengage.com

Printed in Mexcio
1 2 3 4 5 6 7 18 17 16 15 14

ADDITIONAL COPYRIGHT INFORMATION

CONTENTS

★ ★ ★ ★ ★

Murder Stalks the
Fur Trails

★ ★ ★ ★ ★

The author sold seven stories on his own before becoming a client of the August Lenniger Literary Agency. "Murder Stalks the Fur Trails" was the third of these early stories. It appeared in *Dime Western* (8/43). Les Savage, Jr.'s records of the stories he wrote, where they were published, and how much he was paid were destroyed after his death. The copies of magazines containing stories he wrote were given away to a relative by his widow and eventually were junked. The records of what Savage's titles were and when the stories were received by his agent and to whom they were sold can only be charted from the Lenniger Agency pay books where the first entry is dated September 3, 1943.

I

Lee Brand was set for trouble as he swung down the slope toward the seething commotion of trappers, Indians, and traders in Jackson's Hole. At the end of each season, the mountain men brought their harvest of beaver furs to this valley, just west of the Wind River Mountains. And up from St. Louis came the traders to buy the pelts and to re-outfit the trappers for next year. Friction between trapper and trader had been growing with each rendezvous, and Brand knew the blow off was soon due.

He wasn't a handsome man, this Lee Brand, but six months of trapping in the lonely fastness of Yellowstone had given his bony, lantern-jawed face an Indian-dark look that was quite striking against the thick mane of yellow hair that showed beneath his battered, black hat. Around his grease-daubed buckskin leggings was a Navajo gun belt, studded with tarnished silver bosses, and sagging with the weight of a .44 Walker Dragoon Colt. The way that gun was hung and the way his big capable-looking hand hovered near it gave him a look of having more skill with a short gun than a trapper should.

"*Parbleu*," said the little man striding beside him, "eet ees good to see Jackson Hole again, an' eet ees bad. We 'ave to sell our plews to Clegg, an' he weel cheat us from our eyeteeth. How much longair you gonna stan' eet, Bran'."

A slow grin caught at Brand's wide mouth, and he looked down at the volatile, moody French-Canadian who had worked the trap lines with him for five years. Jacques Radiseau's blue-chinned face was covered by the scars from a hundred river battles, for he had been a *voyageur*, a river man. He still wore the *voyageur*'s wolf-skin hat and dirty white coat, and from one of his square-toed boots protruded the black hilt of a sizable Bowie.

"Clegg is a sly one, all right," allowed Brand. "And I don't like his ways any more'n you. But there ain't no use bucking a man as big as him, unless you have to."

Radiseau laughed. "You don' fool me. You'd buck twenty mama grizzlies eef someone jus' drop zair hat."

Brand's grin faded a little. Maybe Radiseau was right. And maybe someone would drop his hat this time. He was due to cut Clegg's trail soon now. A fur trader was known as a *bourgeois*, and Arno Clegg was the biggest *bourgeois* of them all, half owner of Stony Mountain Fur, a ruthless man who had no friends among the trappers from whom he bought his furs.

Brand and the French-Canadian were passing through the skin lodges of a tribe of friendly Flathead Indians who had gathered at the Hole for the week's debauch. Gambling games were in full swing—old sledge, casino, monte. Bearded trappers in greasy elk hides sat cross-legged on fallow-deer robes, horse-hide cards in trap-scarred hands, their battered felt hats full of silver.

Some stentorian mountain man was roaring an Indian chant in time to the beat of a tom-tom and a scraping fiddle, thumping his belly to jerk out the vocables more forcibly. And everywhere drunken trappers lurched through the milling crowds, fighting, singing tipsy ditties. Brand had seen it too many times, and it made him sick to watch the hapless mountain men losing their hard-earned silver to Clegg's whiskey drummers, and the professional gamblers he brought with him.

The real business was going on over by the river. Long lines of pack horses stood hipshot in the sandy bottoms. They were loaded with beaver pelts, lashed into mountain packsaddles, the apishamores of the Taos muleteers. Trappers stood around in little groups, watching Clegg's little *bourgeoisie* go up and down, appraising the pelts. As Brand neared, he sensed the sullen tension pervading those knots of trappers.

A pile of trade goods stood to one side—traps lashed in leather trap sacks, new buckskins displayed gaudily near sacks of chewing tobacco and flour, Pass brandy in flat kegs to fit the apishamores. One or two mountain men were glumly trying on new leggings, fingering the pigs of Galena lead.

Clegg stood beside the trade goods, heavy-lidded eyes missing nothing. The greed evidenced in his business dealings showed clearly in his lean, avaricious face with its ruthless beak of a nose, its jump-trap jaw. His mobile, slack-lipped mouth had the faculty of hiding that avariciousness if he chose, twisting into an easy, indolent smile that was dangerous because it was so disarming.

"Hello, Brand," he said softly. "Bring me some prime beaver plews this year?"

Brand matched his soft tone with an easy drawl. "I left my pack horses up in the grove with Grimes till I found out if what I heard was true. Met a trapper up by Henry's Fork who said you're only paying four dollars the plew this season."

"Why, yes, Brand," said Clegg. "The trip up from Saint Looey is gittin' right dangerous. I have to have some compensation, don't I?"

The trappers had ceased to handle the trade goods. The little *bourgeoisie* had quit appraising the furs and were moving in closer to Clegg.

Brand ignored them, saying evenly: "You sell those plews for sixty bucks apiece in Saint Looey. You were making nine hundred percent profit when you only paid us six dollars a pelt.

13

Even at that rate, there wasn't a trapper north of Taos with two bits in his jeans."

Clegg didn't permit himself to become angry. "Now, towhead, aren't you gittin' too big for your leggings? I'm the only fur agent up here . . . American Fur and Missouri Fur couldn't stand the gaff. If I want to lower my price to four dollars, I don't reckon there's much you can do about it."

"I'll take my furs down to Saint Looey myself before I sell at that price," said Brand, an edge to his voice.

Clegg gave a sudden, impatient laugh. "Let's quit this, Brand. You'll never take your furs down to Saint Looey. You couldn't get through." He turned to one of his *engagés*. "Show this trapper the trade stock and let him pick out his year's outfit."

Brand shot an indifferent glance at the *engagé*, Billings by name, a thick-bellied specimen whose nervous hands held one of Sam Colt's revolving rifles from Paterson, New Jersey, the cylinder set to revolve with each cock of the hammer. Billings's eyes were bloodshot and shifty in a dissipated, joweled face, and he didn't look directly at Brand when he spoke.

"Shore, trapper, what'll you have? We got some new jump traps that'll take the leg offen a grizzly . . . regular hand-worked Delaware buckskin jackets with more fringe on 'em than liars in a holler. . . ."

Yes, thought Brand, *everything a trapper could want—and all at mountain prices.* The mountain men had to have these things, the pigs of lead and the Dupont powder, the flour and black-strap sorghum and chewing tobacco, the Green River blades and heavy, saw-tooth beaver traps. They had to have them, and they had to pay Arno Clegg ten times what they would pay in St. Louis.

Brand could feel the anger brawling up from away down inside him, from five years of battling with this trader. But his voice still held to that easy drawl. "I told you I wasn't selling for

14

four dollars, Clegg. It's been so long since anybody stood up to you that you can't realize I'm not joshing."

"That's tellin' 'em, Brand!" said a trapper. "It's the way we all feel, but we hain't had the guts to say it."

The other trappers mumbled agreement, a sullen tension evident in their uneasily shifting figures, their angry eyes.

Clegg stiffened, anger suddenly twisting his mouth out of that masking smile. "You're right, I haven't been bucked in a long time. And no long-legged towhead weasel-bear of a trapper is gonna buck me now. You know as well as I do that you can't do nothin' else but deal with me. The only reason I come through from Saint Looey alive is that I bring a small army and have some influence with the Indians. You poor fool, what chance'd you have? Your hair'd be hung on a Blackfoot scalp belt before you got through South Pass."

The other *engagé* had moved away from the pack horses and now stood behind Clegg. La Roche, he was, a French-Canadian like Radiseau—a big, slow-moving barrel of a man, thick-chested beneath his red wool shirt.

Brand hitched a thumb into his silver-studded belt, and there was a menace to his slow deliberate words. "I don't like to be called a weasel-bear, Clegg. It ain't the kind of a name a man'd cotton to."

"Well I'm tellin' you, by God," snarled Clegg, taking a sudden step that brought him belly-up to Brand. "And you'd better back down right now and go up and get your furs, or I'll take your hide off with a Green River and stretch it on a skinnin' frame like a prime beaver plew!"

Brand shoved a palm against the front of Clegg's beaded hunting shirt and heaved him backward, hard. As the *bourgeois* stumbled, trying to regain his balance, Brand stepped aside so he could hit Billings when he got his Walker free. But Billings already had that Paterson coming up, carrying the hammer back with a thick thumb, and Brand knew he was too late. Then something whirred past his shoulder, and Billings's shot went wild because he was grabbing at the big Bowie, buried hilt deep in his shoulder. If Clegg or La Roche intended to keep things going then, they didn't, because Brand's Dragoon was free of leather. Radiseau walked around him and pulled the knife out of Billings.

"Ees a pretty good start for our treep to Saint Looey." He grinned.

Clegg had lost face to the blond trapper, and there was a deep, hateful burn in his heavy-lidded eyes that said, plainer than any words, that he would never forgive Brand. "Yeah, Brand, just try to reach Saint Looey. You won't stand any more chance than a beaver in a grizzly trap. And when I pass your bodies on my way back, I'll take along that fancy belt to show all your trapper friends what a damn' fool you were."

The implacable hate in that voice sent a strange chill through Brand as he backed away, still covering them, and he had a feeling that if the Indians didn't stop him, Clegg would make a mighty good try at it, and soon.

Later, driving three loaded pack horses ahead of them, Brand and Radiseau worked up the slope toward the grove where they'd left the furs. Guarding them was old A.A. Grimes, a trapper who had thrown in with Brand to make the trek. It had taken them several hours to rustle what they needed for the journey to St. Louis. Friends had willingly donated extra blankets and powder and horses, and a sougan full of hardtack and dried venison.

"You should 'ave put some lead t'rough Clegg's belly when you 'ad ze chance," grumbled Radiseau. "We'll see more of heem before Saint Looey."

Brand was only half listening. Of course, Clegg would do

everything in his power to stop them. If Brand proved the trip could be made by a small group of free trappers, then all the mountain men west of Fort Laramie would be taking their own furs to St. Louis instead of selling them to Clegg. Stony Mountain Fur Company wouldn't have any business left. But the strange new thrill that was running through Brand made Clegg's threat insignificant. There was something awesome about the trip ahead of them. Other men had been through the vast new land between Jackson's Hole and the Missouri River, of course, but Brand would be blazing a new kind of trail through that wilderness, a trail for all the free trappers in the Rockies to follow.

They were near the grove, and his musing was cut off by the cracked voice of old Grimes, coming from the trees, cursing a blue streak, then choking off.

As Brand broke into a run through the Utah junipers, he could see their train of pack horses milling about in the clearing, whinnying and snorting. A dim figure of a man was galloping around the frenzied animals, driving them into a stampede with his roaring short gun. Brand hauled his Walker out and threw down on the horsebacker. But as his thumb carried the hammer back for a first shot, he stumbled over the body of Grimes, half hidden there in the blue root, and fell flat on his face.

When he rose, spitting out dirt and grass, the rider had disappeared, and with him half the pack train. Their hoof beats now were only a distant thunder on the far side of the grove.

Radiseau was already racing for his saddle horse, picketed with Brand's horse, apart from the pack animals. He leaped into leather and pounded by.

"I'll get the horses!" he shouted. "You take care of *gran' père!*"

Grimes was coming around, groaning weakly, and Brand

helped him to sit up. He was an old whang hide, stringy gray hair falling down over a seamed leathery face, hands marked by the teeth of a thousand traps. His boast was that he had the greasiest elk hides south of Yellowstone, and that his beaver hat had more cooties in it than a varmint hole.

"Tarnation," he cackled faintly, "iffen they didn't put one over on old A.A. that time."

"I'll give you my share of the plews if that wasn't Clegg's work," muttered Brand. He looked bitterly at the remaining pack horses, only now quieting down. Their apishamores had been ripped open or unhitched. Some were dragging on the ground; others had spilled their loads of swart beaver peltries in heaps across the clearing.

"It war a little redhead in a calfskin vest and fancy Mex leggings," said Grimes, "He tried to git away with the hull string of horses, but I augured a mite, an' he hit me on the haid with his short gun. Why should it be Clegg's work?"

Brand told him what had happened in Jackson Hole, and how they were going to St. Louis with the furs. Then he rose, scooping up his gun, his lantern jaw hard set. Grimes lurched erect and grabbed his arm.

"You ain't goin' back down to the Hole?"

"Clegg can't get away with this," said Brand.

"Naow, cool your haid, younker," said the old man. "You had it out with him oncet. An' no real harm was done up hyar. Radiseau'll git the pack hosses back. If we're goin' to Saint Looey, we better start afore anythin' else happens."

Brand's voice eased back into his slow drawl, a faint grin crossing his face. "I guess you're right . . . you always are. I wouldn't gain anything by starting another row, would I?"

"No sirree," said the old whang hide. Then he cackled. "By gonies, Saint Looey. That's a long way, ain't it? Reckon I better git me a extra plug of chewin' tobaccy."

II

They had followed the Green River northward for two days, then turned east to South Pass, rising higher and higher in the pine-clad fastness of the Wind River mountain range. Radiseau hadn't been able to catch the redhead, but he had recovered their stampeded pack horses. Brand rode at the head of those horses now.

He made an impressive picture, sitting his taffy-maned palomino with a grace that belied the awkward, lanky look of his body. Across the pommel of his high-cantled California saddle he carried a big Hawkins mountain rifle, brass-mounted and stocking thirty-two balls to the pound. From his shoulder belt were slung a cat-tail bullet pouch and powder horn, an awl with a deer-horn handle, the worm for cleaning his rifle, and under these his squatty bullet-mold, handles guarded by strips of buckskin to keep his hands from burning when running balls.

On the flank rode Radiseau, forking a skittish little mustang uneasily, because he would always be more a river man than a horseman. A.A. Grimes brought up the rear, riding his bony nag, Molasses, big Crow saddle studded with brass tacks, silver-plated pommel large as a dinner plate. He sat with his seamed face craned forward on a scrawny neck, nothing hidden from his piercing blue eyes, wind-wrinkled at the corners from twenty years in the snows and winds of these mountains.

Brand planned to take the horses as far as Fort Laramie, then to build bull boats and float the plews down the Platte into the Missouri, down the Missouri to the Mississippi, and thence south to St. Louis.

He couldn't help thrilling to this vast, mysterious land into which he was riding. All about him towered the gigantic Douglas firs, red pistillate spikes and orange blossoms giving each tree the appearance of a flaming spire. The bright spring color of the firs was backed up against the dark green of lodgepole pines, climbing up and up the jagged peaks on all sides. And the awesome silence was broken only now and then by the churring of a red squirrel or the cocky squawk of a whiskey jack. He knew how Clark must have felt when he first sighted the Big Stonies, or how Fitzpatrick must have thrilled to standing in the saddle between Twin Peaks and gazing southward to the Great Salt Lake, thinking, perhaps, that he was the first white man to see it.

Brand felt this was his country, somehow. He had come West a long time ago, from Kentucky, bringing his slow drawl and his deadly long rifle, taking the Santa Fe Trail as far as Bent's Fort, where he'd met Radiseau and Grimes. Now they'd been together five years, and each year their bond of friendship growing stronger. The trapper reined his palomino in suddenly, the saddle's rawhide lacing snicking beneath his leggings as he slid to the ground, bending low.

Radiseau cantered up and leaned from the saddle for a look. "Ze firs' wan, eh? From now on, we better tie our hair down tight."

Brand stood, kicking at the bit of beadwork that must have rubbed free of some Indian's moccasin, the hoof prints that led into the forest. He swung back into leather and started up the slope again.

He had expected it, of course. It was as inevitable as the wind or the rain, because this was their hunting ground. But somehow, finding that first sign of an Indian's trail always gave him a strange tight feeling, not a fear or an apprehension, only a certain excitement. And now his watching became a conscious thing, a waiting thing.

They made camp that night in a draw at the west end of South Pass, juniper and lodgepole rising all about them in dark, soughing stands. They unhitched the apishamores, the mountain packsaddles, and piled them against one side of the draw, watering the horses in the Sweetwater, only a few hundred yards away.

Brand took some hardtack and jerky from his saddlebags and hunkered down against the beaver plews. Radiseau drew his dirty white coat around him, muttering: "*Parbleu,* a fire would feel good."

Grimes cackled. "Light a fire an' ye'd have ever' Blackfoot in the teeratory on your neck, let alone them as are follerin' us."

"Oh," said Brand, "there's someone following us?"

"Yup," said the old whang hide. "I seen 'em when we's climbin' the slope . . . sun shinin' on gun metal in the valley, an' sich."

"Clegg," said Radiseau. "Bran', I tol' you to put some lead t'rough hees belly when you 'ad the chance."

Brand might have answered, but Grimes was suddenly rising, and the little Frenchman's bearded face was turned upward in a startled way.

A man sat a stocking-footed horse with black Arab spots there under the lodgepoles, a leering man with greasy black hair stringing from under his flat-topped Stetson. He wore a heavy buffalo coat, and Indian leggings with fringe that looked suspiciously like human hair.

Brand stood carefully, keeping his hands away from his gun, only too aware of the other horsemen crowding in behind the first.

"Well, Smith," said the trapper, "I thought we covered our trail better than that."

The horsebacker's leer broadened until his gold teeth showed. "Nobody else could 'a' follered your trail, Brand, I'll give ye credit fer that. But my dog soldiers are the best trackers in the world,"

He swung from his silver-mounted saddle, showing himself to be a short stocky man, catty on his feet, beaded moccasins making no sound. He was known from Mexico to Canada as Cheyenne Smith, a white man who had lived with the Indians so long that he was one of them, taking scalps and keeping three squaws and trading with the Blackfeet and the Crows and the Cheyennes as well as with the men of his own race. Brand had cut his trail before, and knew him to be as cruel and ruthless as Clegg, though not so powerful.

"I was headin' down Santy Fe way fer the winter," said Smith. "Looks like we'll have real weather up hyar this y'ar."

Radiseau had taken the black-handled Bowie from his boot and was tossing it end over end in the air, letting the hilt slap hard into his palm. But Smith ignored the little Frenchman, turning to give a string of orders in Cheyenne to his Indians, hard young men of the famous Cheyenne soldier society whose pledge was to die rather than retreat in battle.

There were half a dozen of them, hickory short bows slung across bare backs, eagle feathers nodding from roaches above beak-nosed, impassive faces. They dismounted silently. The girl had been behind them, hidden until then.

At first Brand thought she was Cheyenne, her dark hair long, braided over the right shoulder, her face as wooden as the braves. But as she dismounted, split Crow skirt swirling around bare legs, he saw that her hair was brown rather than black, and he sensed something more than Indian in the straightness of her nose, the oval of her face.

Smith didn't bother to introduce her; he simply gave her an indifferent backhand slap, growling: *"Shiu-shiu, kyesh thiek Sha-hi-yena."*

She backed away, then turned and began gathering wood. Brand took a half step forward with his face darkening. Though he was familiar with the Indians' treatment of their women, he couldn't help the anger that rose in him suddenly. Grimes eased up beside him.

"Easy, younker," he said in a low voice. "She's only a squaw." Then, turning to Smith: "Set yore hocks down, Cheyenne. I ain't seed you since we got drunk with Chief White Hair up in the Big Horns."

The girl had a fire going, and Brand lowered himself till he sat, cross-legged, in the circle of men. His anger was gone, yet he still felt the tension along his nerves, sensing something not quite right.

Nothing showed in the Indians' faces; they sat like so many reddish-brown images, firelight playing on the harsh planes of their mask-like faces, catching the hawk beak of their noses, the highness to their cheek bones. And whatever Smith was thinking, he hid behind that enigmatic grin. Perhaps it was the girl who made Brand uncomfortable.

She was gathering wood over by the horses, and she kept looking at him in a strange, studying way. He knew it would be a mistake to evidence interest in her, but he couldn't help it. He kept his voice casual.

"Who's the woman, Smith?"

Smith eyed him, then pulled his buffalo coat back to warm his belly. Stuck in a broad, beaded wampum belt were two bone-butted Paterson cap-and-ball revolvers, handles pointed inward for a cross-arm draw.

"Like the gal, Brand?" He laughed. "She's an armful, all right. Her mother's the daughter of a Blackfoot chief, her father's a white trader. I paid him two hunnert hosses fer the squaw. Right big price, but I guess she's wu'th it. Fights like a painter, an' I like 'em that way."

He laughed again, eyes still on Brand. The blond youth managed to keep his face expressionless. He knew why he'd sensed something more than Indian in her.

"I hear you got some prime plews this y'ar," said the trader. "Mebbe we could make a little hoss trade."

Brand didn't need any more horses, but he rose and walked to the apishamores because the girl was over by them, picking up dead juniper. He chose a packsaddle close to her and bent to undo the diamond hitch.

Her words were low and tense—and in English: "Have you got whiskey?"

He nodded, not looking at her.

"Get it an' feed it to Smith," she muttered. "It's the only thing that'll save your life tonight."

He stayed bent over that way a long moment, fumbling with the rich brown furs. Then, not knowing quite why he did it, he stepped to another apishamore and drew out a half a dozen kegs of Pass brandy, carrying both the pelts and the liquor back to the fire.

A strange, almost fearful look crossed Smith's face as he saw the kegs, and he said quickly: "Right sociable of you, Brand, breakin' out that trade stuff. But I don't think my bucks better hev it. Be dangerous fer a man to git lit up in this country."

"Oh, come on, Smith." Brand grinned, opening the first keg and passing it to the brave sitting nearest him. "Men gotta drink together when they ain't seen each other in three years."

Cheyenne Smith made a half motion to stop the Indian from drinking, but the young buck was already tipping it high.

"Wal, mebbe a few pulls fer my boys, but not me."

The kegs went around and around the circle, and with every trip Smith's effort at abstinence became more painful. He licked his lips, eyes flickering time and time again to the brandy, grin becoming forced. Brand made a great show of drinking deep, but he let most of the liquor back through his teeth into the keg.

Radiseau seemed to understand what was going on, because he didn't get drunk, and his lips were peeled back from his white teeth in that mirthless wolf grin. But Grimes had a predilection to liquor that had gotten him into trouble more times than not, and he was tipping the keg as high as any Indian buck.

Finally Cheyenne Smith broke, taking a keg from the dog soldier sitting next to him. "Hell, I guess I kin take one swig fer old times sake, eh, A.A.?"

"Tha's right," cackled the old trapper, weaving backward and forward. "Our weakness ish likker. To hell with the Injuns. I kin fight 'em, drunk or sober."

Smith's Adam's apple bobbed up and down his thick neck as he threw his head back to empty the keg in one pull. Brand shot a look at the woman, and there was a strange triumph in her eyes.

Brand made another trip to the apishamores, then another. One by one the dog soldiers were drooping into a sodden, drunken slumber. The trader was rambling thickly through an account of his deal with the girl's father, his head bending forward, farther and farther, until finally his voice trailed off and his face hung between his knees.

"Look at that," said Grimes. "I drank 'em all under the table . . . ."

Brand rose swiftly and stepped to the girl, grabbing her arm. "Now. What is this?"

"I knew Smith couldn't resist the brandy," she said. "I had to stop him, somehow. He was going to kill you while you slept. We met one of Clegg's Flathead runners a day's journey north of here an' he told Smith that Clegg would give a thousand dollar to anyone who stopped you. When Smith learned you were taking your furs through, he said he didn't care much about the thousand dollar Clegg offered. He'd rather have your beaver."

"So Clegg's already sent word out," muttered Brand, "and we've already had one caller for our furs. But how do you fit in? I thought you were Smith's squaw."

She flung a look of unutterable hatred at the trader, still bent forward and snoring. Brand remembered the blow, the Cheyenne curses. It would be easy to hate a man like that.

The girl's eyes came back to Brand's, and there was a sudden plea in them. "Take me with you. I can't stand Smith any longer. I'm not his woman. I never will be."

Perhaps it was the marks on her face that had come from a man's fist, or perhaps it was the strange attraction Brand felt for her. "Yeah," he said. "Yeah, we couldn't leave you here now, could we?"

"*Sacre bleu,*" muttered Radiseau. "Isn't eet enough zat we 'ave Clegg behin' us an' hees Flathead runners spreading the word in front of us? Do we 'ave to take zees girl an' get Cheyenne Smith on our tail, too? He'd follow us t'rough hell to get back w'at he pay two hundred horses for."

"Seems like 'most everybody in the territory is dead set on heading us off, anyway," said Brand, that slow grin spreading over his face. "What difference does one squawman trader more or less make? Let's hurry and get the horses loaded."

Grimes was quite drunk, and when he'd finished helping to load the apishamores, he went around the campfire to get Molasses. He was coming back, just opposite Smith, when the nag shied at the snapping fire. Hanging onto the reins, the old whang hide was yanked violently forward, and he stumbled over the snoring trader.

Smith's snore broke off, and he sat up suddenly, looking around with blank eyes. He could see them all—Grimes and Brand and Radiseau, and the loaded pack animals. The only one he couldn't see was the girl as she unhitched her horse from a tree directly behind him.

Cheyenne Smith was a dangerous man even in his cups. Before anyone could recover from their surprise, he shoved his buffalo coat back and cross-armed out those Patersons.

He rose carefully, thumbs carrying back the big single action hammers with a hollow clicking sound that was loud against the silence, that made Brand realize his life hung on Smith's drunken whim. "Wal naow," leered the trader. "You warn't gonna run out on pore old Cheyenne, war you?"

Even as he spoke, the girl was fumbling something from her beaded saddlebags. Her hand came out with a big six-gun and she stepped forward swiftly, decisively, the weapon describing a shining arc above Smith's head.

He didn't even grunt—just collapsed over on his face with his twin revolvers hitting the ground a little before his body. And the girl turned, swinging gracefully into the saddle.

"Well," she asked the trappers, "are you going to stand there gaping at him all night?"

III

They covered their trail by riding the shallows of the Sweetwater through South Pass, then crossing through a low saddle in the Green Mountains and following the crescent curve of their southern flank, through great forests of lodgepole pines, clustered so thickly that the sun rarely filtered through to the forest floor. They ate breakfast in the saddle, and rode on.

Brand found himself watching the girl more and more. She had a marvelous endurance that more than matched the men's; by afternoon, her seat in the saddle was as easy and graceful as it had been when they started. The blond trapper wouldn't deny the attraction she held for him. Mixed blood was usually a stigma, and a half-breed was looked down upon as inferior. Yet, there was no reason for that. Most men were of mixed blood, really. Radiseau, for instance, French and Canadian. Even himself, Lee Brand, Scotch and English and Yankee. Maybe even a little Chinese or Spanish, away back—who knew?

The girl bore herself with an unconscious pride; the delicate strength of her face had more natural aristocracy in it than most of the touted blue bloods Brand had come across in Kentucky. What matter if she were of mixed races . . . ? Then he laughed at himself for trying to justify her. It was like trying to justify a wild, beautiful animal whose very existence was its own justification. She *is,* that was enough.

She sensed his watching her, and finally she turned, smiling faintly. "My Indian name is Rising Moon, but I lived many years with my father at Westport. He called me Marie. We moved north to the Blackfeet last year, an' when Smith came, my father sold me to him."

It revolted Brand to think of a white man selling his daughter like a horse or a blanket. She saw it in his face and laughed softly.

"I've lived with the Indians, Lee Brand, and that is their way. I didn't mind so much the fact that I was sold. It was the man I was sold to." And she touched the marks on her face, that hate darkeneing her eyes.

They made camp in a thick grove of cottonwoods on Lost Creek, Brand and Grimes going back to obliterate a mile of their trail. Brand was erasing the last hoof prints before turning back to the camp, grunting with the feeling of a job well done.

"Not even those dog soldiers can track us now," he said.

"Mebbe Clegg's got better trackers," answered Grimes.

The little muscles around Brand's big mouth tightened as he looked up. "Clegg?"

"Remember how I was tellin' you I saw the sun shinin' on gun metal in the valley, afore Smith come?"

"But that *was* Smith," said Brand.

Grimes spat tobacco. "The only guns in Cheyenne Smith's party was them he had under his buff'lar coat, an' the sun wouldn't shine on them, now, would it?"

Brand slipped a moccasin into the big wooden stirrup and

swung aboard his palomino heavily, sitting there for a long moment. So Clegg hadn't been satisfied with sending out his Flathead runners; he'd put someone else on their trail to make sure—La Roche, or Billings, perhaps. Or even Clegg himself.

He had about finished his buying at the Hole. Brand could easily imagine the dark, saturnine *bourgeois* sending his fur train on ahead, and following the man he hated so much himself. He was the kind to make sure Brand didn't get through.

"I hope it *is* Clegg," said Brand, more answering his thoughts than talking to Grimes. "Next time I get my sights on that *kyesh* I'll do what Radiseau wanted me to do."

Grimes cackled. "That air Clegg didn't know what a stubborn cuss he was up ag'in' when he called you a weasel-b'ar."

They might have gained a few hours by cutting straight through the Great Divide Basin, an endless plateau of greasewood and short grass. But Brand took the long way around, following the southern slopes of the Seminole Range. And he was glad he hadn't taken to that open country, for early in the morning they sighted a war party, filing across the greasewood flats of the Basin, a long line of riders, roaches nodding, bronzed skin whitened by alkali.

Brand drew his pack train into the thick timber and halted, waiting for the Indians to go by. They were just one of many war parties that would be hunting him by now, he knew. Clegg's Flathead runners had been a day ahead of Brand when they'd met Cheyenne Smith; by now all the Indians between Fort Laramie, and South Pass probably knew of the blond trapper's coming.

So Brand tightened his march, letting Grimes scout ahead, stopping every hour or so to scan their back trail, pushing the horses, riding before dawn and not halting till long after dark.

Seven days east of South Pass and somewhere far north of the Medicine Bow River, they were riding through the sunless tunnels of a white pine forest that grew densely on the deep-soiled southern slopes; there was no sound but the softly falling hoof beats, muffled in the thick carpet of needles, the occasional snort of a horse. All around them was a strangely foreboding semidarkness and a vast, all-enveloping gloom.

Then, suddenly, they rode from the semidarkness into brilliant sunlight. It was like stepping into another world, a world that should have been bright and living with all that sun. But it was dead; it was a place where nothing lived but a few scraggy patches of greasewood. Brand reined his palomino up in surprise.

Everywhere he looked was nothing but those huge stony formations, spreading over the slopes and into the coulées, covering the mountainside and the valley below. It looked as if sometime long ago, all the trees in this region had fallen, and had turned to stone.

He slipped from his saddle and approached the first strange formation hesitantly, skin crawling. It was surely a tree trunk; it bore the furrowed outside that was prevalent in the bark of the Douglas fir, the rings that told a tree's age, the different stratas of white wood and core. Yet it was hard as stone to the touch. And all around they were the same, huge fallen trunks, shorn of foliage, lying in their eternal, petrified preservation.

The girl's voice shook a little with awe. "The Blackfeet have legends about this place. They call it the Dead Forest an' say that no man can look upon it without dying."

Brand was just straightening from the examination, realizing how exposed they were, when the shot rang out, echoing flatly down the slope. And Grimes gasped, reeling from his saddle, his old nag breaking from under him and galloping back into the trees.

As Brand whirled and ran toward him, the second shot cracked the echoes of the first, bullet kicking up dark soil where the trapper had stood a moment before.

Radiseau was already milling the pack train back into the pines, lying flat on his mustang's cockle-burred mane. Brand heaved Grimes across the saddle of his own palomino and slapped the horse.

"Get the gal and Grimes and the horses down into the valley and work east along the river!" he yelled at Radiseau. "If I don't catch up with you by night, keep right on going to Laramie!"

He was down on his belly before he'd finished shouting, crawling from one huge petrified trunk to another, working up toward the ridge with the sound of the galloping pack train and Radiseau's curses receding into the forest. And he suddenly felt very alone.

Heat waves rose from the furrowed bark of the strange stone-like trees. The sun beat down on a dead silence, for there were no birds here, no animals. He worked up toward the ridge, dragging his Hawkins, pausing now and then to search the hillside for the gunman.

Finally he spotted his bushwhacker enemy. All three of them were moving in a crouch downhill, and evidently they hadn't seen him. Well, he hadn't expected them to—A.A. Grimes had taught him how to stalk better than most Indians. A.A. Grimes had taught him a lot.

Billings led, his Paterson rifle held in both hands, making heavy work of it through that weird place. Behind was La Roche in his red shirt and square-toed boots. There was a tall man bringing up the rear, a man who Brand hadn't seen at Jackson Hole, but who Brand knew very well. Ewing Calder was another *engagé* of Stony Mountain Fur, and the most deadly of these three, because he had been a trapper before he became Clegg's man, and he had a trapper's skill with the long rifle.

But Brand was a trapper, too. He had a certain fame for his talent with the short gun. Yet, long before he'd packed that

Walker Dragoon, he'd carried a Kentucky rifle. And now he poked his Jake Hawkins out over the tree trunk with a certain grim satisfaction, shifting it until the front sight bore squarely on the greasy elk-hide shirt covering Calder's scrawny chest.

This was for Grimes, because Calder was the marksman, and it would have been he who picked off the old man at such a distance. Somehow, though, Brand couldn't do it in cold blood.

Knowing he was a fool, he called out: "Calder!"

The only surprise the trapper showed was in the sudden twist of his lean body toward Brand's voice. He had his gun almost raised when Brand's ball caught him where it had been aimed to catch him, and he pitched over forward on his pain-twisted face.

Billings threw himself to the ground, emptying a shattering fire of .44 lead from his revolving rifle. The slugs cast a rain of chipped rock over Brand, but that was all the harm they did, because he was hunched down behind the dead tree, shifting his cat-tail pouch around for another load. Swiftly, efficiently he dumped a measure of powder down the barrel, ramming home the half-ounce ball.

When he poked the Hawkins out again, only Calder's body was in sight. And Brand lay there, watching for movement in the greasewood or along the rimrock, waiting for the glint of metal or the shadowy movement of a hidden gunman.

The sun was hot and he began to perspire and the haze continued to rise before his eyes. The silence was a tense, waiting thing. Brand felt his flesh begin to crawl, felt his breath coming harder. La Roche was out there somewhere, moving cautiously into position with his big-bored Northwest fusil; Billings was out there, swift, nervous, skilful hands reloading that Paterson rifle.

A gun racketed suddenly. Lead tore through Brand's elbow. Pain shooting up his left arm, he twisted around and fired his

Hawkins with one hand at the puff of smoke rising from the rimrock, and knew he'd missed. Before the sound of his shot was dead, boots made a dull pounding thud behind him, and he jerked around again, clawing at his Walker.

When he was turned far enough to see Billings coming slantwise down the slope, he squeezed his first lead out. With that bullet through his thick middle, Billings tried desperately to bring his rifle to bear, hugging it in close and staggering on forward. But his shot only thudded into the ground at Brand's feet, because Brand's second slug jarred him over forward, and Brand's third slug caught him in the face as he fell.

Greasewood snapped and the blond trapper tightened his finger on the trigger again, thinking: *Dammit, how many of them are there?*

Radiseau's scarred, blue-chinned face showed above the trunk, and he grinned that peculiar wolf grin with his lips sliding back from white teeth. "*Parbleu,* eet look lak I ees the whole show, eh?"

"I told you to get away with Grimes!" said Brand harshly.

The Frenchman shrugged. "The girl, she wouldn't go. An', anyway, eef we had been en opposite places, you an' I, would you 'ave lef' me?"

A strange warmth pervaded Brand; he grinned. "OK, Frenchie, OK. La Roche is still up there somewhere, but he won't be very dangerous with Billings and Calder out of the way."

They worked back down the slope to where Grimes was lying, propped up against a pine. The girl looked up from where she'd been kneeling beside him, eyes glistening. Brand hunkered down by the old whang hide, the pain of his wound forgotten. He couldn't speak for a long time, because he saw how it was.

"We traveled a long trail t'gether, didn't we, younker?" said Grimes, and when he cackled afterward, blood leaked from his mouth. "Git the furs through. Show that *kyesh,* Clegg, what kinder grizzly b'ar he's playin' with. An' when you git to Saint Looey, take a big chaw on that Algonquin chewin' t'baccy fer me."

His head lolled to one side and his piercing blue eyes lost their keenness, and they closed.

Brand remembered all the misty mornings they'd gone out to the trap lines together, remembered the thousand campfires they'd sat beside, the mysterious ranges they'd explored. . . .

He stood up, taking a deep, shuddering breath, and there was something terrible in his voice when he finally spoke. "Clegg did this. Calder did the shooting, but Clegg just as much as pulled that trigger. It's something I owe him next time we meet.

IV

They followed the Laramie River through the last range between them and the North Platte. Brand's arm wasn't healing right; it was swollen and the wound had an ugly, discolored look.

They were cantering through a grove of cottonwoods in the bottoms east of the fort when Marie reined her horse in around Brand, forcing him to stop.

"Brand" she said, "for the last time, you've got to stop at Laramie an' have that arm looked at. There must be a doctor there."

Brand shook his head. "You know as well as I do that Laramie's a Stony Mountain tradin' post. It's a good bet that Clegg's runners beat us there. I'm not gonna risk your lives as well as mine for a little scratch."

"You fool," she flamed. "It isn't a scratch. I've seen gunshot wounds like that before. If you don't have it fixed up right, you'll be as dead as Grimes in a week!"

He shook his head again, nudging his horse up against hers, trying to move by. But her superb horsemanship wouldn't brook that; she skillfully backed her mount in the way again.

"We're through arguing with you," she said, her eyes flashing. "Once more, will you go to Laramie?"

"No," he said impatiently. "I tell you. . . ."

Radiseau must have been behind him, because saddle leather creaked, then a ton of something hit him on the head and he knew only the empty, bottomless sensation of falling. . . .

Rude, undressed logs showed above him when he opened his eyes. His head throbbed dully, and the feel of a bandage on his arm turned his head. A little rotund man bent over him, his head pinkly bald. Behind huge, horn-rimmed glasses, his eyes appeared bleary, bloodshot, and his nose had the veined, bulbous look of a man who liked his spirits.

"Well," he said thickly, "looks like ol' Doc Sawyer hashn't losht the touch, after all."

He hiccoughed suddenly, then straightened and looked gravely around the room. Radiseau and Marie stood behind him. Then the French-Canadian's lips peeled back and he said sheepishly: "Eet was necessary, *parbleu*, but eet was, Bran'. *M'sieu le docteur* say you would 'ave 'ad gangrene if we hadn' brought you here."

"Yesh," mumbled the doctor. "Gangrene."

Brand tried to sit up, head swimming, but the little man shoved pudgy hands on his chest.

"No, no. You mustn't get up yet. . . ."

"Aw, shut up, you old rum-pot. Let the feller git up if he wants."

Brand became aware of the others in the room. The man who had spoken was big and bluff-looking, his generous-lipped mouth spread in a broad grin. He wore heavy river boots and black wool pants, buckskin jacket gaudy with red and yellow beadwork, epaulets heavily fringed. There was another behind him, a square little man in a calfskin vest and Mexican leggings, short gun thonged down low, hair a flaming red.

The sight of him tantalized Brand with something he should have remembered but couldn't. He shrugged it off, saying: "Thanks for fixing my arm, anyway, Doc."

Doc Sawyer's eyes opened wide. "He called me 'Doc'! Didja hear that? He called me 'Doc'!"

"I tol' you to shut up, dammit!" said the big bluff man, shoving him indifferently aside, then turning to Brand. "Muh name's Williams, Ken Williams. The little fella with the burnin' hair we call Red."

Brand took the proffered hand.

"I see yo're loaded down with plews," continued Williams. "I'm a fur trader o' small proportions myself, an' as long as yo're goin' to Saint Looey. . . ."

"Where did you get that idea?" asked Brand.

"Why, I jist took it fer granted," slurred the other, grinning. "Yeah. An' as I was sayin', I'm goin' to Saint Looey myself. We might as well jine parties. The Injuns atween here an' the Missouri been raisin' a lot o' hair. Be safer, travelin' together."

"Now, look here," said Brand. "I'm taking my furs downriver by bull boat, and. . . ."

"Suits me," said Williams. "I kin knock my Murphy wagins up an' use the oak in yore boats."

Since the beginnings of the West, it had been an unwritten law on the trail that one party could claim the added protection of another if they were traveling the same way. And though Brand didn't especially want to join with Williams, he sensed the other would press the point and take advantage of that law, if need be. So he agreed reluctantly.

Then he got unsteadily to his feet and walked out, casting a last puzzled glance at the redhead.

Laramie was a typical stockade, two blockhouses at diagonal

corners, a cupola above the big iron-bound gates. Brand found the *bourgeois* of the fort in one of the low-roofed buildings that surrounded the inner courtyard.

He was a heavy-bearded Yankee named Anderson, and his sly, shrewd eyes proclaimed him a trader of Clegg's ilk. Brand asked about Williams, and didn't get anything out of Anderson. He was more careful after that. He couldn't determine from the *bourgeois*'s manner whether Clegg's runners had reached Laramie yet or not; it made him uneasy and not a little worried.

Brand traded the string of pack horses for much needed supplies to make the long river journey. The buffalo country was two days' ride east. There he would obtain the hides to make his bull boats, and could send the empty horses back to Anderson. The trader reluctantly agreed to send an *engagé* along to bring back the animals.

The whole fort was Stony Mountain Fur, of course, and Brand wanted to get away fast. If they didn't already know Clegg wanted him stopped, they would soon. And always on the back trail was the threat of Cheyenne Smith, who wouldn't be one to forget what Brand had stolen from him.

Marie and Radiseau were already mounted, waiting. He swung aboard his horse and urged the pack animals out through the gate, past the half dozen ration Indians, standing around in the sun.

Williams's two Murphies were parked outside, mules standing hipshot against the hames. Beside the red-shirted driver on the high box seat of the lead wagon sat Doc Sawyer, black fustian over his pin-striped vest, huge gold watch chain stretching across his comfortable paunch. He was tighter than when Brand had seen him last, and, when the teamster cracked his whip and the wagon lurched into movement, the doctor almost fell from his perch.

"I didn't know the doctor was with your party," Brand told

Williams, when the big man reined up his glossy stallion. "I thought he would be with Stony Mountain Fur."

"No," said Williams. "Oh, no. The doc's been with me for some years. Need 'im now and then when a hoss gits sick."

He broke into a hearty laugh, and Brand kneed his palomino forward, not caring for the laugh, or Williams, still thinking that the doc should have been with Stony Mountain.

Rugged pine-clad mountains gave way to gentle foothills, then the foothills rolled into the prairie, stretching east in an endless blanket of gray-green short grass—buffalo country.

That night, they made camp by the broad Platte, gathering buffalo chips instead of wood for the fire, splitting half a dozen prairie hens Brand had shot with his Hawkins. The two Missouri teamsters were huge, strapping fellows in the square-toed boots and hickory jackets of their calling. The *engagé* that Anderson had sent was an inscrutable Crow Indian, wearing a white man's blue shirt, tails flapping around his buckskins.

"Tomorrow," said Brand, "we start making the boats. Everybody has a job. I'll need your muleskinners, Williams, and the wagons, to carry the hides. You and Red are elected to cut willow shoots for the frame. . . ."

"Now, lookee here, Brand," bridled Williams. "I'm no woodcutter."

Brand's voice was slow and easy, but that light the fire caught in his eyes might have been a rising anger. "You look like a better woodcutter than a hunter, Williams, and, as I remember it, you were the anxious one to come along. Everybody has a job to do."

Maybe Williams had seen that light; he laughed. "Shore, shore, I would make a better woodcutter at that, Brand."

Doc Sawyer stood very gravely, holding his equilibrium with an effort. "Everybodish gotta job but me. Whadda I do, Brand, whadda I do?"

"Ah, shut up," snarled Red, rising to his feet. "You ain't no good for nothin' but that rotgut coffin varnish."

Sawyer drew himself up like a ruffled peacock. "Now see here, Red, just because Stony Mountain. . . ."

With a savage curse, Red whirled, catching him by the lapel of his fustian, hitting him again and again across the face with an open palm. Then he shoved him violently backward. Almost crying with rage, the rotund doctor stumbled and fell flat.

Brand didn't know exactly why he did it; perhaps something about Sawyer reminded him of Grimes. But when Red turned around, he found himself face to face with the tall blond trapper whose strange slow smile had suddenly become very deadly. Brand didn't say anything, and the sudden back-hand blow he gave Red looked almost casual, long arm shooting out without much apparent effort.

Yet Red staggered back as if he'd been kicked by a mule, slamming up against the wagon box so hard that an oak panel cracked. He recovered himself, and for that one, hanging instant, he looked about to slap leather, hand clawing above his thonged-down gun, face twisted in rage.

Brand made no move. He stood with his long buckskinned legs spread wide, thumb hitched into the silver-studded belt, very close to the Walker.

Maybe Red had heard of Brand's talent, or maybe he was a coward. He let his breath out suddenly, his body relaxed, and his hand flattened out against his calfskin vest.

"That's better," said Brand. "Now, is there anybody else who doesn't understand how things stand?"

Williams laughed. "By damn, you're a cold devil, Brand. That's the fust time I've ever seen anybody face Red down. I guess he was the only one that didn't understand things, and I guess he understands 'em now. That right, Red?"

The redhead snarled something unintelligible. Still grinning mirthlessly, Brand helped the doctor up.

"If you want to do something, Doc, you can help the teamsters load the hides tomorrow."

Shock and anger had done a lot to sober the doctor, and there was a gratitude in his eyes. "You . . . you don't know how much I appreciate that, Lee Brand."

He turned and stumbled to the rear wagon where he slept. Red headed for his blanket roll, too. And watching him go, Brand knew it would be a mistake ever to turn his back on that man again.

The buffalo were migrating south in great herds that swept across the shallow places in the Platte and covered the plains with a brown mass of heavy-shouldered, small-hocked beasts. The next morning, Brand and Radiseau led the wagons half a mile south of camp to the fringe of one of those herds.

It was ticklish business, riding hell-for-leather after a bull weighing a ton or more, reining the galloping horse in close, and taking a fifty-fifty chance that the .44 lead would strike home. The buffalo bulls had tremendous vitality, and more often than not they would rumble to a stop after being shot, standing there with head lowering, blood dripping into the short grass, grimly fighting the death that should have been theirs minutes before.

Radiseau was skillful with his big Bowie. When the bulls had fallen, he made short work of the skinning, and after stripping the hides free, he cut off the hump rib and many strips of back fat. It would be a long trip down the river, and Brand wanted the meat almost as badly as the hides.

They returned in the afternoon to find that Williams and Red had done their job, cutting willow shoots as thick as a man's wrist, from the grove upriver. Radiseau had been a *voyageur*, and it was his job from then on. He showed them how to set the butts of the willow shoots into the ground in a twelve foot circle—as wide as the boat's beam—and how to bend them over, lashing smaller branches to the rounded framework.

Marie sewed the hides together with Brand's awl, flesh side to flesh side, until she had two large sheets, each big enough to cover one of the boats. It took all of them to stretch the hides over the frame and lash them to the gunwales. Brand had buffalo tallow melted in a big pot over the fire. After they'd set the bull boats bottom side up, he helped Radiseau smear the seams and skins with grease, forming a watertight pitch when smoked and dried.

That night after supper, Brand lay in his worn Navajo sougan, listening to the eerie howl of a loafer wolf out in the darkness. Somehow, it made him think of Arno Clegg. The saturnine Stony Mountain *bourgeois* was out there, somewhere, either on their back trail or ahead of them, and, like the wolf, he mocked Brand with the threat of his presence.

The next day they finished the boats, knocking down the wagons and using their stout oak beds for bulkheads, taking the osnaberg sheeting for tarps to cover the precious bales of beaver plews. Brand loaded his pelts, still lashed into their apishamores, into a bull boat.

Williams had almost as many furs as Brand, and he filled the second craft with them. Then they hitched the wagon wheels and harness and spare gear onto several pack horses. The *engagé* picked Brand's palomino to ride back, and though Brand had packed his California saddle in among the furs, he felt a lump rise in his throat as the wooden-faced Crow swung aboard the buckskin-colored little horse with its taffy mane. It had to be done, of course. They couldn't take any cayuses with them downriver.

Radiseau came over to Brand and drew him aside, pointing a white-coated arm toward the prairie to the west of them.

Already the file of Indians, riding hard through the roll of short grass, was near enough so Brand could see their leader clearly. He wore a heavy buffalo coat and Indian leggings with fringe that looked suspiciously like human hair.

"I guess it's about time to shove off," said Brand.

V

This was the way, the only way. Turgid water passing beneath bull-hide bows, cottonwoods and aspens and stretches of autumn prairie flitting by on either side. Sky and clouds, and Radiseau, singing the songs of the *voyageurs* from the next boat, the songs of the little white-coated Frenchmen who spent most of their lives on rivers like this, riding the white water of the Saginaw or coasting down the broad Missouri to St. Louis.

Smith and his dog soldiers had ridden hard. But Brand had gotten his boats launched and was away down the river by the time the trader reached their dying campfires. Still, now and then, Brand could look back and see dust rising behind. It would be a fairly even race until the horses tired.

Smith and his Cheyennes always led two or three extra horses apiece, and they could shift to fresh horses all through the day, and still Brand was confident he could beat them. The swift current carried the boats at a pace that would, in time, outdistance flesh and blood.

Radiseau's voice carried back with the wind, twisted oddly, singing:

> *Nous irons sur l'eau, nous promenar.*
> *Nous irons jouer en l'île.*

The trapper was surprised to hear Doc Sawyer translating the words. "We shall go on the water for a boat ride, we shall play on the island. . . ."

"You must 'a' been quite a guy once, Doc." Brand smiled.

Sawyer turned a wistful smile from his place amidships. "Oh, yes, my boy. I haven't always maintained myself on such a deplorable liquid diet. I used to have the respect due any man. But I'm afraid I didn't fight very hard when it came time for courage and strength. She was a beautiful woman. It was like losing my own soul. And then, drink. . . ."

He trailed off, and Brand saw that to press the man would be painful. There were other things drawing his attention, anyway. They were entering a narrower, swifter section of the river, and to the north, tall grim thunderheads were piling up in a threatening storm. Brand didn't know this country, but if the storms struck anything like Big Horn blizzards, it was high time they get out of the river.

Marie sat in front of the doctor, both of them amidships, and in the bow squatted Red, not very skillful with his pole, not trying very hard. Williams and the teamsters rode with Radiseau; the big fur trader seemed to enjoy the French-Canadian's gay songs, for every now and then his hearty laugh would float back.

The sullen roll of thunder decided Brand. He cupped his hands and yelled at Radiseau: "Beach yore boat on this sand spit ahead, Frenchie!"

The *voyageur* stood up. "I t'ink it's about time, by gar."

Wind was whipping at the water, and the rudderless bull boats were becoming hard to manage, yawing and rolling until the river slopped in over the thwarts. Brand shouted to Red: "Drive your pole in hard when we get opposite the spit, Red! It'll swing us in stern first."

Radiseau had already maneuvered his boat inshore and was driving for the beach. But Red's efforts at turning their stern were futile and half-hearted. And finally the doctor crawled past Marie to help him. Brand couldn't hear their voices above the

43

howling wind, but he saw Red turn with a snarl and push Sawyer violently out of his way. The doc tried to save himself, but the boat yawed wildly, and he went over the gunwale into the foamy water. For one awful moment he was within easy reach of Red's pole, if the man would have thrust it out. But Red only glanced at the struggling figure indifferently.

Then Sawyer was a flopping, bobbing bundle of kicking boots and floating fustian, sweeping past the stern. Brand made a wild jab at him with his ten-foot willow pole. Sawyer was too far gone to grab at it.

"Take my place and get ashore, Marie!" shouted Brand.

He slid the pole toward her along the gunwales, then turned and dived into the water. The current caught savagely at him and it took all his strength just to stay afloat. He saw Sawyer's coattails, rising and falling in the choppy crosscurrent, and fought his way toward them.

The storm broke suddenly, sweeping over the river like a black pall, blotting everything from Brand's sight but the whipping water rising before his eyes and the stinging slant of driving rain that came from the dark clouds above.

Brand had hold of the doctor, then; he was a dead weight, threatening to pull both of them under. Slipping one hand beneath the pudgy double chin, the trapper struck out with the other, frog-kicking against the terrific pull of sucking water. He was sobbing with the pain of utter exhaustion when the shoreline hove up ahead—dim shapes of wind-bent cottonwoods and a rising blot of sandy beach. He would never know how he made that final stretch of pitching river. There was a steel band around his chest that cut into him every time he drew a breath; his muscles were numb and loggy; his body refused to answer his brain. But finally he felt the shifting sand underfoot, and staggered shoreward with the soggy bundle of Doc Sawyer dragging behind.

He threw himself on the beach and lay stretched full length for a long time, rain beating down on him. Then, with an effort, he set about reviving Sawyer, dragging the man to a fallen cottonwood, throwing his body across the big trunk, rolling and pumping the water from his lungs.

The little doctor groaned after a while, sat up, and rocked back and forth, holding his head. Finally he looked at Brand, eyes focusing with an effort. The trapper swayed there on long legs, blond hair plastered against his hatless head, water dripping from every fringe on his buckskins.

"I might've known it would be you," muttered Sawyer. "No one else'd have bothered."

"We'd best be hunting the boats as soon as you're able," said Brand, turning.

The other caught at his arm. "Wait, Brand, wait. I should have told you a long time ago, but I just couldn't. I've been working for Williams so long . . . he had me so cowed, he and Red. But you were the first one to call me 'Doc' in I don't know how many years, the first one to treat me like a man. And now that you've saved my life, I owe it to you more than ever."

"Owe me what?" said Brand gruffly. "What're you talking about?"

Sawyer took a deep breath. "Williams and Clegg are partners in Stony Mountain."

Brand hunkered down slowly, heedless of the rain, whistling softly. "Then he knew who I was, all along?"

Sawyer nodded. "Clegg knew Williams would be waiting to join him at Laramie. He'd already sent his runners out, but he didn't want any slip, so he sent the redhead, too. That man rode three good horses to death, beating you. Clegg sent word for Williams to stop you if you got through the Indians, and if Billings and his bunch missed you."

Brand knew suddenly what had tantalized him so about Red.

It had been a redhead in Mexican leggings and calfskin vest who had slugged Grimes and run off their pack horses at Jackson Hole.

"If Williams was going to stop us," he grunted, "why didn't he just shoot us down at Laramie?"

"A greedy man, Williams," said Sawyer. "You have a small fortune in furs, Brand, and he didn't want to split it with Clegg. If he'd done you in at the fort, everyone would have known it . . . the *bourgeois*, the *engagés*, even the ration Indians. And Clegg would have known Williams had the furs. But out here, who's to know what happened? He can get rid of Red, who's Clegg's man. He can get rid of you and Radiseau and the girl, and sell the furs quietly at Westport or Saint Joe. And when he tells Clegg you got through, what else can Clegg do but believe him?"

"I seem to draw the dirtiest bunch of double-crossing cutthroats in the Rockies." Brand grinned. "But, hell, we can't stand here in the rain, gabbing. Let's find Williams before he gives the business to Frenchie and the girl."

The storm had ceased as suddenly as it had begun, and the bottom land swam with a thick mist that steamed up out of the mud and the swamp grass and the bogs. Brand and the doctor stumbled through a demi-world of ghostly shapes, twisted, stunted hackberry trees, clawing briers, waving dodder.

Suddenly a flat shot cracked the silence. Then another, and another.

Brand broke into a slogging run through a motte of dripping cottonwoods, out onto the spit of sand that disappeared into the fog, shredding over the river. There were two men lying on the shore. Radiseau was a heap of white coat and twisted legs. Farther out lay Red, flat on his back, sightless eyes staring upward. Williams had done his work, then, and those dimly flitting shapes out on the river were the bull boats being grunted into the current by the trader and his teamsters. Brand felt a fear clawing at him as he looked frantically around for the girl. She was nowhere to be seen.

He seldom betrayed much emotion, because that was his way. But now, he ran down the spit and into the river until the muddy water churned around his waist, cursing Williams, yanking his Dragoon out, and firing a volley after the ghostly shapes.

The gun only made a series of hollow clicks, of course. The river and the rain had soaked the powder. He stood helplessly there in the muddy Platte, realizing for the first time how total was his loss.

Radiseau's wound was a bad one, through his shoulder, but Doc Sawyer had a bottle of his inevitable Pass brandy in the pocket of his dripping fustian. While he cut the coat away from the wound, Radiseau told them what had happened.

"I get my boat ashore," he ground out. "Zen ze girl come shooting in. Williams tell the teamsters they might as well do it now, an', before I know what happen, zat beeg devil shoot Red t'ree time in ze ches' an' turn hees gun on me. I theenk maybe I die when ze slug go trough me. She's a beeg bullet, eh, Doc?"

Sawyer said: "You'll be poling a bull boat inside of two weeks, Frenchie. They don't make the slug that could stop a man like you."

The sun broke wanly through the mists about two hours later, and Brand set about to dry his powder, and the others to dry their clothes. The blond trapper's dark face showed none of his defeat, but he had lost everything now—the boats, his furs, Marie.

The doctor removed his fustian and hung it on a limb. It wasn't a watch fastened to that big gold chain. It was a snub-nosed Derringer, chain attached to a ring in its nickel-plated butt. He grinned faintly. "Wouldn't think I was a desperate character, would you? But that's the kind of crowd Stony

Mountain hires, gunmen like Billings and Red and Calder. And I was one of them, you know."

Brand eyed him thoughtfully. Now that the effect of alcohol had dissipated somewhat, there was a certain whimsical debonair manner about the rotund little man. He was a Stony Mountain man, drunkard, maybe even handy with that Derringer—yet Brand couldn't help liking him, and he knew why now. There had been another man who laughed with that same twinkle to his wise old eyes, a man with the same predilection for liquor. Yes, though Sawyer wore a fustian, and Grimes had worn greasy elk hides, they were surprisingly alike.

It took them a week to stalk enough buffalo to build another bull boat. Radiseau painfully carved the willow shoots down with his knife, and cut hide into strips for the lashings. Finally they had it finished, not as big as the others, but adequate. They dried some sheets of buffalo meat and loaded it aboard and pushed off, seven days after the renegade Williams had left.

There were only three of them now, coasting down the Platte where it was too deep to pole, covering seventy-five miles a day. Brand was even quieter and more laconic than usual. Radiseau was the only one to show signs of gaiety, because the river ran swiftly and the days were bright with the last fading of summer, and because his moods weren't very logical, anyway.

VI

About two days' journey downriver, they found the other bull boats. They were riding through the broad channel under a lowering afternoon sun that cast deep shadows along the dark-timbered bank. Radiseau was forward, as usual, and he turned to call: "By gar, Bran', I see ze ozair boats!"

Brand's head turned, and he could see them, too. Uprooted cottonwoods had swept down the river to this point, catching on a promontory, banking up, catching briers and plum thickets and silt, forming a high drift. Smashed up against the drift were two twisted shapes, hides torn and ripped, broken frames showing through. Radiseau levered their craft inshore, nosing it against the tangled growth.

Williams sprawled on the small beach formed by the silt. He must have put up some kind of a fight, for his gun was out and empty, and his other hand clutched the bunched arrows through his chest. The teamsters were in the boats, the same slender shafts studding their bodies.

Brand only had to examine one of those shafts to know they were Cheyenne—the yellow scarified marks from head to notch, the triple ring of prairie indigo just beneath the feathers, and the long, slender, barbless heads of the dog soldier society. Brand straightened slowly, the picture forming in his mind. Cheyenne Smith had passed them in the storm, had laid his ambush here, laid it with his patient leer, his little eyes glittering with the knowledge that he would have Marie back once more. Yes, he would have Marie back once more. The thought gave Brand's face a singular bleak, hopeless look.

Sawyer must have understood. He took Brand's arm and said softly: "It was high water, son. Maybe her body was washed downriver. Let's think it was, anyway. That would have been better than being taken again by that devil."

They buried the four men in the sand and pushed away quickly, because the place smelled of death. Late that afternoon they reached Fort Childs, beaching the boat on the shore near the western end of Grand Island.

A grove of giant cottonwoods surrounded the adobe-walled post. It was the first fort east of Laramie, and Radiseau and Sawyer couldn't hide their eagerness to mix with men again, to drink the undiluted Monongahela from St. Louis, to get the news of the frontier.

Brand told them he would re-pitch the boat. They saw the

dull look to his eyes and they didn't protest. He set about gathering buffalo chips for a fire to heat the tallow. Every day the boat had to be smeared anew with that pitch. The hides became soggy and water-logged, and if the craft had a draft of four or five inches at the beginning of the day, it was sure to have nine or ten at the end.

He was almost finished when Sawyer and Radiseau came back with some flour and a side of bacon. There was an odd set to the French-Canadian's face.

"Any news?" asked Brand.

"*Mais oui*," said Radiseau. "A lot. Ever'one at the fort has heard of our coming. Arno Clegg passed t'rough here t'ree day ago, asking for a party of trappers een a bull boat."

"Well," said Brand, "seems Clegg and Smith didn't get together. Guess Cheyenne'd rather have the twenty thousand dollars he can get for my furs than the thousand Clegg would give him for proof he stopped me."

Radiseau laughed. "*Oui.* Smith keel Williams, an' Williams was Clegg's partner. I theenk he keel Clegg, too, eef they meet. Ever'body want your furs, Bran'."

"They're all somewhere down the river now," said Brand. "Smith'll head for Saint Looey, and so will Clegg. If they meet before Saint Looey, it'll be a big showdown, won't it? And if we get in on it, it'll be a bigger showdown." He turned to Sawyer. "Doc, that's what I'm going to do, get in on that showdown. I owe it to Clegg, and to Smith. You'd better stay here at Fort Childs. It'll be a bloody business, and it won't be yours."

Sawyer drew himself up. "Oh, no, Lee Brand. I've come this far, and, by damn, I'm not going to miss the end."

A slow grin spread over Brand's face. "I knew an old trapper named A.A. Grimes that would have liked you a heap, Doc."

★ ★ ★ ★ ★

Plattesmouth was a fur trading post at the confluence of the Platte and the Missouri. There, Brand heard the same thing. Clegg had ridden through a few days before, asking for a party of trappers in bull boats. Evidently he was still unaware that Smith had the furs.

Brand kept a sharper watch now, coasting down the broad Missouri past Council Bluffs, coasting through the stretches of monotonous prairie that stretched away from either bank. Sunfish and bullheads supplemented their dried meat and flour and bacon, but even with the fish, Radiseau was beginning to show signs of scurvy. They stopped at Saint Joe, as they were stopping at every town, poling their craft ashore beside the big Mackinaw boats that ran downriver.

It was a sprawling slattern of a town, Saint Joe, built on the bluffs above the river, named after Uncle Joe Robidioux who had established a Stony Mountain trading post here earlier in the century. Yes, it was a Stony Mountain post, and a Stony Mountain town, where the *engagés* and the *voyageurs* of the fur company gathered.

Poulin Street was full of the bizarre frontier crowds. Pottawatamies and Delawares hunkered down with their backs to rude log walls, bright blankets catching the sun. A train of big swagger-boxed Conestogas stood in front of a settler's store, emigrants bound for Santa Fe, milling around in the mud or sitting on high box seats, gaping at the crowds.

Farther on was the Bucket of Blood, hitch racks full of tethered horses. A line of pack animals stood there in the ruts, too, guarded by an Indian. There were many pack trains like this in the river towns at the end of the fur seasons, and Brand wouldn't have paid any attention to it but for the saddle horses standing ground-hitched nearby.

"Look at that pony on the end, Doc," he said. "Seen it

anywhere before?"

Sawyer frowned thoughtfully. "The palmetto with the Arab spots? Can't say that I have."

"Well, I have," said Brand. "I've seen it somewhere."

"You've probably seen a lot of horses you'd recognize. . . ."

"Cheyenne Smith," said Brand flatly.

He remembered very clearly now—the draw just west of South Pass, the sudden sight of a man sitting that palmetto with the Arab spots, sitting with a leer that showed his gold teeth, dog soldiers crowding behind, and the girl.

"He's here," said Brand harshly. "Smith's here with our furs, and . . . and. . . ."

He was moving toward the Bucket of Blood then, because he had never really believed the girl had been washed down the river.

He rounded the line of horses and saw her about the same time she saw him. She stood in a group of other squaws, blue and yellow blanket covering her head to foot. The marks on her face might have come from a man's fist; her eyes opened wide at sight of the trapper.

"Brand, Lee Brand!"

"Marie!"

She broke loose from the Indian women and ran toward him, blanket trailing off into the mud. "I knew you'd come," she sobbed, face against his chest. "Nothing could stop you. Not Clegg or Williams or Smith or all the Indians in the Platte Purchase."

With his hands still splayed out against the back of her quilled jacket, he saw Cheyenne Smith come out of the Bucket of Blood, four dog soldiers crowding behind through the batwing doors. The trader might have been drinking, but he wasn't in his cups this time, and he took it all in with one swift glance.

"Well, Brand," he said. "I thought the river got you. But

mebbe this way's better."

Brand was hampered by the girl. He tried to shove her around behind him and dive for his gun at the same time. Even as he slapped leather, he saw it had given Smith the edge, saw that he was outgunned.

Sawyer must have seen it, too, for as the buffalo-coated trader cross-armed his Patersons out, the doc threw himself in front of Brand, and both shots caught him squarely. As the rotund little man went down in a coughing, huddled way, Brand triggered out his first shot, because he had his gun free by then.

Cheyenne Smith took a staggering step backward, evil face twisted with the pain of that big slug through his chest. He made a clatter, falling on the plank sidewalk.

Menacing the bunch of dog soldiers with his smoking Walker, Brand kneeled beside Sawyer, trying to help him up.

"I owed you that one, didn't I, boy?" Sawyer sighed. "No, no, don't bother with me. Smith dusted me on both sides. Get your furs, Brand, get your furs. . . ."

He slid into the muddy street, eyes closing behind his horn-rimmed glasses. Brand's throat was choked with emotion when he rose and he hoped the Indians would make a break, because he wanted to shoot somebody very badly. But they stood quiescently before the threat of his gun, grouped together, sullenly eyeing their dead leader.

"Get our plews down to the river, Frenchie," said Brand. "I'll hold these *kyeshes*."

Radiseau grabbed the palmetto's drooping reins and swung aboard. The Indian who had guarded the pack train moved out of his way, eyes on Brand's gun, and the French-Canadian cursed the animals into motion.

When the last horse had galloped past, splattering mud over his worn buckskins, Brand began backing down the street, keeping the girl behind him. He was almost to the bluffs when the dog soldiers scattered, diving for cover, notching arrows to their short bows.

Brand snapped a couple of shots at them, knocking one sprawling. Then he and Marie were racing down the path after Radiseau, and the last thing Brand saw in Poulin Street was the body of Doc Sawyer, huddled there in the viscid mud of the wheel ruts.

They loaded the furs into the bull boat as before, apishamores and all. Brand was glad to find his Jake Hawkins lashed to one packsaddle. Smith had taken everything he could lay his hands on. The trapper slipped the Kentucky rifle beneath the willow braces. They were almost finished when Marie cried out.

"Brand! On the bluffs. There's Clegg!"

Arno Clegg was in the lead, running down the trail. He didn't have Billings or Calder any more. But the Stony Mountain *voyageurs* made a howling pack behind him, and La Roche's red shirt showed in the crowd.

"Eef we fight heem here," yelled Radiseau, "we fight ze whole town! Eef we make zem chase us een ze Mackinaw boats, ze odds will be smaller, *non?*"

Brand nodded, and they scrambled aboard, Radiseau climbing over the cargo to the bow. The trapper shoved the boat off the sand and into the shallows. Someone was firing and the slugs thudded into bull hide, one plucking at Brand's buckskins. Then they were in the channel and shooting downriver.

Brand turned to see Clegg crowding the *voyageurs* and *engagés* aboard one of the Mackinaws, a big boat, fifty feet long and made entirely of wood. Four river men took the oars in the bow, half a dozen clustered into the empty cargo space amidships. Clegg took his place at the sweep astern.

The oarsmen settled into a steady, driving pace, singing that river song:

Nous irons sur l'eau. . . .

Brand saw there was no chance of outdistancing Clegg. He punched the empty shells from his Walker and slipped in fresh ones. Then he drew his rifle.

The *voyageurs* in the Mackinaw boat were armed with short-barreled London fusils, and they sprawled behind the bulkheads and the wooden knees that supported the boat's sides, sending a ragged volley at the bull boat.

Brand felt a certain grim satisfaction as he shifted his cat-tail around for the first half-ounce ball of Galena lead. A good man could pour and load and fire five times a minute. Brand must have bettered that record, laying a cool, deadly barrage that created havoc aboard the other boat. His first ball knocked a rifleman over backward into the river; his second spun an oarsman away from his seat.

Clegg crouched behind the aft bulkhead, leaving the sweep untended, emptying his Colt .44 vainly at Brand. The others had forsaken their posts and were huddled behind the protecting sides.

Even without the drive of oars, the Mackinaw was sweeping down on the bull boat, and Brand saw the race was over.

"Swing our bow around into 'em, Frenchie!" he called. "We'll meet 'em head-on!"

"Mais oui, mon ami!" yelled Radiseau, lips peeling back in that wolf-grin.

His willow pole bent under the weight of the boat, driving deep into the muddy bottom. The craft swung broadside, yawed, then the stern carried around. Radiseau yanked his pole free, holding it across his belly with both hands, rising to stand, spread-legged, in the bow. He had been a river man before turning trapper, and those scars on his face came from a hundred battles such as this.

The boats were nearing quickly and there was no time for reloading. The *voyageurs* in the Mackinaw boat struggled erect from where they'd sprawled, scrambling over the dead and wounded and crowding forward. Three of them clubbed their oars. The others flashed big knives.

Then the bows struck, and the bull boat shivered from stem to stern, supple willow frame bending and shrieking. The lanky trapper threw himself into that bunch of Stony Mountain men, Jake Hawkins clubbed. And right beside him was the little blue-chinned Frenchman.

It was all a howling struggling madness to Brand in those next few seconds. His only thought was to get through to Clegg. He brained a heavy-bearded *engagé* and saw him go down with blood all over his face, and jumped over him to jam his rifle butt in the pit of a big *voyageur*'s stomach. A half-breed lunged at him with a Green River blade.

Brand took the knife in his shoulder, going right on in and tossing the man over his back into the river. He'd lost his rifle somehow, but when a strapping Frenchman went for him, he pulled the knife from his shoulder with a sick grunt and let the man spit himself on the already bloody blade.

Then Brand was through the tangled, yelling men, clawing for his Walker because Clegg had come up from the stern and was standing on the amidships bulkhead with his Colt throwing down on the blond trapper he had come so far to kill.

Brand had waited a long time for this. He owed it to Clegg for the old whang hide who lay in a shallow grave back there in the Dead Forest. Their shots were simultaneous.

Clegg's .44 slug burned through the trapper's thigh and knocked him forward. But as he fell, Brand emptied out his other five slugs into Clegg's body, until the Walker clicked empty.

Face down on the wet deck boards, Brand heard Clegg fall from the bulkhead with a dull thud, heard the man's Colt clatter on wood. His wounds made him sick and weak and apathetic, and when someone made a sound behind him, he couldn't find the will to turn and fight.

But it was the girl. She kneeled beside him and held his head in her buckskin lap. And swaying above her was Radiseau, dripping blood from a big cut in his forehead, grinning.

"Parbleu," he said. "Zat girl, she's a reg'lar wil'cat. She save my life twice. She stick La Roche like you would a peeg, an' she knock a man in ze rivair w'en he would 'ave slit my t'roat wez ees Green Rivair. *Sacre bleu!"*

Brand looked up at Marie, and he didn't say anything, but that slow grin spread across his Indian-dark face.

The Mackinaw boat was behind them. Other river men from St. Joe had probably recovered it with its cargo of dead and wounded. Ahead of them was St. Louis where the streets were full of cursing, drinking trappers and Indians and hunters twenty-four hours a day, where the French quarter was called the Vide Poche because the *voyageurs* always had empty pockets, and where each beaver plew was worth sixty shining silver dollars.

Billings was long dead, and Williams was dead, and Smith, and Clegg. And Brand was very weary. It seemed he had been fighting all of his life. All he wanted to do was lay back against the swart beaver pelts and listen to Radiseau singing up in the bow, and let the girl swab his wounds with Pass brandy.

"It mus' be a marvelous place, Saint Looey," she said. "I've never been there."

"Neither have I," he said. "We'll have to see it together. There's a lot we'll have to see together."

★ ★ ★ ★ ★

CROW-BAIT CARAVAN

★ ★ ★ ★ ★

The author's title for this story was "Bullwhip Trail". Malcolm Reiss (pronounced Reese), the editorial manager who bought it for $125.00, changed the title to "Crow-Bait Caravan" for its appearance in *Frontier Stories* (Spring, 44). Reiss was so impressed with Savage's writing that he asked his agent to submit more stories to be published in Fiction House magazines.

I

The pair of men stepped just inside the door of the Kaycee Freight Company's clapboard office, and there was something ominous in the way the late afternoon sun cast their two shadows across Kaycee Garrett, sitting there with his long legs propped up on the scarred top of the rickety desk. Kaycee turned his head, and when he recognized who it was, his voice was sardonic.

"Well, don't tell me you gents have some freight you want me to haul."

Neither of them answered right away. They sent a swift glance around the room as if to make sure Kaycee was the only one there. And Kaycee couldn't help the sidelong look he sent at his gun and holster, wrapped in the cartridge belt and stuck in a pigeonhole of the desk.

These men worked in Montana, usually, but they were known well enough down here in Singletree, the Wyoming shipping point for the Montana mines. Glenrock was the smaller of the two, his Holstein calfskin vest hanging from square shoulders, Bisley .44 strapped around square hips, the whole look of him compact and forceful and potent. He had singular, almost color-less eyes that never seemed to focus on any particular object.

The other man was bigger, heavier, slow and deliberate in his movements. The front of his weathered Mackinaw coat was spread apart a little by his sizable paunch, and by the gun he wore beneath it. He was known in Singletree as Peso Peters, and Kaycee had always figured that he had been known in other places by other names.

"Bad year for the Bozeman Trail," said Peters, looking finally at Kaycee. "I hear nobody's sending any freight north this season, what with the Sioux, and the cholera epidemic."

"That's what I hear," said Kaycee carefully. "Dudley's last train was wiped out by the cholera up past the Powder."

When he said the name of Dudley, his lips puckered a little as if he'd tasted something bad. For years, a bitter war had been raging between the powerful Dudley Shippers Incorporated and Kaycee's one-horse outfit. Jason Dudley had driven every other shoestring company out of business, but somehow Kaycee had managed to hold on, running just enough freight north on the Bozeman Trail to keep his dilapidated yards going, to pay the feed bill of his crow-bait mules, and meet the wages of what few teamsters would whip for him.

Such a long, unequal battle might have made some men discouraged, or bitter. But Kaycee was hard to discourage, and too young for any permanent bitterness. Perhaps his reaction was the sardonic streak that had cropped up in him. It showed now in the dry, unperturbed smile he turned toward Peters.

He was well over six feet tall, Kaycee, and he could have looked awkward but for his eyes. Nobody could look awkward with eyes like that. Their color matched the sunburned brown of his hair, and they had a terrible shrewdness for such a young man—wary, worldly wise lights coming and going behind narrowed lids. Peters was watching those eyes, and when he spoke again, his voice had lost its edge of confidence.

"If you were to get a good offer, Kaycee, would you send a train up the Bozeman?" asked the heavy man from Montana.

"I might," said Kaycee. "I might."

"Britten O'Hare will be in soon," said Peters slowly. "She'll want you to take a load of hydraulic equipment to the O'Hare mines north of Virginia City. There's five thousand dollars in it for you if you refuse."

Kaycee took his long legs carefully off the desk and stood up. Deliberately he took the holstered Paterson five-shot from the pigeonhole, unwrapping the cartridge belt, and lifting the tails of his black frock coat so he could buckle the gun around his lean hips. He looked at Peters's unshaven face with its beetling brows and thick lips and didn't like it, and didn't try to keep the dislike from his voice. "Who are you fronting for, Peters?"

Glenrock's tone was hollow and flat: "You shouldn't ask that, Kaycee."

"I've done about as bad as any man could in the shipping business," said Kaycee. "But then I've always been particular how I did my business, and who I did it with."

Peters shifted nervous boots on the unpainted floor. He wasn't the kind of a man to enjoy fencing like this, and he said impatiently: "That much money would buy a lot of new Murphy wagons for you, Kaycee, and you can't keep going much longer on those old Conestogas of yours."

Kaycee had guessed why these men had been sent rather than an ordinary go-between, and he had a good idea what his refusal would bring. He shoved his frock coat back from the bone butt of his Paterson with an elbow, and put his left hand on the back of the chair.

"If your boss had come himself and made the offer as a simple business proposition, I might have considered it. But sending a couple of *hombres* like you looks to me like a threat. And I don't like to be threatened. It raises my back hair."

Peters had been keeping his impatience down, but it broke over his face now, along with the dull flush of anger. "There's notches on my gun for men who talked like you're talking. It would be unhealthy for you not to take this five thousand."

Kaycee had a certain skill with his Paterson, but he knew he couldn't hope to match these two men, who were paid for what they could do with their guns. His left hand gripped the chair's back tighter, and he set himself to draw, more to focus their attention on his gun hand than anything else. Then he said harshly: "Whoever sent you here told you to do something if I refused the money. Now either do it, or get out, fast!"

Perhaps Glenrock and Peters had expected it, knowing Kaycee as they did. But for a moment after he spoke, their faces were blank with surprise. Then Peters's mouth twisted with vicious anger, telegraphing what was coming.

"All right, you damn' fool," he snarled, and dived for his gun.

Glenrock drew, too, no expression on his face, or in his eyes. But Kaycee had seen it coming, and even as he slapped his own leather, knowing both men would be faster, he was swinging that chair up around behind him in a hurtling arc.

All Glenrock's concentration was on beating Kaycee's draw, and he did beat it. But before his thumb had quite eared back the hammer of his .44, the chair slammed into the gun, knocking it from his hand and clear across the room. Peters tried to jerk backward and shoot at the same time, and it marred his aim. The slug he got out went wild. He didn't get out another, because he hadn't stepped back quite far enough, and the leg of the chair slammed across his wrist. Peters's howl of pain was followed by the heavy clang of his gun on the floor.

Kaycee let go of the chair, and it followed its arc on around, crashing up against the wall. He had his gun out by then.

"All right," he said, "you can go now. And if you want your guns back, you'll have to send your boss after them."

The startled anger had fled from Glenrock's face almost before it appeared, and he stood there with his strange eyes not seeming to look at Kaycee. But Peso Peters's face was dark, and his mouth worked a moment before he got his words out.

"I've heard you were a stubborn devil, but I didn't think you were a fool to boot, Garrett. I guess you know what you've started now, don't you? If you take that O'Hare shipment, you won't even leave Singletree alive, much less reach the Bozeman with it."

Kaycee's lips drew back from his teeth in a wolf snarl. "Get out!"

Glenrock went first, backing through the door. And as Peters followed, the hate in his eyes made it plain to Kaycee just what he could expect when the big deliberate man got another gun.

Britten O'Hare must have passed the two Montana gunmen on her way to the office. She was standing in the door when Kaycee turned from putting the two six-shooters away in his desk drawer.

"Those men looked mad," she said. "What happened?"

"They offered me five thousand dollars not to take your hydraulic equipment up the Bozeman, Miss O'Hare. And they didn't like it when I refused the offer."

The girl's face took on a pale, confused look. "Why should anyone want to make that kind of an offer?"

He shrugged without answering. The girl had been in Singletree enough times, and they were on speaking terms, Kaycee and Britten O'Hare. But he had never actually seen her up close like this. The whole effect was striking—taffy-blonde hair that hung wind-blown about her shoulders, framing a face that was highly colored from the outdoors. Ever since her father had died two years before, she had run the O'Hare mines north of Virginia City, and had taken to wearing a man's clothes. On her, somehow, the plaid shirt and slick leather leggings lost all their masculinity. Strapped around her slim waist was one of Sam Colt's new .45s, and it was said she had more skill with it than any girl should rightly possess. Kaycee picked up the smashed chair, soberly taking off the back of it, then setting it on the floor, straightening a leg.

"Won't you sit down?" he said dryly.

She looked at it a moment, not sure if he was joking. Then, suddenly, she almost collapsed into it. Her face was strained, and she seemed to be fighting back tears.

Kaycee didn't look at her when she spoke, because she affected him more than he liked, and he hated to see women cry anyway.

"I suppose you know I won't be able to get any regular muleskinners," he said. "It's been hard enough for me to get a decent crew in the past, what with Jason Dudley offering higher wages and undercutting my prices and roughing up what few men I'm able to hire. Now, with this cholera on the rampage, and the Sioux threat. . . ."

"I've got to get those hydraulic monitors to the mines," she broke in. "Dad borrowed money from the Embar Mining Corporation two years ago, when we weren't getting out enough yellow to run our diggings, and the mortgage is due this September. We've hit a vein that will pay off that mortgage a thousand times, but we have to get the gold out with water. And if I can't get those monitors working in time, Embar will foreclose. Alex Hanson's company hauled the stuff from the Mississippi to here, but they won't take it any farther up the Bozeman. I went to Dudley, and he said he couldn't do it, either. You're my last hope."

He would have liked to discuss with her further why anyone should want her shipment stopped, but he could see the strain she had been under, so he shrugged it off.

"I'll see what I can do, Miss O'Hare. You have Hanson's wagon boss pull his train into my yards and unload the equipment from his wagons. I know where I can get some sort of a crew . . . not the best muleskinners in the world, but at least able to snap a bullwhip."

II

The Kaycee yards were directly behind his clapboard office—a big open space, criss-crossed with wheel ruts, and a pair of sagging, hip-roof barns with a hayrack in between them. Hanson's wagon boss had unloaded the monitors in sections the evening before, and pulled out. Kaycee spent the better part of that same evening rounding up his crew and, early the next morning, set them to work loading the O'Hare equipment into his own wagons. He was standing beside one of his big, weatherbeaten barns when Britten O'Hare cantered in on her taffymaned palomino. Her spirits seemed to have risen a little, and, as she swung easily down beside Kaycee, her smile wasn't quite so strained as it had been the day before.

"About ready to go?" she asked.

He nodded toward the wagons. "Only a few more sections of piping and we'll be set."

The girl turned toward the eight big freighters lined up on one side of the wheel-rutted yard. The smile on her face faded. They were ancient wagons, huge clumsy Conestogas of Santa Fe Trail vintage, swagger boxes split and paint peeled, canvas tilts patched and sagging between the hoops. The teams were no better—spavined, stove-up mules standing resignedly in battered hames. A sardonic twist had come into Kaycee's mouth as he saw the expression on her face.

This was what he had been fighting Dudley with for so long—1830 Conestogas against Dudley's bright new Murphy wagons; mules that would collapse if their traces didn't hold them up, against Dudley's sleek fat young animals. And the teamsters—that sardonic twist grew as he saw she had become aware of them.

Sweating over a huge steel nozzle was Blacksnake Brae, river man, trapper, hunter, muleskinner—and primarily drunkard. He was a burly, thick-set barrel of a man, ugly and dirty in a soiled red wool shirt and muddy black river boots. His eyes were bloodshot beneath beetling brows, and his black-bearded face was puffy, still flushed with a sullen resentment at having been sobered up for the first time in six weeks. He cast a surly glance at Kaycee, spat disgustedly, and turned back to curse as he pushed the nozzle into the Conestoga.

Green River Jones and Tomosak, the half-breed son of a squawman, were levering a long section of pipe into the bed of the next wagon down. Jones was a dried-up little whang hide whose greasy tattered elk hides made believable his boast that he didn't change clothes till they rotted off of him. Through the strip of rawhide that supported his frayed blanket leggings were thrust four huge Green River skinning knives.

Backing a pair of wheelers into their traces, one on either side of the tongue, was Sevier, the huge French-Canadian, his cracking bullwhip punctuating a stream of volatile Gallic curses. There was talk of a murder in his past—but if any man could match Blacksnake Brae's skill with a whip, it was Sevier, and Kaycee could overlook the whispers of the Frenchman's unsavory past in favor of his talent with a Missouri bullwhip.

Drunkards, barflies, murderers—the dregs of Singletree. And though the girl was used to her rough miners, used to the brutal, cursing bullwhackers, she couldn't hide the curling of her lips. Her voice held a disappointment, and an irritation.

"You told me none of the regular teamsters would go because of the Indians, and the cholera. But there. . . ."

"What did you expect?" he asked harshly. "A bunch of parsons? This is the best I can offer, and it wasn't any picnic gathering them in."

She glanced at his cut lip, his swelling eye, and for a moment there was apology in her face. Then she turned quickly and mounted her palomino, settling into the silver-mounted Brazos saddle with an ease and grace that would have shamed many a man. She couldn't keep the almost frightened anger from her voice.

"I suppose you did the best you could, but I don't like it. These men don't look any more like muleskinners than a bunch of coyotes would. I've never seen such an ugly bunch."

Kaycee turned his back and walked to his big raw-boned mare, tightening the latigo viciously, standing there till his anger faded a little. He shouldn't feel mad, really—she was just under a strain and she couldn't help it. But he'd had one hell of a time getting these men sobered up and whipped into shape, and he was under a strain, too.

He was outriding, and he had changed his black frock coat for a heavy Mackinaw, his white shirt for a red wool one. The men had hitched up the last team, and by the time he called to them, he had managed to fight down his anger.

"Let's go, you 'skinners. Sevier, you're on the first wagon. Brae, on the tail. Tomosak, you take the cavayard. We'll try to reach Salt Flats by tonight."

Jason Street was Singletree's main thoroughfare, a broad wheel-rutted way, stretching between the double row of false-front buildings, a plank walk running down each side, sagging hitch racks standing at the curb. Kaycee headed his train out of town that way, passing the saloon of Rotgut Farnum, between First and Second, the favorite haunt for most of Dudley's swaggering muleskinners. With Glenrock and Peters still at the back of his mind, Kaycee was expecting trouble before he left town, but he didn't connect it with the crowd of men that had collected in front of Farnum's. Matt Farrow was standing in the street, a little in front of the crowd, one of Dudley's unshaven, hickory-jacketed wagon bosses. As Kaycee's lead wagon rolled by, he threw back his head and laughed nastily.

"Look at that cussed fool, Kaycee . . . two trains wiped out by cholera on the Bozeman, and the Sioux on the warpath, and

Kaycee thinks he'll get to Montana with them Santa Fe relics for wagons."

"Ah, you beeg *paillard!*" shouted Sevier violently. "We could take these Conestogas to the moon and back with barefoot teams!"

Kaycee spurred his mare up beside Sevier's lead wagon. "Shut up, Sevier, and keep on going."

Laughter sifted through the crowd on the sidewalk, and one of them ran out into the street, poking at a flea-bit mule drawing the second wagon.

"Look, it's alive!" yelled the man.

The laughter grew, and it had an ugly quality. Kaycee held the anger that flushed his lean-jawed face, tightening the grip on his reins till his knuckles gleamed white. He had sensed something deliberate in this gathering, and suddenly he was moved to look for Glenrock or Peters. But neither of the Montana gunslicks was to be seen. His horse had passed the crowd, and he wheeled around, sidling back until the horse stood between the men on the walk and his rumbling line of Conestogas.

The batwing doors of Rotgut Farnum's saloon swung open and the crowd gave way before Jason Dudley. He wore a gaudy purple fustian and a furred stove-pipe hat, sideburns running from beneath it and down the sides of his fat red cheeks. Good food and rich living had made a big-bellied, pompous man of Dudley, but beneath the roll of his jowls, his chin still held some of the ruthless strength it had taken to make such an eminent place for himself on this wild, raw frontier.

"I always said you were a loco *hombre,* Kaycee," said Dudley, moving around in front of a hitch rack. "Nobody else would be fool enough to take a train up the Bozeman this year. But then a lot of Sioux pass through Singletree. We'll probably see your hair along about next year, hanging from some buck's scalp belt."

He turned to the crowd, chuckling, and they laughed again, hooting at Kaycee, jeering him. Anger whipped to a froth inside him, Kaycee couldn't help kneeing his horse in close to the pompous Jason Dudley.

"Did you give Glenrock and Peters some new guns, Dudley," he asked, "or were you planning on getting the old ones out of my desk drawer after I left?"

Dudley's face paled, then flooded red with anger. A vein began to pulse in his fat neck, just above his white choker collar. A couple of hard-faced muleskinners had moved in behind him, big calloused hands hanging above heavy Army Colts. It was unusual to find them armed that way in town. It made Kaycee shove his coat back a little farther from the white bone butt of his Paterson five-shot.

"I know what happened in your office, Kaycee," said Dudley angrily. "Most folks do, by now. And there isn't a man in Singletree fool enough to accuse me of backing a play like that. You'd better not be the exception."

"It seems I've always been the exception when it came to bucking you," said Kaycee. "Only you never came so much out in the open before. Careless of you, Jason, to hire a couple of known gunnies to cut me down right here in town. Or were you in a hurry?"

Consumed with rage, Dudley turned halfway around, and the men behind him leaned forward in an eager, waiting way. Matt Farrow's bellowing voice stopped whatever order Dudley would have flung at his teamsters. The wagon boss had spotted Blacksnake Brae riding the tail Conestoga, and he yelled: "If it ain't the old Blacksnake himself! Thinks he's a muleskinner. Thinks he's going to Montany driving them crow-bait carcasses he calls mules. Don't fall off that seat, Blacksnake." He threw back his head and laughed in that nasty thundering way.

Brae didn't bother to stop his wagon. He jumped from the high seat and landed with short legs spread, bent at the knees, whip uncoiling.

"No stinking Dudley jackass can talk that way without tasting my leather, Matt Farrow!" he bellowed.

And before he'd finished yelling, his twenty feet of braided Missouri bullwhip was snarling back of his head. Farrow tried to dodge aside. But Brae's forearm reversed and his snake howled out from behind him, cracking like a gunshot as it lashed across Farrow's face. The Dudley wagon boss screamed, lurching back against the men behind him, hands pawing at his face.

Before Brae's whip had dropped from Farrow's face, Kaycee's muleskinners were jumping from their wagons—Green River Jones snaking two of his blades from the thong supporting his leggings, Escelante Baca, the Mexican, grabbing a sawed-off shotgun from the boot beside his seat. It was what the crowd on the sidewalk had been waiting for, and there was a sudden eddying move as they surged into the street, spreading apart. But they had waited an instant too long.

The moment Brae had dropped off his wagon, Kaycee had realized why there were so many of Dudley's men in the crowd, realized they had gathered here by no mere chance. And he had already begun his play before the crowd started to move. As Blacksnake Brae pulled his whip back and even before Matt Farrow's scream was dead, Kaycee spurred his mare's flank and drew his gun at the same time.

The horse danced sideways under Kaycee's hard rein and slammed into Brae, knocking him over into the dust with a startled curse. Drowning that curse was the single crashing shot Kaycee sent above the heads of the crowd. Its stunning detonation dropped a sudden silence over everything.

The two hardcases behind Dudley, who had been in the very

act of drawing their guns, didn't draw them. Their faces were turned up to Kaycee, blank with surprise. The other teamsters, just beginning their forward surge to meet Kaycee's crew, halted like a bunch of snubbed horses. Some had one foot on the plank sidewalk and the other in the street. And the only one with a gun unleathered was Kaycee, sitting tall and angry there on his big mare, smoking Paterson Colt commanding the whole scene. He spoke to Brae from the side of his mouth, eyes still on the others.

"Get back to your wagon, Brae. I'm not having any rum-pot muleskinner start a fight that would end with my whole crew shot to rags. I'm not giving Jason Dudley that chance."

Brae struggled to his feet, standing there a moment with his face livid, his chest heaving. But Kaycee's own dark face had a harsh, granite look to it, and Brae knew Kaycee well enough to have seen that look before, and to know what it meant.

With a muttered curse, Brae picked up his whip, then turned back to the wagon. Kaycee ordered the rest of his crew back in that same hard, flat voice. Dudley's crowd began to shift. Kaycee sidled his horse toward them.

"Anybody wants a slug through his brisket, just make the wrong move. All right, Sevier, *str-i-i-ng out!*"

The last was a yell, and the lead wagon lurched into movement, jerking as each span of mules leaned forward against the hames. Kaycee sat his horse there till they were well down the street, meeting Dudley's apoplectic gaze with a sardonic smile. When he finally wheeled his mare to follow, he sat turned in the saddle so that he covered the crowd all the way down Jason Street, knowing what would happen if he put his back to them, knowing this was only the beginning of the thing that would stalk him all the way up the Bozeman.

III

Once past the Salt Flats, they rolled beyond the Dry Fork of the Cheyenne, days of creaking wagons and dust, and of constantly muttering men, the threat of cholera putting them under a terrific strain. Blacksnake Brae was worst of all. He hadn't wanted to come in the first place, because of cholera, and Indians, and because he knew he wouldn't see a drop of liquor between Singletree and Virginia City. Kaycee had only deepened his resentment by knocking him over back there in Jason Street and making him lose face to the Dudley men.

The third morning out of Singletree was chilled and foggy. The men rose from their damp sougans in an ugly mood, streaming out to get their teams from the cavayard, where they browsed in the blue lupine and stirrup-high wheat grass. Kaycee followed them as far as the ring of wagons, listening to the crack of whips, the violent cursing.

Driving the third wagon was a cocky little old man named Eph who Kaycee had found dead drunk in the back room of Rotgut Farnum's. He was trying, now, to back one of his mules from a patch of wheat grass. Nearby Brae had rounded up his three spans and was driving them past Eph. The old man whacked his mule with five feet of bullwhip, shouting in a cracked voice.

"Git outta there, damn 'ee ornery varmint, outta there!"

Reacting to the whip with a loud bray, the mule backed right into Blacksnake's team, kicking and bucking. Brae's mules milled and crowded into each other excitedly, breaking into a run, scattering. The black-bearded rum-pot tried to stop them, cursing, running this way and that. But they were already gone in half a dozen different directions.

Blacksnake Brae turned to Eph, snarling. "What the hell are you trying to do? It took me ten minutes to collect my team,

74

and then you whip your old jackass, right smack into the middle of them."

Cursing with rage, he grabbed Eph by the front of his buckskins, holding him there while he smashed him brutally in the face. Kaycee broke into a run for them. Brae had clouted the old man for the third time when Kaycee caught his solid shoulder and spun him around, causing him to release his grip on Eph and let him slide down into the dust.

"That'll do, Brae," he said flatly. "Go get your mules."

"No damn' prospector has a right handling a bullwhip anyway," growled Brae. "He scattered my team on purpose. You saw it."

"You know he didn't do it deliberately," said Kaycee. "You've just been aching for a chance to take a swipe at somebody. I guess I didn't make it clear back in Singletree that you aren't going to make any trouble in this crew."

For a moment Brae stood there, hairy hands opening and closing spasmodically. Kaycee could see the haze of rage in his bloodshot eyes. Some of the teamsters had gathered, muttering in a sullen way. They were turned as skittish as a snake-startled horse by the fear of cholera. Brae was their acknowledged leader, the strongest among them, and there would be no telling what they'd do if he blew off the lid now. Knowing that, Kaycee settled himself, muscles tight across his belly, and he spoke in that flat voice again.

"I said . . . go and get your team hitched up, Brae."

Brae's whole body grew taut as stretched rawhide, and he seemed to gather himself. Kaycee's elbow twitched his Mackinaw away from the Paterson buckled around his waist. Brae's own hand curled above his six-gun. But he was no gunslinger, and he knew it. His eyes met Kaycee's for a hard moment. Then he relaxed, and his voice shook with the effort to control his anger.

"All right, Garrett, maybe this just ain't the time."

Kaycee waited for the other men to scatter, then bent to help Eph up. "Did he hurt you much, Eph?"

The old man cackled weakly. "Not much. But he would have done me in sure if you hadn't stopped him. I've seen him in that kind of mood before when he beat men to a pulp. I reckon you're about the only one I ever seen face him down."

"He isn't afraid of me," said Kaycee. "He isn't afraid of anything. And when the time comes, we'll lock horns proper. What was eating that mule of yours, anyway?"

Eph nodded at the animal, standing over by the patch of wheat grass, its belly bloating, its muzzle frothed—then he pointed to the bunch of blood-red locoweed growing in the grass.

"He's been browsing that locoweed. Makes 'em sicker than a gaunted coach-whip snake with the scours, and nobody can handle 'em for about a week."

"Have to put him in with the sore-back mules," said Kaycee. "Get yourself an extra animal from the cavvy. By the way, didn't Brae say something about you being a prospector?"

"Yeah, I been one in my time."

"Know Montana?"

"Know every gully. Why?" asked Eph.

"I've always thought our cook looked more like a miner than a muleskinner. Maybe you saw him in Montana sometime."

Eph looked toward the wagons. The cook was loading his skillets and kettle into a Conestoga. His chest and shoulders beneath his tight red shirt had the knotted bulky appearance that comes to a man who has swung a pick for his living.

"Sure," said Eph. "I know Lespards. He used to work for the Embar Mining Corporation."

"Oh," said Kaycee. "And maybe you also know a pair of men by the handles of Glenrock and Peso Peters."

Eph scratched stringy gray hair. "I seem to remember a couple of triggermen who went by those names. Seems to me they were on the Embar payroll, too."

"I suppose you know all about Miss O'Hare's diggings?"

"Sure do," said Eph. "Word travels fast when anybody hits a vein as full of yellow as she did. All she needs to do is get those monitors working and she'll be able to pay off that mortgage in a day."

"Tell me one more thing," said Kaycee. "Just who owns the Embar Mining Corporation . . . silent partners as well as otherwise?"

IV

It was Sioux country now, past Pumpkin Buttes, past the hook turn in the Powder River where it stopped flowing south and curved sharply west, up where Dudley's last train had been hit by cholera. It was the girl who woke Kaycee that morning, shaking his shoulder. Dawn threw a dim light over the circle of swagger-boxed Conestogas. Somewhere a man was groaning.

"The men are sick, Kaycee," said Britten O'Hare. "I don't feel very well myself. . . ."

He was suddenly very wide-awake. He stooped out from under the wagon where he had slept and moved through the mist that curled across the open space in milky shreds, gathering softly around the group of men by the ashes of the dead campfire. Several of them were lying down, knees drawn up as if in a cramp. Blacksnake Brae rose from where he had hunkered down beside Green River Jones.

"He started griping like this about half an hour ago. Me, I got a bellyache, too."

Garrett looked around. "Where's Lespards?"

"What's Lespards got to do with it?" growled Brae. "This is cholera. I've seen it before. You get a bellyache first, and then you cramp up, and finally you get weaker than a drink of water."

Kaycee could see the fear in the men's faces, a growing, animal fear of the thing that had haunted them from the beginning of this trip, a thing they couldn't touch or see or fight with their hands. There wasn't much difference between them and a herd of mules just before a stampede. They shifted nervously, sweat bathing pale foreheads, eyes on Brae, waiting. Everything hinged on the stocky, black-haired rum-pot now, and he sensed it.

"We're getting out, Garrett," he said. "We aren't staying here any longer. You kept us as long as you can, but you can't make us die like a bunch of rats here with the cholera."

Kaycee's forehead grew damp with sweat. At first he thought it was only a growing excitement at what was coming. Then nausea swept up from his stomach. The fingers of his hands began to curl uncontrollably. And he knew the perspiration wasn't from any excitement. But this thing between him and Brae had started a long time ago, and he was going to finish it now, whether he had cholera or not.

"Don't be a fool, Brae," snapped Kaycee, his voice strong with the bitter resolve inside him. "If you have the cholera, it won't do any good to slope out now. Chances are you'd never reach Singletree alive. And if you did, you'd only spread it through the town."

Brae shook out a coil of his twenty-foot whip. "Get out of our way, Garrett."

The men began to move forward, crowding one another, voices rising. Brae shook out another coil. And Kaycee knew whatever he said now didn't matter. They were filled with a reasonless animal fear, and all they could think of was running somewhere, anywhere, away from the cholera.

The whole length of Brae's whip lay on the ground, and his forearm rippled as he tensed his grip. "Get out of the way,

Garrett, or I'll whip you out!"

The muscles along Garrett's lean jaw ridged as he ground his teeth shut against the nausea sweeping him, and he spread his legs, and that hard set came into the lines of his face. Roaring a muleskinner's gargantuan oath, Brae snapped his whip behind his head. The men behind him surged forward, yelling, shouting, grabbing for their guns.

Brae had an incredibly swift skill with his blacksnake, and though Garrett had seen it coming, nausea slowed his reflexes. His gun had barely cleared leather when that howling whip crashed across his wrist, knocking the Paterson flying. He grunted with the sudden sharp pain, taking an instinctive step backward. Then they were on him, the whole shouting, swearing bunch of them, Blacksnake Brae's leering, black-whiskered face looming up out of the press, grin triumphant.

The sheer weight of them forced Kaycee to his knees. But he was a big man, and he was hell-mad, and he wasn't finished yet. As the big French-Canadian lurched hard into him, he drove upward, grabbing the man's thick torso and using his momentum to toss him on over his shoulder. With Sevier still flying through the air behind him, Kaycee lunged forward, smashing Escelante Baca fully in the face. The Mexican dropped his gun and fell backward, tripping up the wrangler and a couple of others, who stumbled over his body and fell across him.

Even as Kaycee hit Baca, he twisted sideways and caught Brae with his left arm. Then he lunged his shoulder into the shorter man and heaved him backward. Losing his balance, Brae fell among the rushing men, knocking one aside, crashing into another pair and halting them. It stopped their forward surge in that instant, and Kaycee took a swift step back so there was a little cleared space between him and Brae. Already Blacksnake had struggled free of the men, and, roaring madly, he brought his whip behind his head again.

The gunshot crashed loudly above the shouts and yells. Brae's hand stopped there behind his head, and a blank look crowded the anger from his flushed face. Then he brought his hand back around so he could see it.

The bullet had cut the twenty-foot lash neatly from the whip stock, and all Brae held in his fingers was that foot of braided handle; the rest of the whip lay behind him where it had fallen. Britten O'Hare stood from where she had shot, her new Sam Colt still smoking in her small hand. Her voice had a cool, unshaken sound.

"This fight between you and Kaycee has been building ever since we left Singletree, Brae, and we won't have any peace till it's over. But it's going to be fair."

They shifted away from Brae, and they wouldn't make any wrong moves, not with anyone who could shoot like that. Britten cast a single glance at Kaycee, and in it was all the plea of a girl who knew her only chance of saving everything she had lay in his beating Blacksnake Brae.

Brae dropped what was left of his whip stock and set himself with a sullen growl, a heavy, broad man with a grizzly's strength in his sloping shoulders beneath the dirty red shirt. Kaycee took a breath, and wondered if Brae was as sick as he. Then he moved forward, bending a little to meet the shock of Brae's rush, stripping off his Mackinaw and throwing it aside. And Brae moved forward.

To the sudden scuffle of their boots, and the puff of dust they made, the two men crashed together, bodies meeting with a singular, giving, fleshy thud. Brae had his knee up as he came. Kaycee took it in the groin, his sick grunt lashing out above the sound of their struggle. Brae bent in and got his thick arms around the taller man. All the skill of a hundred barroom brawls was in his sudden vice-like squeeze, his jerking movement to the side.

Kaycee heard the crack of his ribs, stiffened to the sudden shooting pain through his spine. Then he got his long arms going. Right and left, like pistons shooting out from the breadth of his shoulders, pumping into Brae's face. The shorter man's head snapped back to a left, and his grip around Kaycee's waist was pulled free. His head snapped back again to a right, and he reeled away. Kaycee followed, doubling him over with a jab under the heart, then straightening him with a right that howled in and caught Brae on the jaw bone, knocking him over into the dust, flat on his back. He rolled, though, and seemed to bounce up, dancing away and shaking his black head, roaring curses. Then he wasn't moving away any more, and they locked.

Britten O'Hare stood with her face pale and set, her Colt steady on the crowd. The men spread out, shouting encouragement to Brae, jeering Kaycee, forgetting their fear in the excitement of seeing these two hard men smash each other to pulp.

Brae doubled over suddenly in Kaycee's grasp, butting. The air exploded from Kaycee and he sank down like a deflated balloon. Brae's thick hands were on his face, thumbs seeking his eyes. The burly man's heavy river boot smashed into Kaycee's side. Drawing a choked, ragged breath into his lungs, Kaycee fought upward, jerking his head away from Brae's hands, driving out with a weak left into Brae's belly. Then a stronger right. And he stood erect again, smashing his fists into the shorter man, salty blood in his eyes, agony searing him every time he breathed.

Brae took the blows, grunting thickly to the first, and taking a step backward, grunting to the second, and stepping back. The third one put him over on his back.

This time he was a little slower getting up. He shook his head like the stubborn bull he was, and moved in. He ducked a right and shot in with his arms out, taking Kaycee's left jab so he could grapple. What happened after that was a little too fast for the crowd to follow. Kaycee's long leg snaked behind Brae's knee, and they rolled into the dust. Gagged and blinded, Kaycee couldn't tell whether he was above or below. Finally he heaved up, getting a leg under him, throwing Brae away. His head rocked as Brae's boot caught him across the ear. Then Kaycee was striking out again, following Brae back relentlessly. He caught the man on his jaw with a right. Brae lurched, stopped himself from falling. A left sank into his belly, drawing a wheeze. The right slammed him in the face again, and he sprawled full length on the ground.

Kaycee swayed there above the black-bearded man, shirt ripped off his shoulders and hanging from his belt, blood dripping from his chin. Silence held the crowd as they waited for Brae to get up that third time. It took an eternity for him to rise on his elbow, another to raise himself to a sitting position. He spat some teeth, and some blood. Then he tried to get to his feet, failed miserably, sinking back to his elbow.

He was brutal and vicious and a hopeless drunkard, Blacksnake Brae, but a man. There was no rancor in his voice. "All right, Kaycee, I guess it's all over now. Not many men can say they whipped Blacksnake Brae. I get awful mad sometimes, but nobody can say I hold a grudge against a man just because he proved he's better'n me."

Kaycee turned to the others, gasping. "Anybody else think they're sloping out?"

There was indecision in the men's faces, and they wouldn't meet Kaycee's burning gaze.

"Then we'll start from scratch again," said Kaycee. "Lespards didn't desert because he was afraid of the cholera, or the Sioux. I figure he'll be back soon, with Jason Dudley and a crew of his teamsters, and some gents named Glenrock and Peso Peters. Maybe Lespards thought you'd desert when the cholera hit, maybe he thought there wouldn't be anybody here when he came back. And maybe he'll be surprised."

V

The Conestogas stood alone in the little valley, canvas tilts gleaming a little in the late afternoon sun, shadows sprawled across the ashes of dead campfires. There was no cavayard browsing in the grass, no sign of men. The whole scene had a certain desolation to it.

The file of dusty horsemen came down the rutted Bozeman Trail from the direction of Singletree, slowing warily as they sighted the Conestogas. Lespards was in the lead, forking a big dun he had stolen from the cavayard.

Dudley must have been waiting with his men somewhere on the back trail. He sat a stout Morgan, his pompous face dripping sweat, his fustian grayed by dust and bulged at the hip by the six-gun he wore on rare occasions such as this. Matt Farrow was there, too, the Dudley wagon boss, his thick-featured face still bearing the scar of Brae's deadly bullwhip. And Glenrock and Peters riding together, and some twenty Dudley muleskinners, all packing short guns, all hugging the scabbards of their saddle guns under their left knees. Lespards led on confidently, and his voice was loud enough to reach the wagons.

"What'd I tell you, not a man in sight! I'll bet they scattered like a bunch of schoolma'ams from a polecat when they woke up this morning with a bellyache and thought it was cholera."

Dudley reined in his Morgan, looking at the circle of Conestogas suspiciously. "I don't know, Lespards. I don't trust that Garrett. Under any other man, those derelicts would have deserted the first day."

"They didn't leave a single horse in the cavvy," said Lespards sullenly. "The whole camp is empty. What else could you ask for? We had rabbit stew last night, and I spiked it with enough locoweed to make a whole cavvy sick for a week. They thought

83

it tasted funny, but I said maybe I put too much seasoning in it, and everybody but me ate some. That locoweed acts just like cholera. And I'm telling you, not even Kaycee Garrett could stop those fools if they thought they had cholera."

Dudley turned to Farrow. "Have your boys got the axes?"

Farrow nodded. "When we get through smashing those monitors, there won't be piping left to pump a drink of water."

"Get your guns out then, and keep your eyes peeled," said Dudley. "I've been fighting Kaycee too long to take any chances."

The soft thud of hoofs was the only sound. A strained line came into the men's bodies, sitting their horses stiffly. Even Lespards shifted uneasily in his saddle. Finally Dudley halted near the wagons, nodding at Farrow. The wagon boss swung from his mount, unstrapping the big double-bitted axe from the whangs on the skirt. The other teamsters followed suit, gathering around him, eyeing the wagons reluctantly.

"Well, damn it, let's go," snarled Farrow, stepping forward.

Two men followed him. The others spread out in twos and threes, each group going toward a wagon. Farrow slowed as he reached the first Conestoga. Then, with an impatient curse, he reached up and grabbed the chain on the tailgate, raising his boot to swing aboard.

The shout that broke the strained silence came from within the wagon, and it was Kaycee's voice. "Up and at 'em, damn you! You're a bunch of yellow dogs who wouldn't know guts if they were thrown in your face, but you're going out there now if I have to carry you myself!"

The tailgate slammed down, catching Farrow in the face. He sank to the ground with a hoarse sob. And standing there in the rear of the wagon was Kaycee, shoving Escelante Baca, the Mexican, out in front of him, giving Green River Jones a kick that sent him sprawling from the wagon bed. Still yelling, Kaycee followed them, throwing himself on the nearest of the teamsters who had come in behind Farrow.

Kaycee had guessed Dudley would come from the back trail, and had chosen a wagon nearest that approach. All of his crew was sick as dogs, nauseated, cramped. And though he had beaten Brae, though the derelicts had given in to him, Kaycee still couldn't trust them. As his body struck that Dudley teamster, carrying him to the ground, Kaycee still didn't know whether his men would back him, or whether he was alone.

He rose up on his knees, straddling the man's body, clubbing with his Paterson. On the second blow the big teamster collapsed.

Farrow had regained his feet. And as Kaycee rose, he caught sight of the man's blurred figure to the side. The wagon boss had his axe up over his head, already beginning the downward swing that would cleave Kaycee like splitting a rail. Whirling, desperately trying to thumb back his hammer for a shot, Kaycee knew he would never be in time.

Farrow lunged forward, but the axe in his hands dropped down his back instead of arcing over his head into Kaycee. Startled, Kaycee stepped away from the falling body. As Farrow hit the ground, Kaycee saw Britten O'Hare standing in a wagon opening, with her smoking .45 already aiming at another.

Green River Jones stood where he had landed after being booted from the wagon, and he was standing over a gutted teamster and pulling another skinning knife from the rawhide thong holding up his leggings.

Only then did Dudley and his groups of teamsters begin to recover from their stunned surprise. The whole thing had happened in one blinding flash, and had been so unexpected. But now they were whirling, grabbing for guns, dropping axes. Dudley wheeled his horse, fumbling beneath his fustian for his six-shooter. Kaycee cast a desperate glance at the other Conestogas. He had planted Brae and the rest of his crew in those wagons. If they failed him now. . . .

Then Brae's roar sounded from the tilt of an ancient wagon. "Come on, you rotgut boot-hill muleskinners! Kaycee's our boss now, and I said I didn't hold no grudge against him, and you're going to prove it. Get out there and show those teamsters how real 'skinners can fight!"

Sevier tumbled over a tailgate as if he'd been kicked out, and another man followed him the same way. Then Brae leaped out and on top of a hapless Dudley man. The whole circle of wagons erupted then, drunks and barflies and outlaws and even murderers, all sick as dogs, but all following Brae, following Kaycee.

Peso Peters suddenly loomed in front of Kaycee, running for his horse. They saw each other about the same time. Peters raised his gun, hatred twisting his mouth. Kaycee's whole body stiffened as he thumbed back his hammer for a shot from the hip. Then he caught the hammer before it fell because another man had rushed in between him and Peters.

Sevier, the French-Canadian, yelling deep-throated curses and cutting Peso Peters down with a wild, slamming volley. A big, red-shirted teamster shot Sevier in the belly before Peters had hit the ground, and the French-Canadian staggered to a halt, bent over, sagged onto his face. Escelante Baca let both barrels go on his sawed-off shotgun and the red-shirted teamster followed Sevier down with his face blown off.

Kaycee stumbled over Peters's body, and Sevier's body, hunting for Dudley. But the battle had raged in front of the man, hiding him from Kaycee for a moment.

Something pounded into Kaycee's leg. He staggered, throwing a snap shot at the half seen figure in the dust and smoke, and only after he saw the man go down did he realize he was shot in the leg. He lurched to a knee, trying to rise back up again, seeing Brae where he had risen from the man he'd jumped down on.

A pair of Dudley teamsters came through the smoke, running for their horses. Brae was in their way, and they began shooting fast, still going forward. Brae whirled, his six-shooter bucking from the hip.

But all his skill was with a bullwhip, and he had to empty every shot from his gun before one of these Dudley men went down. The other kept right on coming, shooting. Brae staggered back, clutching at his side as a slug caught him.

He must have known how much chance he had, facing that blazing six-shooter with his empty iron. Yet he steadied himself and bent forward to meet the man's charge, roaring defiantly in the teeth of hot lead.

Kaycee was on his feet by then. He took a lurching step forward, throwing down on the Dudley teamster charging Brae. His gun bucked in his hand, and the sound was lost in the roar of battle, and he knew he had missed. His second shot was lost, too, in the raging sound, but it struck home. The running man faltered, slid to his knees, flopped over on his face.

Still clutching his side, Brae turned. When he saw Kaycee standing there with the smoking Paterson, a grin split his black beard. Then, on past Brae, Kaycee saw Dudley.

The pompous man hadn't been known to leave the environs of Singletree in years. He must have wanted to stop Britten O'Hare's shipment pretty desperately to come this far north himself. Desperately enough so that if he couldn't smash it, he'd burn it up.

His Morgan was standing nervously by one of the wagons on the far side of the circle. And stooping to light a pile of brush that laid against the wagon wheel was Jason Dudley. Glenrock stood to one side. He had an empty tar bucket in one hand, the bucket that hung on the tailgate of every wagon, filled with a mixture of resin, tar, and tallow that the teamsters used to grease their axles. It was inflammable enough, and while the fire it started wouldn't do much damage to the steel piping and nozzles of the monitors, it would certainly burn the dry old wagons to the ground, and keep the girl from getting her equipment to Montana. Kaycee had lost sight of Britten in the smoke and dust, but thought of her helped him to break into a limping run, passing Farrow's body, jumping an outspanned wagon tongue, landing so hard on his wounded leg that he sank to his knees again. He gasped with the agony, fought upward.

This was no pot-shooting at a bunch of wild teamsters who couldn't hit a mule at three paces with a scatter-gun. Glenrock made his living by his skill with a gun. And Dudley had always won before.

Knowing that, Kaycee stumbled forward. Flame leaped up the side of the wagon, and Dudley stood. Kaycee brought up his Paterson. But Dudley saw him, and ducked around the wagon, moving incredibly fast for such a bulk. Kaycee's shot hit wooden sideboards where Dudley had been an instant before. Then Dudley was behind the wagon and only Glenrock stood there, settling into a habitual crouch, so sure of his skill that he let Kaycee fire first. He must have known that Kaycee couldn't hit anything, running forward like that with a game leg that made him jerk every time it hit the ground, throwing his aim all off. Kaycee found it out after his third shot.

Then Glenrock fired, and the slug hit Kaycee in the shoulder, and he had to stop anyway. Glenrock's second slug missed him because he had staggered and was falling sideways.

He didn't go clear down, though. He caught himself with his good leg, straightened, holding his Paterson carefully out in front of him. Glenrock might have had his hammer eared back for his third shot, because he was that fast, but he didn't let it drop. Kaycee's big five-shot boomed with a finality. Kaycee saw the dust puff from Glenrock's vest above the heart. Then Glenrock was falling forward.

The fire was licking up the side of the wagon. Kaycee knew once it reached the canvas there would be no stopping it. He stumbled to the Conestoga, kicked dirt at the flames, tore his shirt off, and beat at them. He reached up and ripped a piece of canvas from the hoops before it could catch fire. His hands were burned and his chest was blistered when he finally realized the fire was out. His right hand was so bad that he had to put up his left to help hold the gun.

He punched a couple of exploded rim-fires out and fumbled two fresh ones from his belt. Then, holding the Paterson in both hands, he moved toward the wagon tongue. Dudley's Morgan was still fiddling around on the inside of the circle. Kaycee knew Dudley wouldn't try to get away on foot—he knew this country better than that. He would be waiting, then, on the other side of the Conestoga. The lines in Kaycee's face had taken on that terrible granite harshness. Dudley, now, the man he had been fighting so long and so bitterly, the man who had always won before, in any game he played. . . .

Kaycee crouched over the tongue, waiting for a second at the corner of the high wagon box. Just as he remembered that Dudley could see his legs beneath the bed, there came a small thumping sound around the corner. He leaped out, turning, hammer carried back under his left thumb, nerves screaming for the release of his booming shot.

He was looking at a small round stone that had bounced off the wagon wheel and was just rolling to a stop. Jason Dudley had thrown it. Knowing how he had been trapped, knowing what was behind him, Kaycee let his body keep right on going, its own momentum carrying it over. Dudley's shot crashed out from back of him, the bullet clipping at the holster on Kaycee's hip, clacking into the wooden side of a Conestoga.

Twisting as he fell, Kaycee was facing Dudley when he hit

the ground. His Paterson was still cocked, still held out in two hands like that. It bucked once.

Dudley took the bullet squarely and went down with all his weight, a big pompous man who had wanted too much out of life and who was dead before he hit the ground.

Kaycee was doing a bad job of trying to rise when the girl's soft arms slipped around him, helping him up.

"I thought I told you to stay in the wagon," he said.

"Brae and the others have sent Dudley's teamsters packing and it's all over," she murmured, casting a glance at Dudley. "How in the world did you know Lespards would come back with Dudley?"

"I half suspected Dudley at first," said Kaycee. "He had good enough reason for not wanting me to go up the Bozeman. If I got through with your stuff, I'd get all the contracts he couldn't meet this year because of the cholera. But when I talked with Eph, I found Dudley had an even bigger iron in the fire than that. Not many people know it, but Jason Dudley is silent partner in the Embar Mining Corporation, owning a controlling share."

The girl saw it then. "And he would much rather have had my mine than the money I'd pay on that mortgage. Then it was Dudley who imported Glenrock and Peters to kill you, and that mess in Jason Street was deliberate, trying to start a riot so he could shoot up your crew."

Kaycee nodded. "Lespards was an ace in the hole. I found him in a saloon and had to sober him up, just like some of the others. But Dudley had planted him. Even when I found out from Eph that Lespards had worked for Embar, and that Dudley owned Embar, I couldn't come right out and accuse Lespards of being a Dudley man until I had more proof. And we've got it now. I guess you heard him say what he put in the stew?"

"I'm glad it's locoweed instead of cholera," she said.

"If I didn't have such a big stomach ache, I'd ask you something," he muttered.

"Ask me anyway."

"Have they got a parson in Virginia City?"

She didn't answer. But she didn't have to, because suddenly she was in his arms, taffy hair soft against his burned chest. He forgot the pain of his wounded shoulder, and his leg. Blacksnake Brae had come into the open space between the wagons, still holding his side, hand blood-soaked. Several others were behind him, all gaping at Kaycee and the girl.

But Kaycee didn't mind that, really. It seemed fitting that they should be present. After all, they were his crew now.

★ ★ ★ ★ ★

Wild Men of the Fur Frontier

★ ★ ★ ★ ★

Under the title "Trail of Lonely Bear", Les Savage, Jr., completed this story early in September, 1944, and sent it to his agent. It was sold quickly to Mike Tilden at Popular Publications who changed the title to "Wild Men of the Fur Frontier" when it appeared in *Star Western* (1/45). The author was paid $255.

I

Dobie Burton began hearing about the crazy Scotsman as soon as he reached the Rocky Mountain House. In 1827, this was the rendezvous of every trapper who came to St. Louis to sell his season's harvest of beaver pelts. It was a huge taproom near the Vide Poche, with a row of gleaming mahogany center columns supporting its high hand-hewn beams that looked down on the oppressive stink of sweat and buckskin and tobacco and gunpowder emanating from the jostling crowd of trappers and mountain men and *voyageurs*. A bunch was sitting, cross-legged, around a buffalo robe near the wall, playing the inevitable old sledge, and the very youthful Dobie halted there a moment.

The man dealing was a picture of dissipation, his belly overflowing the rawhide hackamore he wore for a belt, his long black hair as greasy as the elk-hide leggings he wore. Unshaven jowls puffed around slack, sensuous lips, and his dissolute eyes were heavy-lidded and bloodshot.

"I seen it, I tell you," he growled, jamming his big Green River knife to a more comfortable position between his tremendous thighs. "Ain't much can scare Hooker Spanial, see, but I couldn't eat supper that night. Two American Fur men, up on the Big Dry. No telling how long they'd been dead. Nothing but that Scotsman's sword could have done it. One of them was chopped 'most in two at the waist."

"Sledge," said a hatchet-faced French *voyageur*, slapping a horse-hide card down and raking in the pot. The prodigious Hooker Spanial counted five silver pieces from his felt hat upturned on the floor, and threw them to the center of the robe. The other trappers anted, and the Frenchman began shuffling.

"The Scotchman?" he said. "Ian Kenmore, *non? Oui.* He was here in Saint Looey about 'Twenty-One. Never saw such a big man. Seven feet tall maybe. And that sword he carried. *Sacre bleu!* As long as him. They say he went crazy when American Fur shoved Baffin Bay Company out of the Three Forks country."

Dobie Burton moved closer, intrigued. Spanial lost the second hand, and cursed bitterly. He counted out another pile of silver, took a deep pull at the horn of Monongahela.

"They say a lot of things," he muttered sullenly, shifting his Green River again. "They say some American Fur trappers stole Kenmore's daughter and sold her to the Indians for their help in burning Kenmore's Big Dry post. Fine, educated girl, that daughter. Must 'a' driven Kenmore wild. They say Kenmore had a hundred thousand dollars' worth of furs cached somewhere on the Teton River."

"Sledge!" cried the Frenchman, slapping down his card. "A hundred thousand in beaver plews on the Teton? Why not? Kenmore was chief factor for all the Baffin Bay posts north of Colter's Hell. Maybe you go crazy, too, if someone took all that away from you and sold your daughter to the Indians besides. Maybe you want to chop up all the American Fur men on the Mizzou, and poach their furs in the bargain."

"I'll want to poach your furs if you win another pot," growled Hooker. Then he became aware of Dobie Burton, standing there behind him, and turned his bloodshot gaze upward. "Let your eyes bug out any farther, greenhorn, and I'll knock 'em off. What are you doing there?"

Dobie wiped a big hand nervously against the tattered leg of his homespuns. He had slept in a ditch the night before and his blond thatch stood, stiff and dirty, above a pale, gaunt face. His wide blue eyes held the innocence of youth, but his flannel shirt was strained a little by his heavy shoulders.

"Nothing," said Dobie. "Just watching."

The huge man turned his greasy black head to the Frenchman. "Watching is right. That why you won so many pots, Terrebonne? You plant the greenhorn behind me?"

"*Parbleu*," said the *voyageur*. "*Non,* Hooker. . . ."

"*Non,* hell," snarled Hooker Spanial, and was on his feet with an amazing ease for such a ponderous hulk. He turned and grabbed Dobie's shirt in a fat, hairy fist. "You been watching my cards and signalin' them to Terrebonne!"

"No," said Dobie, and reached up automatically to grab Hooker's fist. "Take your hands off me."

The surprise in the fat man's face twisted suddenly to pain. Still grasping Hooker's hand in both big fists, Dobie tore it off his shirt and used it to shove the huge man backward. Spanial tripped over a squatting trapper and fell onto the buffalo robe with a force that shook the floor, scattering cards and silver with his flailing boots. Again he jumped lithely to his feet, his wicked Green River whipping out of its long brass-studded scabbard. "Damn' greenhorn!" he bellowed. "I'll split your gizzard four ways from the middle and make you eat each piece whole."

"Take it easy, Hooker."

Spanial stopped himself with a visible effort, standing there with the skinning knife held out, low. The soft voice had come from behind Dobie, and Dobie turned, following the fat man's surprised gaze to where the speaker stood.

He was tall and skinny as a split rail; his eyes were sleepy and humorous in a long face the color of cured buckskin. Over his tattered elk-hide shirt was slung a belt full of his possibles—

bullet mold and powder horn and tiger-tail bullet pouch and flint-and-steel pack. He had his brown fists on the curly maple butts of two long pistols slung on his broad belt by their brass belt hooks.

"The greenhorn wasn't working with Terrebonne," he said lazily. "You just aren't a very good card player, Hooker."

Hooker's fat jowls turned purple. "Keep out of this, Kentuck."

"Maybe you'd like to see what that Green River can do against a couple of AJ smoothbores," said Kentuck, grinning slowly.

Hooker Spanial's bloodshot eyes dropped to the pistols at Kentuck's belt. For a moment longer he stood there on tiptoe, the knife held out. Then he dropped it, and a smirk twisted his thick lips.

"All right, Kentuck," he said. "Maybe this isn't the time. I sort of been waiting for you to show up here, but perhaps this isn't the time. Later, perhaps."

"I'll be around," said Kentuck indifferently. Then he slapped a horny hand on Dobie's shoulder. "I guess you got stronger hands than Hooker expected, boy, but next time, carry a little better argument. What say we go over and see how the vittles are getting along? Rocky here has a dish of greens and pot likker he cooks from slick thistle and poke shoots that'd make a Kentucky hound stand up on its tail. You look like something a beaver's been chewing on all winter. I'll bet you ain't et in a week. Run away from home?"

He chuckled as Dobie started to protest. "Never mind, never mind. I run away myself. Want to be a trapper, maybe? Want to go out and fight the Arikarees and wear buckskin britches till they get so stiff they'll stand up by themselves and kick you if you try to wash 'em? Where you from?"

"Tennessee," said Dobie, and found himself relaxing under

the drawling voice as they moved away from the card game.

The man saw Dobie's admiring gaze on the pistols, and patted them with a grin. "Spanial didn't want to stack his Green River against 'em, did he? I should think not. Kentucky pistols, boy. Converted 'em from flintlock to percussion myself. Knock a varmint's eye out at a hundred paces. I been cutting beaver sign through all the ice between here and Colter's Hell since last January, and now I'm going to throw a drunk the likes of which Saint Looey ain't seen in a blue 'coon's age. And I need someone to throw it with. You just set down at my table, and we'll fill our bellies before we go to work on that Monongahela. . . ."

He stopped suddenly, with his hand on the chair he was going to pull out from the table near the wall, and he was looking behind Dobie. "All right, boy, you'd better go now."

The sudden change took Dobie by surprise.

"What?"

Kentucky's voice didn't rise, but it took on a startling intensity. "I said you'd better go. Get out!"

Then Dobie saw the ponderous hulk of Hooker Spanial moving through the crowd toward them. "If it's because of him, I won't go."

"He ain't coming because of you," said Kentuck swiftly. "He's got his friends to back him now, and he ain't coming because of you. You're a nice kid. Maybe we'll be meeting again. Get out now."

"No," said Hooker Spanial, coming up from behind Dobie. "No, Kentuck, if the kid is in this, he'd better stay."

Dobie saw the other men moving toward them now. One was the white-coated French *voyageur* Hooker had been playing with—Terrebonne. Another was a Mexican with a big glazed sombrero casting his face into a sharp mordant shadow.

"The kid isn't in it," said Kentuck. "Let him go, Hooker."

"I'd like to have a talk with you, Kentuck," said Hooker. "Both of you, in the back room."

"What about?"

"About Ian Kenmore," said Hooker. "The loco Scotchman who's been hacking those American Fur trappers to death and poaching their pelts. I hear you and Colonel Harvey Gillis was up around the Big Dry this January. You didn't happen to come across those two American Fur men I was telling about?"

"Maybe. Maybe not. What about it?"

"I got an idea that the Scotchman didn't do it," said Hooker. His bloodshot eyes rested a moment on the Frenchman who had moved around to Kentuck's side.

"Then you're the only one," said Kentuck, and turned slightly so he could see Terrebonne as well as Hooker. "What else could work men over like that except Kenmore's sword?"

"Oh, then you did see them?"

"I didn't say that," said Kentuck. "Tell your Mex not to move around by the wall any farther."

"Let's go in the back room," said Hooker.

"Don't think I will," said Kentuck.

"Let's go in the back room," said the man by the wall.

Dobie hadn't seen him. He must have been standing behind one of the mahogany columns all along, and had moved out while their attention was on Hooker and the others. He was little and red-headed with a scar at one side of his mouth that twisted his lips up. He held a big H.T. Cooper pistol in one freckled hand.

"The hell we will," said Kentuck, and dropped suddenly. The Cooper boomed, but Kentuck was already below the level of the table. He heaved up beneath it with one shoulder, both his Kentucky pistols in his hands. The table smashed back into the redhead.

The Mexican threw himself at Kentuck from the far side.

Still bent over from lifting the table, Kentuck fired one of his pistols. The Mexican screamed and doubled over. His momentum carried him into Kentuck.

The man's hurtling weight whirled Kentuck half around, and he staggered back, trying to regain his balance. Spanial leaped on Kentuck from behind, catching him around the neck with one fat arm, the Green River flashing in the air.

Kentuck tried to jerk his unfired pistol from between him and the Mexican, but the man's dead weight held it pinned between them, and the realization that he would never make it was in his face as he looked up toward Hooker's downcoming blade.

Then Dobie's chair smashed into Hooker's head. The boy had swung it clear around from behind him, and it knocked the man off Kentuck and slammed him up against one of the mahogany posts.

"Damn greenhorn!" screamed Hooker. He threw himself away from the column toward Dobie, with the side of his cheek streaming blood.

Dobie stepped in, swinging the chair, and smashed the knife from Hooker's hand. Then he brought what was left of the chair up on the back swing and caught the huge man fully in the face. Hooker crashed back against the column for the second time, and slid down to the floor, pawing at his face and making small sobbing noises.

The redhead had got the table off him and was scrambling over its slanting top. Dobie threw himself bodily, and the both of them slid back down the top and brought up against the wall. The redhead went limp beneath Dobie. Then something hit Dobie on the back of the head, stunningly. The tinkling sound of broken glass followed him into deep darkness.

II

The monotonous creaking was the first thing young Dobie Burton heard when he came to. Then he felt the damp breeze against his cheek. And finally the throbbing pain in his head. Someone was shaking him, and he pawed feebly at the hands holding his shirt. Finally he opened his eyes. He saw the face of the man holding him, and knew he would never forget it as long as he lived.

The softness of that face was almost womanish—or feline. The eyes watching Dobie were filled with little lights, as tawny as the long mustache drooping over the thin, curling upper lip. The hands, too, were pale and soft like a woman's, yet possessed a strength that held Dobie's weight off the boards without apparent effort.

"A greenhorn." The man's voice was contemptuous. "Why in John Colter's Hell did you have to pack him aboard this keelboat, Kentuck?"

Kentuck's lazy drawl came from somewhere to the side. "If it wasn't for the greenhorn, Colonel, I wouldn't be here. Hooker would have slit my gizzard with that Green River if the kid hadn't swatted him off my back with a chair. Hooker thought the kid was with me. They would have finished his pemmican if I hadn't got him out. It was the least I could do."

Dobie was looking at the man above him now, in a strange sort of awe. Colonel? Colonel Harvey Gillis? There was no mountain man more famous—not John Colter or Hugh Glass or Jim Bridger. Even in the remote Tennessee village where he had been born, Dobie had heard the dim legends of this man.

Dobie's cousin had gone north with Ashley's fur brigades in 1823, and had come back full of the stories of Colonel Harvey Gillis. It was hard to reconcile those fabulous myths with this small, square, soft-spoken man—until he looked at the eyes again. Gillis wore a Pawnee jacket with fringed epaulets and beadwork in the front, and his golden sideburns swept from beneath a black wolf-skin hat streaked with white. His only weapon was a singularly long Delaware tomahawk stuck through a belt of Cree wampum.

"Why did you tangle with Hooker?" he asked Kentuck, letting Dobie back down. "I told you not to get drunk. I told you to stay free of that fat weasel-bear."

"Hooker forced it," said Kentuck. "Maybe he knows, or maybe he just made a good guess, but, either way, he forced it."

"Knows what?" asked Dobie.

Colonel Harvey's snarl was soft. "Shut up."

"Oh, leave him alone," said Kentuck.

The tawny-haired man turned sharply toward Kentuck, anger whispering into his voice. "Don't talk that way to me, Kentuck. You had no right mixing him up in this just because he saved your life. You're a sentimental fool and you're worse when you're drunk. Sometimes I could. . . ."

He quit speaking abruptly, and his tawny eyes were turned past Kentuck. Dobie had seen it by then, too, and he felt suddenly cold.

They stood on the wet deck boards of a keelboat, with the shadowy banks of the Missouri passing by on either side. It was a long wooden craft with a cargo box taking up its center, and a narrow walk on either side between box and rail. Dobie knew this walk to be the *passe avant,* upon which stood the polers, twelve red-shirted French *voyageurs* on each passageway, each with a long pole of turned ash. The captain aboard these French riverboats was a *patron,* and he stood up near the bow to give his orders. The *voyageurs* were waiting near the bow, now, in their line, and the *patron*'s voice carried down to Dobie.

"*À bas les perches!*"

The *voyageurs* thrust their poles down into the shallow water until they struck bottom. Then they walked in a line down the *passe avant,* keeping their poles dug into the mud, until they reached the stern.

"Levez les perches!" called the *patron.*

The two lines of Frenchmen lifted their poles, turned, moved back toward the bow down the narrow passage between cargo box and rail. They halted in the bow and awaited the *patron*'s order to lower their poles and begin all over again. But it was the *patron* himself at whom Colonel Harvey was staring. The man had climbed onto the cargo box and was walking back toward the stern. He was huge and gross, perhaps three hundred pounds in his dirty black river boots, yet he walked with a springy, bouncy stride.

"À bas les perches," he said, reaching the end of the box. Then he turned, chuckling. "Well, well, the fabulous Colonel Harvey, the amazing, unbelievable, legendary Colonel Harvey Gillis. How nice to see you."

"What does this mean, Hooker?" said Colonel Harvey. "When I signed on this keelboat for the upriver trip yesterday, Jules Lebaron was *patron.*"

"Something unfortunate happened to Captain Lebaron in Saint Looey," said Hooker. "So now I'm *patron. Levez les perches.*"

In the stern, the *voyageurs* raised their poles and turned to march back. Dobie recognized the man who had been working the long handle of the rudder now. He was little and short and red-headed and his mouth was twisted up at one side by a scar. He carried an H.T. Cooper pistol hooked onto his belt.

Hooker dropped off the cargo box as if he weighed no more than half his actual poundage, grinning. "I see you have tabbed the red-headed gent. He is known as Rudder. He didn't like the way you treated him last night, greenhorn. Your name isn't on the passenger list. I take it you're with Colonel Harvey Gillis and company?"

"No," said the colonel softly. "The greenhorn wasn't with Kentuck last-night and he isn't with us now. Putting his pelts in our apishamore isn't the only mistake you made, Hooker. What you tried to do last night was another mistake. Don't make it again."

Hooker glanced at the man named Rudder, and then at the two lines of *voyageurs* marching sternward with their poles, and chuckled. "It's a long way up the Mizzou, Colonel Harvey."

"Yes," said the colonel sibilantly, "but it won't do you any good. There are just as many free trappers signed on as passengers as you have in your crew of mangy Neds, and I guess you know whose blankets the mountain men will play sledge on if it comes to anything like you have in your mind. Think it over. Then if you still want to continue what you didn't finish last night, why go right ahead. Yes, Hooker, just go right ahead."

Hooker flushed, and didn't answer for a moment. Then he began to chuckle, and his huge belly quivered against the brass-studded scabbard of his Green River. "Of course, Colonel Harvey. You misconstrue me. This greenhorn, now. If he isn't with you, he'll either have to pay his passage or work for it."

"I haven't any money," said Dobie.

Kentuck reached for a fringed pouch slung beneath his bullet mold. "I'll. . . ."

"No," said Colonel Harvey, moving in front of him. "The boy isn't with us."

"Then get along up front, greenhorn," said Hooker. "I'll put you on relief pole."

Dobie moved up the narrow walk between the cargo box and the rail, hearing the deck boards pop wetly to Hooker's bouncing tread behind him. He had reached the bow end of the *passe avant* by the time the polers started back, and moved in front of the box to be out of their way. He was now out of sight of the stern.

"Levez les perches," Hooker growled over his shoulder. "Now, boy, you'd better talk. I know you're with Colonel Harvey, whether he says so or not. You just tell me what you know and you won't get hurt."

"What do you want to know?"

"Don't act dumb," said Hooker, and reached out a fat hand for Dobie's shirt. "You know what I want to know."

Dobie slapped the hand aside and slid from between Hooker and the box so he was in the open, whirling to face the big man. "Keep your hands off me, Hooker. I'll work for my passage, and take orders from you as long as they have to do with that. Just don't make the mistake of laying your hands on me."

Hooker took a step toward Dobie, then stopped. He settled his prodigious torso forward a little, rubbing a hand across the scars showing white against the purple, veined flesh of his unshaven jowl. Finally he spoke, and his voice rasped a little with his effort at control.

"All right, my boy," he said. "This is just the beginning. I have plenty of time to find out what you know, and plenty of ways. You'll talk before we reach the Three Forks. Believe me, you'll talk."

The days were twelve hours of hell for Dobie, and the nights were dead things of sick, exhausted sleep from which he woke unrefreshed. His work on the farm had hardened him, but it had been sheer indolence compared to poling the Missouri. The skin was worn from the palms of his hands by the ash pole until there was nothing but raw, bleeding flesh with no chance to heal. In the morning the blood had frozen and congealed over the wounds, and his body was so stiff some of the *voyageurs* had to lift him from his soggy blanket and stand him on his feet. Then the pole would chafe his palms until the blood streamed down again, and the stiffness of his body turned to a dull, excruciating ache that made it agony to move a muscle.

The pork and lyed corn foisted on the poorly paid Frenchmen made Dobie deathly sick the first meal, and he couldn't eat for several days following. Kentuck gave him a ration of the trappers' jerked buffalo hump, and though he felt no immediate effects, the boy knew it was the only thing that kept him from total collapse.

Hooker drove him unmercifully at the poles, found extra duty for him at night, taking delight in waiting till Dobie had rolled into his fetid blanket and then coming with orders to pitch the bow planks or unload some wetted cargo from the hold to be dried.

But Dobie had left home filled with the burning desire to see the mysterious lands west of the Missouri, and that desire was still in him, driving him on when he wanted to lie down and die.

The change came so gradually that he didn't recognize it himself until that day at Robidoux's Post. Kentuck had been putting a poultice of lard and gunpowder on his raw hands every night, and finally the wounds began to heal, and the skin to grow back and toughen, and the day came when he bled no more on the pole. He was able to rise by himself now, and the stiffness was disappearing.

They reached Robidoux's Post at the end of March, running the keelboat in between a Mackinaw and a train of bull boats moored at the rickety landing below the bluffs where Joe Robidoux had his white-frame trading houses. Colonel Harvey waited till Dobie was alone on the shore to speak with him.

"We decided you're not getting off here, Dobie. From now on you're with Kentuck and me. Your passage will be paid and you won't have to worry about Hooker Spanial any more. We've been watching you upriver and think you have the makings of a trapper. Now you stay down here and watch our outfit while

Kentuck and I go up and see if Joe Robidoux hasn't got a pair of leather leggin's for you. When we head on upriver, you'll be a mountain man for sure."

Dobie felt the warmth flushing his cheeks. To be accepted by the fabulous Colonel Harvey Gillis—he had even hesitated to dream about it. Every man north of St. Louis would have given his Jake Hawkins rifle to join the colonel's party. Watching the colonel and Kentuck go off up the beach, Dobie felt happier than he had ever been before.

"Unloading some trade goods we got in Saint Looey for this post," said Hooker, leaning over the thwarts. "Get in the hold and lend a hand."

"Sure," said Dobie, "for the last time." He laughed at the surprise on Hooker's dissolute face.

Dobie dropped down the ladder into the cargo box and passed the bunks rigged for the trappers at the forward end. The boats sometimes hauled upriver empty and came back down full of pelts, but Robidoux had ordered some whiskey and blankets, and the after end of the box was piled high with the trade goods shipped from St. Louis.

Several men were rolling out a huge iron kettle from between kegs of Monongahela. Dobie had stooped to help with the kettle, when he heard the forward hatch close with a soft, popping sound. He straightened, heard the ladder creaking beneath someone's descent, and then the deck boards echoing to a springy tread behind him.

One of the men straightened from the kettle now, and he saw that it was Rudder. The other man came from behind the kegs of whiskey; he was the hawk-faced Frenchman, Terrebonne.

"Well," said Spanial, and the pop of deck boards ceased beneath his feet as he stopped behind the boy. "So Colonel Harvey and his friend went up to Robidoux's for a while. I told you it was a long way up the Mizzou, boy. I told you there was more ways than one of making you talk."

Dobie shifted until he stood with his back against the port wall, facing them. With Hooker were two more *voyageurs*, little cast-iron men in white coats as grimy as their unshaven faces. Hooker settled his weight forward a little, caressing the leather butt of his wicked Green River.

"Now," he said. "We'll start with Colonel Harvey. Every year, he and Kentuck disappear into the country around the Teton River for three months or so, and come back loaded with more beaver pelts than any other outfit gets all year. Last season, the two of them brought in over fifteen hundred pelts. You're going to tell me how they do it."

"The Teton River?" said Dobie. "That's where the crazy Scotchman is supposed to be, isn't it?"

"Kenmore?" Hooker's glance at Rudder was barely perceptible. "Yes, he had some posts along the Teton."

"And he was supposed to have cached a hundred thousand dollars' worth of pelts in the region," said Dobie. "Back in the Rocky Mountain House, you seemed to think Kentuck had seen those two American Fur men Kenmore was supposed to have murdered on the Big Dry. That's near the Teton, isn't it? Is that what you're interested in, Hooker . . . Kenmore's cache?"

The boards squeaked beneath the hawk-faced Terrebonne as he moved in between Hooker and Rudder. The other two *voyageurs* shifted onto Hooker's other side until they blocked the way toward the front hatch. The air suddenly seemed close and stifling to Dobie, and he heard his own breathing, fast and harsh.

The fat man was chuckling. "You aren't asking the questions, boy. I am. Of course I'm interested in Kenmore. Every man on the river is. Maybe Colonel Harvey has found Kenmore's cache of beaver, maybe he hasn't. It would be one explanation of the amazing harvests he brings in every season. But there are others that might fit better. I want them. Kentuck *did* see those two dead American Fur trappers on the Big Dry last January, didn't he? In fact, he might even have been around when they were killed, eh? That's what I want to know. You'll tell me, won't you, boy?"

The deck above Dobie's head groaned to someone passing forward. There was no use waiting any longer. Dobie understood what would happen if he didn't tell them, and he couldn't tell them, so there was no use waiting. He licked his lips. "No, Hooker, I won't tell you."

A dull red crept up the rolls of fat that formed Hooker's neck. Someone dropped a pole into the bow thwarts with a muffled thud. Hooker began sliding his Green River from its brass-studded case. "You're all alone down here, boy. . . ."

He gasped with the weight of Dobie's body suddenly hurtling out from the wall into his flabby paunch. Dobie had shoved himself with his hands from the boards, and he carried Hooker's bulk on backward to crash against the opposite wall. He put one of his big fists into the man's belly and felt Hooker's grunt explode hot against his face, and grabbed the man's wrist and twisted the knife from his fingers.

He had taken the other four men off guard, and they were just jumping after Dobie as he whirled. He threw himself to meet the first man, with the Green River out. It was the Frenchman, Terrebonne, and the blade went to its leather-bound hilt in his belly.

Rudder jumped to one side for a clear shot at Dobie. The boy left the knife in Terrebonne so he could catch the Frenchman's body with both hands as it fell forward, and heaved it at Rudder with a grunt. The redhead's H.T. Cooper boomed, and the Frenchman's body jerked to the slug that would have taken Dobie, and then smashed on back into the redhead. Rudder fell onto the iron kettle with a metallic crash, the dead Terrebonne sprawled on top of him.

The other two *voyageurs* were on Dobie then, their weight throwing him to his knees. He caught one of them around the waist and heaved upward. He heard the pop of broken ribs and the man's scream, and only then did he realize what it was, in him. He had been strong enough before, from laboring at the plow, but, poling a keelboat twelve hours a day against the wild current of the Missouri was something that would either kill a man or give him a strength almost superhuman. It hadn't killed Dobie. Now he felt the full surge of his savage, animal power, and with an exultant bellow, he stood up from his knees and threw the Frenchman bodily back against the wall. The impact shook the whole boat. The *voyageur* slid to the floor and lay still.

With his amazing agility, Hooker had risen again. But Dobie had already whirled to put his shoulder into the other *voyageur*'s midsection, and his driving legs carried the man across the deck into Hooker. All three of them crashed into the starboard supports.

Sprawled across the two men, Dobie drove a set of knuckles into the *voyageur*'s beard, putting all the weight of his shoulders behind it. The man stiffened, then collapsed, and Dobie rolled him aside with a sweep of one arm to get at Hooker beneath.

"No!" shouted Hooker, trying to roll away. "No, boy, no . . . !"

"This is the way you wanted it, Hooker," snarled Dobie, and stood up, straddling the man, catching his collar. He was surprised how easily the great body heaved up when he pulled. He forced Hooker up against the wall with his body and began slugging him in the belly. Hooker bent over with a sick gasp, feebly trying to catch Dobie's fist. Dobie knocked aside his hand and straightened him with a jab to the face.

He hit the man till his hands were sticky with blood, sinking them into the blubber of his belly until there was no more resistance, battering the fat face into an unrecognizable mess.

At last he stepped back and let the big man slide down the wall to a sedate sitting position, fat thighs spread out, head sinking onto his chest.

Dobie heard a faint clatter and turned. Rudder was climbing out from beneath the dead Frenchman, shaking his red head. Dobie took a step toward the scarred little man. The fog left Rudder's eyes, and he sprawled back against the overturned kettle, holding up his hands with their palms toward Dobie.

"All right," he said desperately, "all right."

"All right." Dobie laughed, panting, and turned to sway toward the forward hatch, kicking one of the unconscious *voyageurs* aside. He was shaking like a blown horse and couldn't seem to draw in enough breath. His shirt was ripped almost off his back. He climbed the ladder heavily and shoved open the hatch, leaning on the edge a moment. Then he saw Colonel Harvey and Kentuck coming across the wet sand at a run. They jumped the thwarts and shoved through the crowd of *voyageurs* who had gathered at the opening.

"What is it?" said the colonel. "Don't tell me. Hooker . . . ?"

"You said I wouldn't have to worry about Hooker any more," said Dobie gustily. "You're right. I won't."

III

The cottonwoods up past Robidoux's Post were greening with the spring, and the black, loamy banks melted into high bluffs that came down to the river. The keelboat reached the Arikaree village near the mouth of the Grand River in early April, running up on the beach among the buffalo-hide canoes bobbing in the shallows and resting on the white sand.

Spanial left most of his *voyageurs* to guard the boat, for this was the tribe that had tried to wipe out Ashley's brigades in 1823, and though they had been peaceable since, the mountain men had yet to trust them.

The village was set up on the chocolate bluffs, surrounded by a high palisade of upright cedar logs. The trappers rested here on their upriver journey, feasting and trading.

Dobie Burton walked with the score of mountain men, and Hooker had four of his *voyageurs*. Some of the youth had been weathered from the boy's face, and his hair was long and bleached white against the ruddy burn of his skin. Work on the poles had put so much solid weight onto his chest and shoulders that they began splitting out his cotton shirt. Kentuck had to get him a new shirt of red wool from the trade goods in the hold. Moving through the cornfields atop the bluffs toward the sullen crowd of Arikarees who had come to meet them, now Dobie walked with his shoulders giving a top-heavy swing to his stride, and Kentuck began to chuckle.

"Colonel Harvey used to be the lady-killer in this passel of trappers, kid, but it looks like you're going to take his place. Those squaws are making doe-eyes at you already. But you want to be careful with the women here. I don't think even you could fight your way out if these Arikarees got peeved."

Inside the palisades there were sixty or seventy huge mound-like lodges, thatched with clay and leaves, the tunnel doorways projecting beyond the main front wall. Standing before the largest lodge was the chief, lean and intense with burning eyes set in a narrow, vicious face and black hair braided long over his rich brown buffalo robe.

"Starapat," Kentuck told Dobie. "It means Little-Hawk-With-Bloody-Claws."

In broken English, Starapat invited Colonel Harvey Gillis and the others into his lodge. With a dozen mongrel dogs yapping and sniffing at his heels, Dobie followed Kentuck, feeling a sudden sense of suffocation as he stooped into the narrow, fetid tunnel that led inside. The inner frame of the lodge was of huge cedar posts set upright, upon which other logs were laid horizontally to form a skeleton square. On this were lashed the willow boughs that gave the building its round shape, and on that the thatching.

The lodge quickly filled with evil-smelling, buffalo-robed warriors, feathers nodding from their braided hair. Dobie was allowed to squat on the inner circle around the fire, and take several puffs on the long red pipe that was passed around. With the unceasing cries of the herald outside almost drowning him out, Starapat began talking to the colonel in Pawnee.

"What's he saying?" Hooker asked nervously.

Colonel Harvey looked around with a strange gleam in his tawny eyes. "More about the crazy Scotchman. Starapat says there's a rumor going the rounds that American Fur has put a confidential agent on Kenmore's trail."

There was a sudden strained silence. A bitter war had always been waged between the free trappers and the mountain men working in the brigades of the large companies. Half these men in the lodge were independent trappers, and they reserved a special hatred for the secret agents hired by American Fur or Baffir Bay to weaken the free trappers' hold on what little beaver country they had left. The Indians, too, had a bitter contempt for the undercover agents, for it was one of these men who had brought about the trouble between the Arikarees and Ashley.

"That's right," repeated Colonel Harvey. "A confidential agent for American Fur. He might be sitting among us right now."

Hooker's spluttering sound broke the uneasy silence. Most of the big man's teeth had been knocked out in that fight in the hold, and he was still eating nothing but gruel and coffee. He wiped a fat, perspiring hand across his battered lips.

"Hell, why let it bother us? The agent's after Kenmore. We haven't anything to do with it."

Colonel Harvey grinned. "Starapat was telling me something else. It seems we have arrived at a very fortunate time. The Arikarees are a branch of the Pawnees, and they make the annual Pawnee sacrifice to the Morning Star, the greatest of heavenly heroes. We shall have the privilege of viewing the ceremony as soon as the star rises."

Food was served by young squaws with bear grease glistening on their plum-brown cheeks and Northwest stroud leggings brushing softly at their doeskin skirts as they walked. Sitting on a willow mat, Dobie stuffed down dry *pemitigon,* the Arikaree pemmican, and bread made from ground corn and beans, and a succulent boiled meat. Dobie licked the juice off his fingers, asking Kentuck: "This venison?"

"No, boiled dog," said Kentuck, and burst out laughing as Dobie spat the meat out with a groan.

After the dog they had roast beaver tail, a delicacy for which any Indian would gladly sell his soul, and then buffalo steaks and baked squash and corn *tiswin* that filled Dobie with a roaring fire from nose to hocks and made the smoky interior of the lodge reel and swim before his eyes.

He didn't know how long the feasting lasted. Once he had to go out and be sick, and after that he slept a while with his back against a cedar post and the buzz of replete braves filling his varicolored dreams. Finally they all staggered out into the chill air. The moon was down and the squaws were carrying bundles of willow withes to a scaffold in the center of the village.

Dobie's reactions had been dulled by the food, and the *tiswin* was burning him up. It took him some time to understand what he saw when three half-naked braves hauled a struggling woman out of a far lodge. He turned to Gillis.

"Sacrifice, you said. Not *human sacrifice?*"

Colonel Harvey belched softly. "What else?"

Dobie made a fumbling move forward, and Kentuck caught

him. "Take it easy, boy. You'll see worse than this in the north country. The Arikarees been doing this since buffaloes had horns. You interfere now and you'll be the death of all of us."

"They capture a virgin from another tribe," said Hooker Spanial heavily, "and keep her nice all winter and give her anything she wants and fatten her up just like a cow for market. Then they tie her to that scaffold, and when the Morning Star rises, a medicine man runs out of his lodge and cuts the girl's heart out. Try and stop it and you'd have a hundred bucks on you quicker'n a beaver can slap his tail."

A tom-tom had begun to throb against the first flush of false dawn, and the Arikarees were shifting into dark crowds among the lodges about the center compound. Dobie could see the men holding deadly, short-barreled London fusils under their buffalo robes.

The heady dizziness of the *tiswin* was swept from him, and he stood stiffly with Kentuck and the colonel still holding his arms, feeling a growing revulsion as he watched the braves drag the girl toward the scaffold. Her screams were shrill and terrified. For an instant she tore loose from one of her captors, turning toward the tight little group of trappers. Dobie caught an impression of lustrous black hair framing a pale, tortured face that only accentuated the luminous fear in her large dark eyes.

Suddenly Dobie jerked free of the men, sending Colonel Harvey Gillis back against the lodge with a spasmodic wave of his arm. He shouted hoarsely: "Kentuck, can't you see, *she's a white girl!*"

She was calling to them now, twisting in the Indian's grasp. "You're white men! Won't you help me? You're white men . . . !"

Kentuck caught Dobie again, and Gillis was on him from behind. Other trappers put their weight in, carrying the fighting boy to the ground. Then Kentuck looked at the girl, and his

116

voice was soft and hollow. "She's white all right, Colonel."

"What does that matter?" said Gillis. "Try to save her now and we'd all be killed. White girl or no, we're not playing fools. You can't be soft, now, Kentuck."

"But don't you recognize her?"

Still struggling with Dobie, the colonel looked at the girl again. They had her up on the scaffold now and were tying her to the frame with rawhide. She was dressed in a long white doeskin gown with red and blue beadwork patterning the waist. There was a necklace of eagle's claws about her neck. The light from a dozen fires turned her face to a glowing twisted mask of terror.

"Hold it, Dobie, hold it," snapped the colonel, and something in his voice stopped the boy from struggling. When Colonel Harvey Gillis spoke again, it was hardly audible. "That's her, all right."

"That's who?" said Hooker.

Colonel Harvey Gillis ignored him. "You game, Kentuck?"

"I am," said Kentuck.

"What about it, Mullen?" said the colonel, turning to the other trappers. "Wade? Fitch?"

Mullen was a big, slow-thinking trapper. He rubbed his graying beard with a trap-scarred hand. "I dunno, Colonel. Suicide. I'd like to, but. . . ."

"I got my Jake Hawkins," said Wade, patting his long rifle.

By the time Starapat had come over with half a dozen of his young bucks, four of the trappers had consented to help Gillis. The chief thrust aside his heavy buffalo robe to wave a sinewy hand at Dobie.

"What is?" he wanted to know.

"Let him up," the colonel said. "Nothing, Little Hawk. Your *tiswin* was just too powerful for such a greenhorn. He thought he was a bald eagle and wanted to fly."

Dobie rose slowly, his eyes on the girl. He held himself in with an effort.

"Listen," Hooker told the chief nervously. "Starapat, listen. I've got some Saint Looey Monongahela down in the boat Joe Robidoux sent up for you. Yes. I'll go get it now so you can really give a Morning Star ceremony. Yes. I'll need some of my men to help carry the kegs up. I'll go get it now, eh?"

"Hooker!" Colonel Harvey Gillis's voice halted the ponderous man as he started to sidle away. "You have the boat ready, understand? If you aren't in this, the least you can do is have the boat ready. We'll be coming down in a little while, and if you aren't there, I'll follow you, Hooker, and the world won't be big enough for you to hide in. So you have the boat ready, understand, Hooker?"

Hooker wiped his sensuous lips. "Sure, Colonel, sure. I'll have the boat ready. Sure. . . ."

The *voyageurs* went with him toward the gates, and Mullen, and the other trappers who weren't willing to make the attempt. Starapat looked after Hooker suspiciously.

"What Big Belly mean, he have boat ready?"

"We're shoving off in the morning, Little Hawk," Gillis told him blandly, then broke into a torrent of Pawnee, gesticulating with his long tomahawk. Finally Little-Hawk-With-Bloody-Claws jerked his narrow black head, and a buck moved off toward the gates. When Hooker and his crowd had passed out, the buck said something to the half dozen warriors standing around the huge doors. The ponderous cedar portals closed with a foreboding creak. Colonel Harvey Gillis watched one of the Arikarees drop a bar into its slots.

"It would seem," said the colonel, "that Starapat doesn't trust us. We are hostages until Hooker returns."

"Which Hooker has no intention of doing," said Kentuck.

Starapat had moved off a little, leaving a group of warriors nearby to watch the mountain men. Colonel Harvey Gillis spoke in a low voice from the side of his mouth: "Three of you get as near the gate as you can, and when we start it here, try to get the doors open and keep them that way. Wade, you got your long gun. You pick off the shaman before he reaches the scaffold. I'll take care of Starapat. He's our prime plew. Kentuck, you and the greenhorn get the girl. Soon as we have it done, start toward the gates. Keep together and don't scatter no matter what happens."

The first lanky trapper began reeling drunkenly toward the gates. He fell on his knees as if too tight to stand, and guffawed thickly, and got up and walked in little circles, moving imperceptibly toward the gates.

Some of the young squaws giggled and pointed at him, but the men looked at one another with suspicion in their painted faces. With the first trapper attracting the Arikarees' attention, the other two began sifting through the crowd almost unnoticed. One started flirting with a girl, and she began coquetting away in the direction of the doors. He followed, pawing drunkenly for her. Kentuck shifted up against Dobie, and the boy felt cold metal pressed into his hand.

"I dumped some powder in your pocket," said Kentuck. "Here's half a dozen balls. Pinch of powder down the barrel and dump a ball right after. No time for a ramrod. Wet your lead so it'll stick and knock the butt of the gun against your free palm. Kentucky sights. Set up a little for long shots. Take your time. Shoot for the middle of the body. All set?"

Dobie hooked his thumb around the brass butt cap of the Kentucky pistol. The tom-tom seemed to be inside of him now, beating his blood through his head with an increasing rhythm.

The Arikarees were shifting restlessly, watching the trappers, and Starapat kept looking into the lightening sky. Colonel Harvey Gillis was the first of the mountain men to see the star. His voice came soft above the tom-tom. "There it is."

The medicine man burst from the big lodge at the instant Dobie saw the Morning Star. A low cry rose from the packed ranks of Indians, and the tom-tom accelerated until it matched the beat of the shaman's running feet across the hard-packed compound toward the girl.

The medicine man's white buffalo robe flapped about his running heels, and the ocher stripes gleamed across his face. He held a bone knife in one hand as he ran headlong for the scaffold. Then Dobie heard the sharp click behind him, and stiffened. Wade's shot deafened him. The white-robed shaman screamed and kept on going two or three steps, and then seemed to crumple like a doll with all the sawdust leaking out, and slid into a heap on the ground.

Dobie didn't see anything after that except the girl. He was dimly aware of his own feet pounding across the dirt and his own hands firing the gun and reloading it as Kentuck had told him, and Kentuck running, long-legged, beside him and shooting and loading and shooting again.

Then he was on the scaffold, tearing the rawhide off the girl's wrists and ankles. The girl's body was rigid against his arms, but soft, too. With the lashings free, he caught her around a slim, lithe waist and whirled to jump down. In that instant, from the height of the platform, he could see the whole scene.

Kentuck had dropped to one knee beside the scaffold, and the two Indians he had shot sprawled halfway between the scaffold and the first lodge. He had his smoking gun leveled across one forearm, but he hadn't needed to fire again. Colonel Harvey Gillis, backing across the open space toward Kentuck, held Starapat in front of him with one buckskinned arm around the chief's neck, and the other holding the tomahawk above Starapat's narrow head. He spoke to the chief, but his voice was loud enough for all to hear.

"Tell your *kyeshes* not to make a move, Little Hawk, or you get this Delaware blade through your skull."

Starapat's voice came loud and clear. Before he was finished, Kentuck jumped erect, shouting: "Damn his red hide! He's telling 'em to go ahead and take us, forget, about him!"

The Indians were shifting restlessly now, and Dobie saw them drop their dark robes to reveal the London fusils traded by the Northwest Company—ugly gleaming smoothbores, deadly at close range. Starapat began struggling in Gillis's hold. The mountain man jerked his arm against the Arikaree's throat, and Starapat made a strangled sound, legs kicking spasmodically.

"Clop him one, Colonel," said Kentuck. "He wants it."

"If I kill him now, we don't have any hold on them," the colonel snarled softly. "He's the only thing keeping them good."

"And he knows it," spat Wade, reloading his Jake Hawkins. "Come on with that girl, Dobie."

They backed across the compound in a little bunch. The tom-tom had stopped, and a strained quiet had settled over the Indians, punctuated by the whisper of a nervously shifting buck here and there, watching Starapat with beady eyes. Then Dobie saw Kentuck turn to look behind them, and was chilled by the expression on the man's long, dark face.

"Colonel," said Kentucky quietly. "They didn't get the gates open."

IV

Dobie saw the three men who were to have taken care of the gates. It must have happened during that first scramble, just after Wade had shot the shaman. A group of Arikarees stood around the one who had simulated drunkenness. He lay with his arms outstretched and his fingertips almost touching the doors he had failed to reach.

The second trapper sat up against the walls with his jaw hanging slackly in death, and a dead Arikaree across his legs. The third was huddled halfway between the last lodge and the gates. The squaw he'd been flirting with had a surprised look on her plump face.

A line of Arikarees stood across the doors, hands gripping their London fusils, and Kentuck was looking at them as he spoke again. "We'll never reach the doors before it blows. They're going to do it, Colonel. Another step and they're going to do it, Little Hawk or no Little Hawk."

Dobie felt his palm sweaty around the maple stock of the Kentucky pistol. The girl had almost fainted with terror, and was a dead weight on his other arm.

"One more step," said Kentuck. "Just one more." He took it.

Starapat suddenly gave a violent jerk, twisting around in Colonel Harvey Gillis's grasp. He broke free and threw himself toward his people, screaming in Pawnee.

"That does it!" said the colonel. Dobie didn't know he had thrown the tomahawk until it was in the air. The deadly weapon turned over once before it struck Starapat between his shoulder blades.

Dobie saw the colonel leap after the fallen chief and bend over to yank the tomahawk out. Then the Indians opened fire. Dobie whirled, with the girl in time to see the flame of Kentuck's pistol, and one of the Arikarees by the gate fell forward. The others formed a sea of twisted, screaming faces in front of Dobie, the red stabs of their exploding fusils blinding him, the bedlam of shouts deafening him. He fired blindly at a yelling mouth and it disappeared. He felt the shock of a bullet strike his leg and throw him back on the girl. He fell to his knees, straddling her body.

The Indians were too close for reloading; they were clubbing their guns, or dropping them for knives and hatchets. Dobie caught the flash of a blade above him and struck out desperately with his pistol. The Indian fell back, clutching a broken arm.

Then Colonel Harvey Gillis came through the howling crowd. All the leashed fury of the man had erupted in his padding run, like a big tawny cat moving with a terrible, blinding speed. "There's one for hell," he snarled softly, and leaned into a swipe that hacked an Arikaree's face off his neck. "And a hot trip down for you!" He struck another blow that split an Indian's skull from forehead to jaw.

Behind him Wade charged, swinging his five-foot Jake Hawkins in a circle that left no man standing within its circumference. Their devastating rush cleared enough space around Dobie for the boy to rise to his feet.

"Forget the gates!" shouted the colonel, hacking at an Indian who threw himself madly at them. "Get on that ladder before they pull it down, and go over the wall!"

The Arikarees from across the compound had reached the others now, and their press was hurtling the first ranks in on the mountain men again. Kentuck jumped at the smaller group of Indians between them and the wall, firing pointblank at the first and clubbing a second before the other had fallen. He grabbed a third by the hair and swung him around into two others, knocking them up against the cedar logs. He kicked free of a last pair of clawing hands and was on the ladder, reloading in swift, sure movements. He climbed the rungs like a monkey and shot an Arikaree off the platform that ran around inside the wall above. He leaped on up to grapple with another, shifting his long legs and heaving him off to fall screaming into the crowd below.

Dobie fought halfway up the ladder with the girl, and Kentuck reached down and got her under the armpits. Colonel Harvey Gillis hacked a last Arikaree down and threw himself at the ladder. It swayed dangerously with his added weight.

Wade came last. As he turned to reach the bottom rungs, the

first of the Arikarees charging from the compound threw themselves on him. He swung his long gun in a desperate arc, and two of them fell. Then the few Arikarees by the gate were jumping at him, too. He made a last desperate try, clawing at the ladder with one hand and kicking them off. Then he must have realized he could never make it. With a strangled, animal cry, he turned and jumped away from the ladder, throwing himself bodily into the pack of Indians with nothing but his bare hands. Dobie saw him get one Indian by the neck, and he was still holding on when he was engulfed by their red, sweating bodies.

Colonel Harvey Gillis dropped over the wall first, alighting like a cat, and caught the girl as Dobie lowered her to arm's length and dropped her. Then Dobie jumped, turning his ankle as he hit. Kentuck was silhouetted atop the sharpened stakes above for a moment. Dobie heard the sharp rattle of fusils from inside. Kentuck had struck the ground before they realized he had fallen, and not jumped.

Already the gates were creaking open. Kentuck gasped from where he lay: "Go on, get out. You'll never make it with me."

The colonel was already halfway down the bluffs on the trail. He shouted back to them: "Kentuck's right, kid! Come on."

"No," said Dobie, and began dragging Kentuck down the trail. The gates burst open and the first ranks of Arikarees surged out. Dobie felt a pistol pressed into his hands.

"Give me the other one now," said Kentuck. "If you're going to be a damn' fool, you might as well do it right."

Grinning, Dobie handed Kentuck the empty gun. Then he squatted down, taking careful aim with the loaded piece Kentuck had given him, and fired over Kentuck's shoulder. The leading Indian shouted and fell onto his face. Dobie had Kentuck under the armpits, dragging him down the trail in a sitting position while the man loaded the other gun. He was surprised to feel the second Kentucky piece pressed into his hand so soon after he had fired the first. He dropped the empty one into Kentuck's lap, took aim over the man's shoulder, and fired again. Another Indian went down.

"Come on!" shouted Colonel Harvey Gillis from down on the beach. "Leave him there! Oh, you damn' fool greenhorn!"

A good man could pour, load, and fire five times a minute, and since Kentuck was only loading, and Dobie was only firing, they must have doubled the record. Dobie was shooting almost as fast as he could drop an empty gun into Kentuck's lap and take the loaded one from the man's hand. He dragged Kentuck a few quick steps, stopped, and fired, then dragged him again.

The running Indians had emptied their fusils, and they had none of the mountain man's skill in reloading. Unable to face that steady, deadly fire, they scattered into cover among the rocks and brush, leaving three of their number sprawled out in the open with Dobie's Galena lead in them.

Then Dobie felt wet sand beneath his feet. He took a last shot at a painted face, saw it sink into the willow shoots. Colonel Harvey Gillis had let the girl drop to the ground, and stood there, looking out past the bull-hide canoes drawn up on the sand or bobbing in the river, to the empty expanse of dirty yellow water where the keelboat had been moored.

"It looks," said the colonel softly, "as if Spanial has left us holding the trap sack."

"And it's plumb full of Arikarees," groaned Kentuck.

North of the Grand, the Missouri was roiling at its banks with the muddy turbulence of spring, sending the last of its melting ice downriver in bobbing white chunks. The aspens were quaking green in the bottoms, and the serviceberries bowed the bushes with their pregnant red clumps.

On up that swollen river the keelboat had gone, leaving them stranded. But the colonel had been expecting as much. He leaped among the buffalo canoes drawn up on the sand, slashing the bottoms of all but one, and pushing that one out into the water.

Before the Indians gained the shore, the three men and the girl were in the deeps. One of the Arikarees tried to paddle a boat out after them, and it sank beneath him. Without their canoes, the Indians could do no more than run along the bank, firing their short fusils, useless at that range.

The colonel turned the canoe downriver and let the swift current carry them out of sight of the Indians. That night they camped in the soggy bottoms without eating. They rose before sunrise, sinking the boat with rocks lashed to its bottom and obliterating all other signs of their presence. Then they turned back northward, passing the Arikaree village on the opposite bank, and circling far to the east. They headed on up the Missouri in a forced march, the colonel driving them from long before dawn to after sundown. Near the Big Heart River the Mandans lived in palisaded villages much like the Arikarees, and there the colonel got horses, disappearing one night from camp and coming back next morning with a string of Mandan pintos.

They had their first cooked food on the Big Dry, three days later. Dobie had shot some prairie hens, and the colonel spitted them over the fire. Kentucky sat, wrapped in a buffalo robe that had been used as a saddle blanket on one of the Mandan ponies. His wound in the chest had been an ugly one, and he was doing badly.

"Some gruel for you, Kentuck," said the colonel, setting a Mandan gourd down in front of him. "Juice from those prairie hens and *chimaja* I found in the bottoms."

Dobie was working on a wing. *"Chimaja?"*

"Wild celery," said the colonel. "Mexicans use it on all their sick. Make Kentuck jump up and do a Virginia Reel."

"Hear you're the one shot those birds today, Dobie," said Kentuck, grinning weakly as he sipped at the gruel. "You're a wonder with those Kentuckies. Did you see the way he picked off them Arikarees, Colonel? Regular Dan'l Boone on a short gun. You like them irons, don't you, boy? Tell you what. You did so well with 'em back at the village, you can give me one, and keep the other for yourself."

For a moment, Dobie couldn't speak. He realized how much Kentuck valued those guns. A strange choked emotion welled up in him, and he held out his hand.

"That's all right, Dobie." Kentuck grinned. "You saved my life twice now. I guess a man can give a friend one of his pistols. You'll be needing an iron. Blackfeet country ahead."

"That means beaver country, doesn't it?" said Dobie. "Shouldn't we hit a post before that? With your old outfits in Hooker's keelboat, you'll need new traps and things. And the girl. . . ."

"We'll leave the girl at the first decent fort we strike, of course," Colonel Harvey Gillis told him. "Far as outfits go, though, we don't need to strike a post. We got a cache of traps and such up in the Highwoods."

The forced march on foot had kept them all so exhausted that they hadn't been interested in much more than swallowing the raw sunfish the colonel had caught and throwing themselves on the ground for a few hours of sleep before rising again to push on. The girl had taken it hardest, moving in a dull apathy most of the time, rarely speaking. But now, with three days of riding behind them, and a hot meal inside her, she showed signs of renewed interest in life.

"Weren't you up at Fort Union several years ago?" she asked, studying Colonel Harvey Gillis with her big dark eyes.

"We've been to Fort Union, yes," said the colonel, then turned to face her fully, smiling. "My, my, gentlemen, we've been so interested in shaking the Arikarees off our tail we didn't have time to see how beautiful this child really is. Will you look at that hair. Glossy as a prime plew."

"You told us your name was Nairn," said Dobie. "That's an odd name. Nairn what?"

A strained look crossed her pale face, and she glanced at the colonel. "Dobie said you recognized me back at the village."

"Yes," said Colonel Harvey Gillis, "recognized you as a white girl. Nairn. That's a pretty name. Your first name?"

He was bending over her now, and the tawny little lights were kindling softly in his eyes. She looked up at him, and the rise and fall of her bosom became more perceptible beneath the grimy white doeskin of her Arikaree dress.

"I was taken by the Arikarees a year ago," she said. "They treated me like a queen all the time. Gave me the best food, clothes, servants. I had no idea what it was leading up to until that last day when they told me. I guess I went a little crazy with fright. And when I saw you there, white men, and thought you weren't going to help me. . . ."

She bit her lip. The colonel hunkered down beside her and took her hand. He began to stroke her dark hair.

"That's all right now. You're among friends. No need to be afraid any more."

The girl stiffened under his hand, perhaps not understanding yet. Then she saw his eyes and pulled away. Dobie stood up, wiping greasy fingers on his pants.

"What's the matter, Nairn?" said the colonel, dragging her back. "I told you we were friends."

She suddenly put both hands against his chest and tried to shove him away. But he was breathing hard, and had both arms around her, and bent her backward with his flushed face lowering to hers. She understood fully now, and began struggling violently.

128

"Stop!"

She didn't say any more; she crouched there with her hands still raised where she had been pushing at Colonel Harvey Gillis's chest, and the fear in her eyes was mingled with surprise as she stared at the colonel where he now lay half a dozen feet from her, sprawled on his back.

It had all happened that fast. Dobie had taken two vicious steps to the colonel, and with one hand on the man's buckskin shoulder had torn him away from the girl and spun him around hard enough to throw him over on his back. Now the boy stood, spread-legged, above Colonel Harvey Gillis, his heavy shoulders swaying a little with that top-heavy look, his face dark against the bleached white of his long hair.

"Wait a minute, Colonel," said Dobie coldly, and the colonel stopped, trying to rise. "Before you get up I want something understood. There won't be any more of that with the girl."

The shock was completely gone from the colonel's soft face now, and his eyes narrowed suddenly with a violent anger. He made another jerky effort to rise. "Why, you. . . ."

"Colonel!" The boy's voice stopped the man again. "If you want to try and get up without reaching that understanding, go ahead. But I won't let you get your feet under you with that tomahawk in your belt. I guess you know what I mean."

Colonel Harvey Gillis lay there a long time, breathing heavily, looking up at Dobie towering above him. He let his hand slide off the tomahawk and reached up to wipe his mouth. His voice was almost inaudible when it finally came.

"All right. Maybe I forgot myself. You may consider that we have reached our understanding." Dobie stepped back, and the colonel got slowly to his feet. "But there is another understanding we should reach before this is finished here. No greenhorn tells me what to do, in my own camp or out of it, and no greenhorn puts his hands on me that way. The next time you do will be the last time, understand?"

V

Up past the Big Dry, the mountains climbed to the sky and tumbled down again in ceaseless undulations of pine-darkened wilderness. The pungent scent of pine needles swept into camp on the milky shrouds of morning ground fog, and the night fell with a sudden awe-inspiring blackness. Dobie was filled with wonder.

On Squaw Creek they began to harvest the beaver, and Dobie's hands suffered once more from the traps. Their few Mandan ponies soon became overloaded, and the youth began packing a buffalo saddle lashed high with swart pelts. It was the Missouri all over again, days filled with staggering exhaustion and new work that his big hands never seemed to learn, and pain from a hundred new sources he had never dreamed existed. Then, at the headwaters of the Squaw, they came across the first American Fur man.

Dobie had worked to the topmost pool of the creek and was staggering downstream under a great pile of water-logged carcasses. The ice-cold water had numbed his feet and legs, and now the sand ground in through the rents in his tattered boots, pricking through the numbness like a thousand malignant needles. Diving in ice water after drowned beaver had settled a cold in his back, and, when he straightened, the stabbing pain through his lumbars made him gasp.

A man came hurriedly toward him through the chokecherry. It was Colonel Harvey Gillis, and that was strange. He was usually silent as an Indian.

"Cut over this way to camp," he said.

"But I left a bunch of carcasses down by the aspens," Dobie told him. Then he stopped, because he had seen past the colonel. He took a step forward, face strained. "Kentuck?"

"No, no," said the colonel, and tried to get in his way. "We'll go back to camp this way."

Dobie dropped his load and broke through the wild cherry. The man lay on his back. His head had been almost severed from his body, and the blood was fresh and wet, spreading beneath his agony-twisted features.

"Know him?" asked Dobie sickly.

The colonel seemed angry. "Not personally. He works with Reeves's American Fur brigade. They have headquarters on Knee Creek."

"The Scotchman?"

"Kenmore, yes," said the colonel. "Who else would hack a man up like that? Pile some rocks on his grave when you bury him so the coyotes won't pester. I'm going to cut for Kenmore's sign. If he's around here, I don't want him catching me like he did this *kyesh*. I'll be back to camp before nightfall."

Dobie had finished with the grave when he entered the camp. Kentuck sat huddled over in his Mandan robe by the cold ashes of the morning's fire; he was weakening rapidly, and the pain of his infected wound was plain on his face. Dobie got him some water, then began setting up the skinning frames. The girl came over, pushing a dark lock of hair from her forehead.

"You looked strange when you came in with the beaver," she said. "What is it?"

"We found an American Fur man down by the creek," said Dobie. "Not dead very long. The Scotchman must be near."

A strained look turned the flesh white around her lips. "You mean . . . Kenmore? No. No. How can you be sure?"

"The trapper was all hacked up," said Dobie. Then he glanced at her sharply. "What do you mean, no? This is where the Scotchman is supposed to be, isn't it? Who else but a crazy man would do that to every man he meets? Hooker found two of them on the Big Dry last January. Just like this one."

"It can't be Kenmore. How can you know? Just because. . . ." She turned away suddenly, and he saw her fists clenched at her sides. Finally she turned back, drawing a ragged breath. She watched him lash the stretchers on the frame for a long time. Finally she said: "I'm sorry. Here, if you want to be a mountain man, you'll have to lash your stretchers tighter than that. You do want to be a mountain man pretty bad, don't you?"

The speculation in her glance made him bridle. "Why not?"

"Don't be like that," she said. "I understand what it is. Nobody can explain it. You can't even explain it to yourself, what the mountains do to you. Some men were just born for it, that's all. And women. When they see the Big Stonies or the Highwoods or the Shoshones, they know they've come home. Only . . . do you think you'll get to be a mountain man like this?"

"What do you mean?"

"With Kentuck and the colonel," she said. "I'll bet they haven't had it so easy in years. They give you every dirty job there is."

"They're my friends," he said, and stiffened with a fierce pride at being able to say that of such men. He glanced at Kentuck. Hard and brutal, perhaps, but every time he remembered how they had fought together at the Arikaree village, he felt a tingling thrill. "Don't talk about them that way."

"Your friends," she scoffed. "You're no better than their slave. They load you down like a pack horse. They make you pitch every camp and gather all the wood and roll out long before they do to have things ready for them in the morning. They make you dive in ice water for drowned beaver, and march all day sopping wet, and clean up the horse droppings behind us when Gillis wants to hide our tracks from Blackfeet. In any ordinary camp, all the men would take turns doing those things. About all Gillis does is eat and sleep and hunt. He hasn't touched a plew yet."

"I've got to learn," he said. "I'm a greenhorn."

"What are you learning?" she demanded. "Are they teaching you anything you want to know? You'll be a greenhorn forever at this rate. Gillis never shows you anything you ask him to, never even bothers to answer most of your questions. Do you learn to trap beaver by carrying the pelts on your back? And just how have you been trapping beaver? You come back with a load every day heavy enough to make you stagger, yet we haven't got a trap in camp."

"Colonel Harvey Gillis told me to leave the traps," said Dobie. "We'll pick them up on our way back."

"Oh, Colonel Harvey Gillis told you," she almost whispered, kneeling beside him now. Watching him, she put her hands on the stretcher. One was soft and warm against his hand, and he realized suddenly that there was more in the world than becoming a mountain man. "Dobie, do you set your traps again after you've taken the beaver out?"

"Set them?"

"Yes. You don't just leave them sprung, do you? They won't catch any beaver that way. Did Gillis tell you to do that, too?"

"He gets results, doesn't he?" said Dobie. "More than any trapper north of Robidoux's Post."

"Yes," said the girl. "The Arikarees talked about that during beaver season when I was in their camp. It struck me as rather strange that two men should bring in more plews than any ten men in the American Fur brigades."

"Nothing strange about it."

"No," she told him. "Maybe there isn't. Maybe it's all very simple. I didn't want to believe it before this. But now . . . you are a greenhorn, aren't you, Dobie? You don't realize what finding that American Fur man here means? Those trappers only work in American Fur territory. *This* is American Fur territory!

And the way we work . . . leaving the traps behind, not having a single trap in our camp, hiding our trail most of the time and not stopping at any of the posts, and pushing our horses as hard and fast as we can without killing them. Don't you see what it means, Dobie? I didn't want to believe it, because you'd saved my life. But now I can't help it. Don't you see what it means?"

Dobie opened his mouth to reply, but just then Colonel Harvey Gillis stepped out of the timber, glancing at them suspiciously. The girl moved away and said nothing more.

Beyond Squaw Creek they hit the frowning gorge of the Missouri, and then the quaking aspens along nameless creeks beneath the dark-timbered crests of the Highwoods. The colonel had stopped the girl from saying anything else back there on the Squaw, and, after that, it seemed Dobie and Nairn never got a chance to talk together without one of the two men being near enough to overhear.

Dobie couldn't divine what she had meant, but it gradually became more apparent to him that she had been right about Gillis not teaching him anything but the most menial tasks. He resolved to learn from the colonel whether the man would teach him consciously or not. All day long on the trail, the boy began to study Gillis's ways with a grim intensity. How the man hid his sign, or read another's; how he listened to the birds constantly for an indication of another human's presence; how he always stopped above a watering place and waited till he was sure it was free; even how he walked, the peculiar swinging stride of a mountain man. And bit by bit Dobie stored away the thousand little skills that Gillis manifested consciously or unconsciously.

They were all walking now, with every horse loaded hocks to withers with pelts, and that was the way they struck Little Coon Creek, coming down through the cottonwoods and out onto the white sand. Kentuck leaned weakly against one of the hipshot pack horses, hanging onto the lead line to keep himself erect. His face was pale and haggard, and a feverish light burned in his eyes, and it was becoming more and more apparent that he didn't have long to go.

There was a series of small islets in mid-stream, covered with dwarf pine. Reaching down the bank of one was a beaver slide, a trap's float bobbing near it. But there was no safety peg in the riverbank, no trap showing in the shadows.

"Greenhorn," said the colonel. "The beaver's pulled out the safety stick and hauled his trap into deep water and drowned himself again. You'll have to dive for him."

Greenhorn! Would they never stop calling him that? Wearily Dobie dropped his load, wrapped his pistol and powder flask in a piece of buckskin, and put them beside a rock. Then he waded out into the deep, icy pool, gulping in a breath and plunging down through the murky chill. He came up for air the first time without the trap. The men were standing on the bank, Gillis staring intently up toward the higher timber. He turned to Dobie suddenly.

"We're going upstream to pitch camp. Get your load and we'll have the skinning frames set up, time you reach us."

Kentuck hurriedly kicked the droop-necked horses into movement, and hung onto the tail of one as they broke into timber. The girl said something to Gillis; he shook his head and took her by the elbow, turning her after Kentuck.

"Colonel!" called Dobie, but they were gone. With a strange foreboding in him, he dived again for the beaver and came up with it this time. He lifted his head from the water, spluttering. A man was standing on the bank. Though he had never seen the man before, he knew who it was instantly.

"Well, laddie," said Ian Kenmore, "will ye come oot an' get

yere just deserts, or shall I wade in an' chop ye doon where ye stond?"

For a moment Dobie stared, unable to speak. The man was huge, nearly seven-feet, with a craggy face topped by a mass of curly black hair. His buckskin jacket and blanket leggings looked bizarre by contrast with the plaid tartan of red and yellow about his thick middle. Slung from his tremendous shoulders by a broad black belt was the biggest, longest sword Dobie had ever seen. It must have been Kenmore who Gillis had spotted. Or maybe it was Hooker Spanial.

The fat man stepped from the thicket a few yards farther down. He was grinning slyly. "Before you lay your claymore to the boy, Kenmore, I'd like a talk with you."

The red-headed Rudder was behind Hooker, and half a dozen French *voyageurs* with London fusils and Jake Hawkins rifles. Kenmore's husky whisper held all his surprise.

"Ye!"

"Yes." Hooker chuckled. "I've come to take you back to Saint Looey for the murder of some dozen American Fur trappers and the poaching of their furs."

The beaver slipped from Dobie's hands with a soft splash, and he began to wade ashore. "*You're* the American Fur agent?" he asked.

"I am," said Hooker. "That was an American Fur keelboat. How else did you think I got on as *patron*? Everybody would expect a secret agent to hide his connection with American Fur. I figured 'em one up. I thought Colonel Gillis was mixed up in this somehow. I thought maybe Kentuck would tell me that night at Rocky Mountain, but you had to butt in. Then, when Gillis signed on the keelboat, American Fur yanked Jules Lebaron and put me in his place as *patron*. I would've found out how Colonel Gillis stood in this sooner or later if we hadn't been forced to part so abruptly at the Arikaree village. But it doesn't matter much now, anyway, does it? I found what I wanted. I took the keelboat on up to Fort Union. Blackfeet there said they'd cut Kenmore's sign in the Highwoods. Been tracking him from there. As I say, Kenmore, I'm here to take you in for the murders. But that's officially. Unofficially other arrangements might be made. Arrangements that would leave you running free as before, if you led me to that hundred-thousand-dollar fur cache you got on the Teton."

"The only arrangement I'll mak' wi' a crowlin' ferlie like ye is wi' ma claymore," growled the Scotsman.

"I have something else in my hand," said Hooker. "Your daughter."

"Nairn?" Dobie saw a strange glitter come into the huge Scotsman's eyes, and he seemed to crouch a little. "What do ye ken of her? Ye're American Fur, Hooker? Then ye were there when they took her. 'Tis the only way ye could ken. Not anither mon in these mountains kens. I've hunted for a year noo, an' not anither man in these mountains could tell me where she is. Ye took her, ye fat reif randie. . . ." He jumped at Hooker suddenly, smashing up against the man with his huge hands clutching Hooker's fat neck. "Where is she? Tell me or I'll break yere neck in twa."

"Not me," choked Hooker, struggling in the giant's grasp. "The boy. Let go! Dobie Burton. He knows where she is. I didn't recognize her at the Arikaree village, but Colonel Harvey Gillis did. Up at Fort Union they told me what she looked like, and I knew then. . . ."

The white-coated *voyageurs* were swarming over Kenmore now, trying to tear him off Hooker Spanial, beating the Scotsman's curly head with their fusils. It gave Dobie his chance to reach the shore.

The rock where he had cached his pistol was to the left of the struggle, and he had almost reached it when Rudder jumped from around the other side of the fight, drawing his H.T. Cooper.

Dobie threw himself bodily at the shore, sand spewing up beneath him as he rolled across the rock, grabbing at his cache. The redhead's Cooper boomed. Stone chipped off into Dobie's face, blinding him as he rolled away from the rock with his Kentucky pistol in his hands. He came belly up, covered with sand, and fired across his stomach with both fists gripping the pistol. Rudder made a choked sound, dropped his gun, and fell softly into the sand.

The Scotsman had heaved himself free of the writhing mob for a moment, staggering under blows from the rifles. Then his sword was out. He was in a rage, bellowing as he swung the terrible claymore with both hands.

"Scots wha hae wi' Wallace bled!" he screamed. "Scots wham Bruce hae aften led"—and his sword split a Frenchman's skull like a ripe melon—"welcome to yere gory bed."—and another *voyageur* staggered away.

A fusil boomed. Kenmore jerked, and swung around to chop at another Frenchman with a terrible roar. A second gun sounded, and Kenmore sank to his knees, putting his blade through another man as he fell, still shouting crazily. "Lay the proud usurpers low, tyrants fall in every foe . . . !"

Hooker had gotten a dead Frenchman's Jake Hawkins, and was dancing back from the struggle, jerking the long gun to bear on Kenmore. Dobie jumped at the fat man from where he had risen to his knees, leaping Rudder's body and catching the rifle by the barrel. Hooker let go the gun and they rolled to the ground in a tangle.

Dobie came up on top, lifting the rifle. Hooker's Green River flashed out and Dobie felt the hot stripe of pain cross his chest, and heard the soft rip of his red wool shirt. Then he had Hooker squarely beneath him, and the heavy gun high over his head. He saw one moment of utter terror on Hooker's dissipated face.

"No, boy," gasped the fat man. "No. . . ."

After that, Dobie got up off the limp hulk, and turned with the Hawkins still in his hands. Kenmore was on his knees, bent forward with one hand on the sand supporting him, the other trying to lift his claymore again. A last Frenchman had jumped back out of range and was dumping powder in his fusil. He dropped a ball of Galena in, struck the butt on the sand, and jerked the gun up. Dobie reversed his Jake Hawkins and squeezed the trigger. He felt the velvety jump of the spring, and the huge rifle almost bucked out of his hand. The Frenchman went over on his back with a sharp grunt, and stayed there.

When Dobie lunged toward the huge Scotsman, Kenmore made a feeble attempt to wield his sword again. Dobie warded off the blow with the Hawkins and caught the man as he dropped the claymore and fell forward. Kenmore struggled weakly in the boy's arms, then his eyes cleared.

"Ye were fighting Hooker. Helping me. . . ."

"Why not?" said Dobie.

"I was going to chop ye doon. Ye were poaching my lines, an' I was going to kill ye."

"Poaching?"

"That's what I said," groaned Kenmore. "I've been a free trapper ever since American Fur forced Baffin Bay oot o' the Three Forks, an' these are the last lines I've got. That's the way ye've been working? I've heard aboot it fro' the Indians. Cleaning oot ony lines ye strike, American Fur or Baffin Bay or free trapper. Who would hae thought it was a bairn like ye? Nae oot-fit o' yere own. Nae traps, nae trap sacks, not e'en a bottle o' beaver medicine."

The girl had said the same thing. Was that what she had tried to tell him? Dobie stiffened. The girl. . . .

"Nairn?" he said. "You said that was your daughter's name?"

Kenmore pawed at his shirt, trying to rise. "The American Fur men took her when they burned ma post at the Big Dry. Ye ken where she is?"

"We took a girl named Nairn from the Arikaree camp down on the Grand," said Dobie. "Black-haired, blue-eyed, skin like milk. . . ."

"That's her," said Kenmore wildly. "Nairn Kenmore. "Where is she? What've ye done wi' her?"

"Colonel Harvey Gillis. . . ."

Kenmore began to thrash about wildly. "She's lost. Gin she's wi' that purrin', poachin', crowlin' ferlie, she's lost. Ye were wi' Gillis? Ye're worse than American Fur, then."

Dobie shook his head. "I didn't realize. They'd recognized her as, your daughter. I thought they were saving her from the Arikarees just because she was a white girl. It all happened so fast, I forget exactly how it went. But they knew she was a white girl before they recognized her as your daughter, and they weren't going to save her then. It was only when they realized she was Nairn Kenmore that they started planning to save her. But why would it have made a difference?"

Kenmore looked at him dazedly, then jerked his head. "The same thing Hooker Spanial was after. Spanial didn't care aboot takin' me in. He only wanted that hundred thousand dollars' worth o' furs I'm supposed to hae cached on the Teton. Gillis thought ma daughter could lead him to that cache."

Dobie felt himself trembling suddenly. "We've been heading for the Teton ever since we left the Big Dry. They haven't touched her yet. Maybe because I got in the colonel's way when he tried that time, maybe because they were waiting till they reached the Teton. Now. . . ."

"Noo they'll hae her alone and they'll be strikin' the Teton in a day or twa," gasped the Scotsman. "They'll force it frae her. I ken their ways. Worse than Indians. And me too weak to lift a blade. Better she had been killed by the Arikarees."

"They haven't gotten a very big start on us," said Dobie.

"Dinna joke wi' me, poacher. Ye wouldna ony mair follow Gillis than ye'd put yere nose in a jump trap."

"I helped you with Hooker," Dobie pointed out.

"Aye." Kenmore frowned, wavering. He shook his head. "I dinna ken where to put ye. E'en if ye *would* follow Gillis, then ye couldn't. Nobody in these mountains could follow Colonel Harvey Gillis if he didna want to be followed. What could a murderin', poachin' greenhorn like yereself expect t'do?"

Dobie's voice was hoarse. "I'll show you. I've been traveling long enough with Colonel Harvey Gillis. I've been watching him long enough. I could follow him across slick rock to hell."

VI

Whatever trail the colonel had made on the shore of Little Coon Creek had been obliterated by the struggle, but Dobie coursed the timber until he found the spot where Colonel Harvey Gillis had dumped enough beaver packs to mount himself, Kentuck, and the girl. Squatting there over the bales of pelts, the boy looked toward the higher timber.

"Ye're a greenhorn," muttered Kenmore. "No mountain mon could skylight himself goin' o'er a ridge top when he can get to the same place goin' doon a valley."

"You don't have to skylight yourself if you go parallel with the ridge," said Dobie. "Gillis always claimed the man on top had the advantage. Anyone traveling in a valley exposes himself to view from either slope. A man riding the hill can see everything without being spotted himself."

Just within the timberline, after another hour's search, a hundred feet below the ridge top, Dobie found one of the signs Gillis had missed—a clump of pine needles lying on the ground.

"Squirrels," growled Kenmore.

Dobie pointed to the branch the needles had been knocked from. "Not at that height. Nothing but a horse. Colonel Harvey Gillis don't often leave that much sign. He must be in a hurry."

Kenmore shook his head groggily. Dobie had applied the mountain man's cure-all of lard and gunpowder to the Scotsman's wounds, but Kenmore was weak with pain and loss of blood.

"So ye found their trail. They're mounted and we're afoot. When do ye sprout yere wings?"

"Them being mounted is the only thing that saves us," said Dobie. "Afoot, Gillis wouldn't leave enough sign for us to trail at all. Now he can't help dropping notice here and there. And we can take short cuts he can't."

They saw that the trail was leading down the ridge to where the Little Coon made a loop around into the next valley, and took the first one of those short cuts, sliding straight down the steep cliffs above the water, because the riders would have to ford the stream at some spot.

Dobie found the scratches leading across a rocky bank and into a deep pool. The two of them came, gasping, to the opposite bank, where four trails leading four different ways showed plainly in the white sand.

"Which one points toward the Teton?" he asked Kenmore.

Kenmore waved vaguely at one leading toward a motte of aspens. "But that isna the one to follow. If a mon makes four fake trails like this to cover his real one, 'tis a certainty his real one isna going to be pointing directly toward the spot he means to arrive at finally. Not even a greenhorn would be that obvious."

"Exactly why the real one does head straight toward the Teton," said Dobie. "Gillis is always one step ahead of everyone else. He knows most trackers would figure just like you did, and look for the real trail to be among the three not heading directly north. So that's the one he takes. Where's the next big water on the way to the Teton?"

"Knee Creek," said Kenmore. "Twenty miles north. American Fur preserves. Anyone striking toward the Teton through there would be bucking Reeves an' his whole Highwood brigade o' American Fur men. Colonel Gillis wouldna be fool enough. . . ." He stopped, turning to Dobie, shaking his head. "All right. So he would. Nobody else would, but *he* would. If that's it, we can cut off ten miles by going as the crow flies. If ye're right, we should catch him before morning. If ye're wrong, this will put us so far behind we'll ne'er see ma lassie again."

They ate serviceberries for supper that only an Indian could swallow with a straight face, and washed them down with water. Dobie still watched the Scotsman narrowly. All up and down the Missouri they had told him Kenmore was insane, and Dobie had seen enough signs to believe them. But Kenmore was so weak that all he could do was stagger along behind Dobie, muttering sullenly.

They traveled all night through murky valleys filled with the frightened voices of quaking aspens, and over cloud-hung crests echoing to the questions of flapping horned owls. Finally when dawn was blushing in the east, they staggered down into the mucky-sweet spring smell of the Knee Creek bottoms, and burst through a popping tangle of chokecherry. They almost stumbled over the body of a man lying with his head in the shallows, the way that American Fur trapper had lain back on the Squaw, all hacked up from chest to waist, the water darkened by his blood. Dobie grabbed the Scotsman's arm suddenly, shoving him off the cutbank.

"Watch it!" he yelled, and leaped after Kenmore, with a bullet kicking up sand where he had stood a moment before. The echoes of the shot trembled into silence farther down among the cottonwoods dripping their morning fog. Lying there, half submerged in the shallows, they heard the man call: "Dobie? How in Colter's Hell did you do it? I never saw anybody else track the colonel before. And we had cayuses. Don't come out."

Slowly Dobie shifted around so he could get his gun unhooked from his belt. He had the picture of Kentuck's lazy grin when the man had given him that gun, and a sick dread seeped through him.

"We *were* poaching, then." Dobie's voice came out half choked. "That's how you and the colonel always got such a big harvest."

Kentuck sounded weary. "That's right, Dobie. Bad and good in every man, I guess. More bad than good in me. We were friends, though, weren't we? That much was good. That's why this is the hell. Please don't try and come out."

Dobie blinked his eyes, dumping out powder that had been wetted till he came to some that had not been reached. He pinched it out of the flask and dumped it into the gun. He remembered Kentuck and himself fighting side-by-side through all the howling Arikarees there on the Grand, and dread was bearing him down now like a physical weight.

"That was you hacking up all those American Fur men and poaching their furs, then, and not Kenmore?"

Dobie was surprised to hear Colonel Harvey Gillis's voice, coming from somewhere farther away than Kentuck's: "Me, greenhorn. With my tomahawk. The one on Squaw Creek had come across me while I was cleaning out his trap lines there. I'd just finished with him when you had to come down. I wasn't hunting Kenmore's sign when I left you to dig the grave. I was hunting for the corpse's partner. Reeves. I didn't find Reeves till today. He had camped here and cut our sign when we started to cross. Got suspicious when he saw all those unskinned carcasses from the Squaw. Using my tomahawk on them that way threw the guilt on Kenmore. That story about the crazy Scotchman swearing vengeance on American Fur fitted in with our plans. We could do whatever we liked, and nobody to suspect it was us."

"Hooker suspected." Dobie had the picture of Kentuck and himself laughing together over a tall tale by a lonely campfire on the Squaw, and cursing together at an ornery pack horse that had pitched its *aparejos* on the Big Dry, and sweating together on the trap lines, and all the other things that lay between them.

"That was him back on Little Coon?" the colonel called. "I spotted someone coming downslope. Kentuck didn't want to leave you, but I couldn't risk a fight, not with the girl."

"That was Hooker," said Dobie. "What made you change your mind back on the Mizzou and take me in?"

"Kentuck was full of Monongahela that night at the Rocky Mountain House," said Gillis, "and couldn't remember just how much he'd told you. If he'd told you what we were doing, I couldn't leave you running around loose, could I? I wanted to get rid of you and throw the blame on Kenmore. Kentuck wouldn't have it. He's a sentimental fool. Next best thing was to take you along. Who's that *kyesh* with you?"

So he didn't know! Dobie rammed his lead into the barrel. He had another picture now, of a dark-haired girl with skin like milk and hair like a prime plew, and he knew it would have to be one or the other.

Dobie could see Gillis. The colonel was backing downstream, but his movement had brought him into view only now. In another moment he would be in the timber. He had the struggling girl held in front of him with one arm, holding the tomahawk with the other. Dobie remembered what had happened to the last person he had held that way.

Gillis must have caught the shift Dobie made as he set himself to rise. "Don't be a damn' fool, greenhorn. Isn't a man north of Saint Looey would go running into Kentuck's smoothbore that way. You'll be like a duck popping up out of water, and Kentuck can knock their peepers out at fifty yards. I'm taking the girl to the Teton now. She'll tell me where that loco Scotchman's cache is, and these few furs we poached will look like a sick varmint beside the pile we'll have then. You just stay down behind that bank and you won't get killed."

Dobie's feet made a soft sound in the sand as he got up, and Kentuck heard the sound. "No, Dobie, don't do it! Harvey left me behind to hold you, that's all. I couldn't have gone much farther anyway. This is about the last plew left in my sack. Don't do it now, Dobie. Stay down and let the colonel get away and everything'll be fine. We're friends, Dobie, you and me."

"I'm coming, Kentuck," said Dobie.

He stood erect and threw himself up the cutbank. The sand sluffed off beneath his boots, and then he was slogging across the shore to where Kentuck sat huddled in his Mandan robe in the somber shadows of two cottonwoods. Kentuck's pistol made a brassy flash.

Dobie had his gun in line, but he kept running forward, his face twisted with the terrible conflict tearing at him. Then he stopped.

Kentuck's pistol was still. He grinned weakly. "I can't," he said. "Go ahead."

"I can't," said Dobie.

"Damn you, Kentuck!" screamed Gillis. He threw the girl from him and started back in that padding run at Dobie. Dobie whirled. He saw Colonel Harvey Gillis's tomahawk flash upward. He fired and dived forward.

Gillis's black wolf-skin cap was plucked off his head. That was the last Dobie saw. He had thrown himself low, knowing the colonel always aimed at a man's chest or head—but not low enough. The head of the tomahawk hissed past, and the end of its long handle struck his head. The handle flew up and the blade down—into the small of his back. He was still in midair, and the sickening blow on his spine knocked him flat.

With his face buried in the sand, he heard Colonel Harvey Gillis's yell, and felt the man's weight strike him. The colonel straddled Dobie and shifted sideways to grab his tomahawk. Then Dobie felt the man's body jerk erect on him, felt the blade come out, and waited for it to descend again.

The gun's bellow came from somewhere to his right. He felt Gillis twitch, and sob, and fall forward against him with the tomahawk flung out in one slack hand. Dobie struggled weakly from beneath the dead man.

"I guess Colonel Harvey was right. I'm just a sentimental fool," murmured Kentuck, and tossed the smoking gun out on the shore toward the boy. He grinned. "You can have the other one now, Dobie." He sagged forward in his Mandan robe with the glaze on his eyes turning to a dead blankness.

The girl kept trembling in Dobie's arms as he led her down to where Ian Kenmore lay behind the cutbank. "On the Big Dry, Colonel Harvey pretended he didn't know who I really was, remember?" she explained feverishly. "And you didn't seem to know me. Everyone on the river thought my father had done those murders. I was afraid you'd turn me over to American Fur if you knew I was Ian Kenmore's daughter. That's why I never told you my last name. You stopped him that night or he would have begun trying to force me to tell him where the pelts were."

"There isna ony fur cache," said Kenmore weakly, as they hauled him out of the shallows. "That's just a rumor some Blackfoot started after he'd pulled too long at a *tiswin* jug. But there's new country out past the Big Stonies nae trapper's ever seen, and there's more beaver there than ye could find in a thousand caches like I was supposed to hae had. These little holes in me will heal up soon enow, noo that Nairn is wi' me.

I'll need some help to start another company in that fresh country. Whoe'er it is will have to be experienced, understond. Nae crowlin' ferlie o' a greenhorn that couldna track his finger across the table."

Nairn Kenmore was watching Dobie, and it was in the girl's wide blue eyes that there would be more than just beaver and trap sacks in that new land for him, if he wanted it. Her voice was soft. "How about it . . . mountain man?"

★ ★ ★ ★ ★

The Buckskin Army Heads South

★ ★ ★ ★ ★

This story was one that the author marketed himself before he engaged an agent. It was his sixth story to appear when it was published in *Star Western* (11/43).

I

Painter Cole led his raw-boned mare into Taos from the old Pecuris Trail, the bloody corpse of Esperanzado Panuela tied face down across the saddle. Cole had sensed something wrong when he had reached the first outlying hovels of the little New Mexican pueblo. Panuela had been a well-known fur trader here for fifteen years, and sight of Cole bringing his dead body into town should have drawn a crowd instantly. Yet the only sign of life was the flash of a terrified face at a doorway, or frightened eyes gleaming from a shadowed window.

Where the trail entered the sun-splashed plaza, Cole halted. Behind him stood his long train of Flathead pack horses, hip-shot and jaded beneath their heavy packsaddles, their occasional snorts the only sound in the foreboding hush.

The sun of late summer shone hotly on Cole's tall, broad-shouldered figure, standing there among the ancient terraced houses. He wore the grease-daubed hunting jacket and elk-hide leggings of the free trapper. At some time in his past he had mixed with a mountain lion—known to the trappers as a painter—and his face had been left terribly scarred. One of his ears was ripped to shreds. Four parallel claw marks started high on his bony forehead, cutting down across the big questing beak of a nose to the corner of his broad mouth, tugging it up into a perpetual, twisted smile. Men had forgotten his Christian name. He was known from Yellowstone to St. Louis as Painter Cole, the ugliest man in all the Rockies.

As the trapper turned to face Don Fernando Avenue where it entered the west side of the plaza, he realized what was the matter with Taos. Cimarron Saunders was in town. The red-haired man was coming out of Don Fernando and across the plaza toward Cole, his cut-throat crew swaggering behind him. This was 1843, and New Mexico was still a northern province of Mexico. There wasn't much law outside of Santa Fe, the capital of the province. And when a man like Cimarron Saunders came to town, the people locked what doors they had, and stayed inside their houses. Saunders's tone was mocking, as he stopped in front of the trapper.

"Hello, Cole. Where did you run acrost Panuela in that fix?"

A smoldering enmity had long existed between these two men since, among other activities, Saunders was a poacher. A free trapper's hate for the men who poached his furs went so deep as to be almost inbred. Cole deliberately let a long moment go by before he answered the red-headed Saunders.

As the uncomfortable silence lengthened, anger flickered through the poacher's eyes. He was a big man, as tall as Cole, with a torso that bulged thickly beneath his blazing red wool shirt. He could handle a gun as well as most, and he packed one of Sam Colt's new Dragoons. But primarily he was a knife man. Stuck through the broad black belt that held up his buckskins was a huge, curved *saca tripas*— gets the guts—the wicked plebian knife of the Mexican peon. His hairy hand had begun to caress its leather-wrapped hilt when Cole finally spoke.

"I come across Panuela yesterday evening, about twenty miles south of here. Some *hombres* had him spread-eagled on the ground and was giving him a good going over," said Cole, indicating the obvious marks of torture on the fur trader's head and face. "They skeedadled when I took after 'em. It was almost dark and I didn't see who they were. But I shot one *hombre*'s gun outen his hand."

The trapper's glance left Saunders and swept among his men, looking for a bandaged hand, or an empty holster. His eyes took in Pablo Rodriguez, a tremendously fat *bandido* whose prodigious physique threatened to burst the seams of the blue, Mexican cavalry coat he wore. Beneath the floppy brim of his sombrero, his little eyes glittered malignantly at Cole. Neither of his pudgy hands was marked, and his .44 was in its usual place, struck through the broad red sash that banded his tremendous girth.

Saunders seemed to hold himself in check, and speculation narrowed his eyes. "Was Panuela alive when you reached him?"

Cole kept on looking at the men. Tanay, the Mescalero Apache, was admittedly a murderer. He cut the ears off the men he killed, and sewed them into his belt. Dangling from each of his own ear-lobes was eight or ten inches of gold watch chain, filched from the body of a hapless victim on the trail.

Cimarron Saunders had a hair-trigger temper, and now he found it difficult to keep his voice from shaking with his growing anger. "I asked you, Cole, if Panuela was alive when you reached him?"

"Yeah," said Cole. "Yeah. Panuela lived a minute after I got to him. . . ."

He knew suddenly that he had talked too much. The speculation slid from Saunders's eyes. He shook his red head from side to side, and his placid mouth spread in a smile. His crew began to spread out around Cole. Enrique Valzabar moved to one side on high-heeled boots; he was the scion of a clan that boasted nothing but *bandidos* and killers in its ranks since Oñate founded Santa Fe in 1608. Claude Tate—a river man from the wild Missouri, his tattered wool pants supported by Yankee galluses, shifted to the other side.

Painter Cole knew how a beaver in a jump trap felt. His eyes flashed to the creamy mud walls of Esperanzado Panuela's *hacienda* on the east side of the plaza, not ten feet behind Saunders. To the right of the dark oak door that led into the house proper was a *socavón*— a tunnel-like passageway leading through the wall and into the inner patio. And in that shadowy *socavón*, behind an iron gate, stood the half-breed, Tomosito, Panuela's partner. He was a clever man, Tomosito, an opportunist who would not put himself in Cimarron Saunders's way for a mere free trapper.

Cole's Paterson five-shot, sagging heavily against his hip, might as well have been left home. Whatever skill he had with a shooting iron wouldn't save his life against the dozen guns of these men who now surrounded him completely.

Still caressing the leather-hafted *saca tripas*, Saunders spoke again harshly, demandingly: "Now, Cole, I want you to answer me another question, quick. What did Panuela tell you afore he died?"

Cole put one of his huge, bony hands up to his ugly chin, rubbing the black bristles almost thoughtfully. There were many variations to the tale of his battle with the painter. But there were even more legends of the incredible strength in his great trap-scarred hands. He knew he had already irritated Saunders to the point where the man's temper was near to exploding. He knew, too, Saunders's penchant for using his knife when that temper did explode. The resolution that now entered Cole's mind was a long chance, but it was the only way he could see out of this thing he had so unwittingly stepped into. When he finally spoke, it was in a stridently contemptuous tone, deliberately calculated to infuriate Cimarron Saunders.

"I've answered enough of your damn' questions, poacher. I don't know why I wasted talk with you in the first place. Now, get out of my way!"

Amazement was in the sag of Saunders's mouth. Then a dull red flush crept up his bull neck and into his heavy-jawed face.

With a throaty curse, he lunged forward, yanking out his *saca tripas.*

Cole met Saunders's lunge almost before the man had started, big hand closing around Saunders's wrist. With a pull and a wrench, he twisted that wrist until the knife was reversed, its sharp point digging into the poacher's belly. Enrique Valzabar had his gun out by then, and Rodriquez had also drawn, his cocked hammer making a sharp, metallic sound.

"Tell your coyotes not to shoot," panted Cole. "Or I'll rip your guts out."

Still trying to jerk backward out of Cole's grip, Saunders gasped: "Don't shoot. He'll rip me, sure's his word." And suddenly he quit struggling, standing very still, breathing harshly. He was a big, heavy man with solid muscle packed into his thick-set torso. Perhaps he could have wrenched loose from that one vise-like hand, using all his strength and weight. But the point of the *saca tripas* was driven so hard against his belly that his red wool shirt had spilt beneath it. One thrust of Cole's incredible hand, and Saunders would spit himself on his own blade.

Cole reached backward for his mare's reins. Still holding Saunders's wrist so the knife was against the man's stomach, the trapper began moving forward, shoving at Saunders with short vicious jabs, moving him back against the wall of Panuela's *hacienda.*

"Open that door, Tomosito!" called Cole. "Get this mare inside. And my pack train, too. I got a year's harvest of beaver plews on them horses, and I don't wanta leave 'em out here with these poachers."

Tomosito had retreated out of sight, and the gate was opened by an impassive *mozo*— one of Panuela's Indian manservants. Over the sound of the pack horses' plodding hoofs, as they followed the mare through the *socavón,* Cole could hear the shuffle of feet in the plaza behind him. Jamming the knife in a little harder, he growled: "Tell your *hombres* to stop right where they are, Saunders."

"Do like he says!" cried Saunders. "And put them guns away. I don't want my belly cut out because somebody's finger slipped!"

Cole's perpetual smile grew a little, mirthlessly. Then all the horses were through the creamy adobe wall with its network of weather cracks. Cole whirled Saunders around until the redhead was in between him and the others. He let go of the man's wrist, shoving him violently, stepping back into the cool shade of the *socavón*. The *mozo* slammed the iron gate shut on Cimarron Saunders's choked curses.

Esperanzado Panuela's *hacienda* was a typical New Mexican house—a sprawling, one-story building, built around the inner patio they called a *placita*. Panuela had carried on his fur trade from here, and to one side of the *placita* was the big fur press, surrounded by a few swart beaver plews. A willow spread its shade over a bright-roofed well, and stables stood to the rear.

A pair of menservants had lifted Panuela off Cole's mare and laid him on a Chimayo blanket spread on the ground. Carmencita Panuela kneeled beside her father, sobbing hopelessly. She was exotic even in her grief, with blue-black hair piled up under a white mantilla, the dark rebozo around her shoulders showing her station by the quality of its weave—as did the corresponding serape of a man.

Beside her stood Tomosito. He was the son of a Spanish soldier and a Pueblo Indian mother. The intelligence and avarice of the Spaniard parent and the grim dogged patience of the Pueblo mother had combined to make a rare man of Tomosito. Seldom was a half-breed so well educated, widely traveled— even more seldom was one so rich. He had carefully cultivated the manners of an aristocrat, and most men had forgotten he had once been a peon.

In deference to the girl's grief, Cole moved over beside his pack horses, nodding for the half-breed to follow.

"What's this all about, Tomosito?" he asked in a low voice. "Why did Saunders try to stop me out there?"

Tomosito ran one buckskin-gloved hand up and down the edge of his red and blue serape, folded across his left shoulder. The silver buttons of his tight, blackened leather leggings were unfastened to the knee, showing his immaculate white drawers beneath. His dark hawk face crowned by queued, jet-black hair was turned to Cole with a faintly ironic smile.

"*Señor* Cole, it is unfortunate that you told Cimarron Saunders my partner was alive when you reached him," he said softly. "Right now, I wouldn't give a single *peso* for your life."

II

The words sent a cold premonition clean through the trapper. And then, because he understood none of this, impatient anger thickened his voice. "Look here, Tomosito, I've been away all season. Make it clear, will you? What have I got that Saunders wants?"

"It isn't only Saunders who wants what you have," said the half-breed. "Word will leak out, and within a week every *maldito*, every cut-throat north of Durango will be seeking you."

He turned to glance at the servants who had lifted Panuela and were carrying him into the house. Carmencita rose, still sobbing softly. She turned and came over to stand beside Tomosito, dark eyes filled with grief. The half-breed turned back to Cole.

"A lot has happened since you left last spring, *Señor* Cole. Some Texan named Mier led a military expedition into Mexico. It so angered *Presidente* Santa Anna that he ordered Governor Armijo to close the Santa Fe Trail to the Yankees. That meant

Esperanzado and I couldn't ship our furs to Saint Looey. The furs kept coming in though, mounting to such alarming proportions that I finally went to Mexico City, trying to find a market there. But the prices were so far below those we get from the Yankees that it was absurd to consider them. While I was gone, Panuela evidently decided to hide the furs. . . ."

"He had to," interrupted the girl in a choked voice. "We had gathered over two hundred thousand dollars' worth of pelts here. Saunders must have found out, somehow. When he came to town, Father knew we weren't even safe in our own house as long as those furs were stored in the *placita*. He began taking loads out at night. He wouldn't even tell me where he was caching the furs. And the servants that went with him were sworn to kill themselves rather than reveal the hiding place."

"They kept their word," said Cole. "I came across their bodies on the Pecuris Trail. They'd all shot themselves. Your father wasn't so lucky. There were signs of a fight, and tracks leading away, so I cached my pack animals and followed 'em. Came across those *hombres* torturing your father just north of the Pecos. They'd been using the garrote. . . ."

He stopped, with the ugly memory of it. The men had used a rawhide hobble for the garrote. They had tied it around Panuela's head above his eyes, thrusting a short length of hickory through it, twisting tighter and tighter until the rawhide had been sunk deep into the old man's flesh. Cole had heard of younger, stronger men than Panuela cracking under the garrote. Yet the old man evidently hadn't divulged his secret, and he'd even retained enough coherence to speak those few words to Cole before he died. Carmencita was making a gallant effort to control her grief, biting her full under lip, twisting her handkerchief.

"My brother," she asked, "you . . . you found him, too?"

"Manuel?" said Cole. "No, I didn't see hide nor hair of him.

And I still don't see how this affects me."

"*Señor* Cole," said Tomosito, "you have sold furs to Panuela for years, have wintered in his *hacienda,* have been one of his best friends. And you told Saunders that he was alive when you reached him. Wouldn't it be logical for Saunders to conclude that Panuela told you where his cache was? In other words, you are, to all intents and purposes, the only man in the world who knows where two hundred thousand dollars worth of beaver pelts are hidden."

For a moment, the only sound was the quiet bubbling of the little rivulet that ran through the *placita.* Then Tomosito leaned forward with that soft smile, and his veiled eyes held a sudden eagerness, almost a greediness.

"Esperanzado Panuela *did* tell you where those furs are, did he not, *Señor* Cole?"

Cole might have answered without hesitation, but his glance had gone beyond Tomosito to the girl. Something else beside grief was in her face. She was staring intently at Cole in a silent plea—or warning.

"Well?" said Tomosito.

Cole untied the arrowhead from one of the whangs that formed the fringe on his leggings. Still trying to fathom that look in the girl's eyes, he held the bit of agatized rock out to To-mosito.

"Esperanzado told me to take this to Carmencita. That's all he could get out before he died."

Cole had expected disappointment in the half-breed. But To-mosito masked whatever he felt, taking the arrowhead, turning it over and over in his gloved hand.

"*Pues,*" said the girl dully, "it's only an arrowhead . . . the kind you can find in any of the deserted pueblos."

Tomosito nodded. "*Si.* Obviously Panuela wouldn't cache his furs in an inhabited pueblo. If this means he hid them in one of those deserted villages, it doesn't help us much. There are hundreds of them throughout the province. It would take us a lifetime to search them all."

"You know how the jewelry and blankets of each pueblo vary slightly," said Cole. "The arrowheads must have some small differences, too. Isn't there some *viejo,* some old man among your people, who would be able to tell that difference?"

Tomosito's face darkened momentarily—he didn't like to be reminded of his Pueblo blood. Then, as swiftly, his soft smile returned. "It is our only chance, isn't it?" he said. "There are some *viejos* at Acoma who might know. It is several days' ride south of here."

The girl moved closer to Cole. "You will go there with us, *señor,* you will help us? It isn't the furs so much. It's Manuel, my brother. He was with Father, and, if you didn't find him, he may still be alive, may still be out there somewhere."

"You are in this as deeply as we, *Señor* Cole," said Tomosito. "For until those furs are found, your life won't be safe one minute of the day."

Cole could see Tomosito's point. Yet it wasn't the furs, really, that drew Cole into this so inextricably. It was the girl.

Carmencita Panuela's vivid Latin beauty was as famous in this northern province as was the strength in Painter Cole's hands. Cole's ugliness set him apart from other men, but his reactions to a beautiful woman were normal enough. Every *caballero* in Santa Fe was in love with Carmencita—why should Painter Cole be an exception? He had never revealed his feelings, knowing too well how she must regard him, she who but with a single smile could have had the handsomest, richest aristocrat in the whole province.

Yet now, with the girl standing there so close to him, her eyes filled with that plea, he knew he was more deeply involved than Tomosito could conceive.

"Yeah," he said. "I'll ride with you."

" *'Sta bueno*," said the half-breed. "We'll start tonight. Perhaps we can give Saunders the slip."

"I'm going, too," said Carmencita.

"One Panuela is already dead," said Tomosito. "You'd better stay here."

Her chin tilted. "My brother is out there somewhere, and they are my furs as much as yours, now, *Señor* Tomosito."

Tomosito didn't raise his voice, but it had suddenly lost its softness. "*Señorita* Panuela, I forbid you to go."

Cole was amazed that the girl had been able to control her grief even this long. All the fight suddenly went out of her. She turned swiftly toward the house, and her shoulders were shaking with sobs beneath the dark rebozo as she went through the door. Tomosito watched her go, and in his smoldering eyes was none of the normal admiration or desire a man should feel for such a woman—only a cold, impersonal speculation. It irritated Cole strangely.

A sickle moon cast eerie yellow light across the plaza. Painter Cole stood in the deep gloom of the *socavón*, behind him Tomosito and the *mozos* he had picked to ride to Acoma.

These New Mexican *haciendas* had been built to act as forts as well as houses. Their exteriors were grim, slit-like windows piercing walls at infrequent intervals, the number of doorways kept to a minimum. Invariably there was only one gateway large enough to permit the passage of horses and the solid-wheeled *carretas*. This *socavón* was the only way out for Cole and the others.

Cimarron Saunders had taken over a house on the south side of the plaza, turning it into his own private *cantina*. Sounds of drunken revelry came to the men standing in the *socavón*— a thick voice singing some obscene ditty of the wild Missouri, a raucous laugh. Tomosito called to the sharp-faced *mozo* who squatted on the roof of a shed, peering over the wall.

"Well, Jarales, can you see any of Saunders's men?"

Jarales had been Tomosito's servant for many years. His vacant, glazed stare and his slack-lipped mouth revealed a weakness for the peyote bean, a drug that was a religion with the Indians, a vice with Jarales.

"*Sí*," he said. "Saunders himself is in the house, drinking. But he has left a whole army of his *demonios* waiting for us. Pablo Rodriguez and that Apache are on the roof of *Don* José's house across the street. Valzabar and some others are hanging around where the Pecuris comes into the plaza. It would be suicide to go out there now."

"Saunders is just the kind of *kyesh* to wait for me all the rest of his natural life. We might as well try to get through tonight as anytime," said Cole, turning to a Navajo servant who stood by the iron door. "Open up when I give the word."

Cole's mare was jaded from the long trip out of the mountains, and Tomosito had given him a magnificent black from the stables. Jamming a Ute moccasin into the stirrup, Cole swung aboard. He settled into the rawhide-rigged Spanish saddle, holding his long Jake Hawkins rifle parallel to the horse so it wouldn't catch in the doorway. Unlashing a braided quirt from the saddle skirt, he waited until the soft creak of leather behind had quit, telling him all were mounted.

He turned to the Navajo. "Open the gate."

The iron hinges creaked, the grille swung back. Cole raised his quirt and laid it into the black. The stallion leaped forward, shooting from the darkness of the *socavón* into the moonlit plaza. Bending low over the huge silver-mounted pommel, Cole swung in rhythm to the pounding hoofs. And suddenly from the roof top across the way came Pablo Rodriguez's hoarse voice: "C-e-e-marron, *está que diablo*, Cole. C-e-e-marron!"

162

Shots followed, loud, thunderous. Lead kicked up red clay all about Cole, plucking at his leggings and whizzing by his head. His mount was in full gallop now, black flanks rippling, magnificent barrel heaving beneath the trapper's tightly held knees. If the horse had as much bottom as it had speed, Cole felt capable of outrunning anything Saunders could fork.

Above the pound of hoofs behind, he could hear the drunken curses of Cimarron Saunders as he lurched out of the house he had taken over, cursing his men for fools and bellowing for horses.

Three men loomed up in front of Cole suddenly, jumping out from behind the terraced house that fronted on the Pecuris Trail. The foremost man raised his London fusil, a deadly weapon at that close range. But Cole had already dropped his quirt, and gripped his Jake Hawkins in both hands, leaning far out in the saddle and swinging viciously.

Flesh and bone pulped beneath Cole's blow. The London fusil exploded harmlessly in the air as the screaming man slammed back against a mud wall. The other two scrambled desperately from beneath the hoofs of that careening black. The trapper caught a flash of Enrique Valzabar's contorted face. Then the youth, whose clan boasted nothing but murderers since Oñate was behind Cole, and the trapper was racing through the narrow lane that led between the last outlying hovels.

Free of the town, Cole eased straighter in the saddle, pulling his horse into a steady gallop, allowing Tomosito to catch up with him.

"*Válgame Dios,*" panted the half-breed. "I thought you wouldn't get through those last three men on the south side."

He put his still-smoking Adams self-cocker back into a tooled holster that rode his blackened leggings in a stiff, unfamiliar way. He had always been the one to let others do the gunning.

"Did we lose any men?" asked Cole.

"One," said Tomosito. "I hope they killed him. I wouldn't want Cimarron Saunders to get him alive."

They rode southward across the plain surrounding Taos, through flats covered by the ubiquitous greasewood. It grew colder as they climbed the pass through the Taos Mountains, wending through stunted cedars, hoofs muted by the grama grass that matted the ancient trail to the Pecuris pueblo.

It was near dawn when they reached the place where Cole had found Panuela's three dead *mozos*. He indicated the rocky mounds where he had buried them.

The trapper knew how useless it would be to try and hide their trail permanently from Tanay and Saunders's other Apache trackers. So he led the little cavalcade through the ford of the Pecos and about a mile beyond. Then he sought hard ground where their hoofs would show less marks, cutting off the Pecuris at right angles, riding a quarter mile up the slope through scrub oak and *palmitos*. There he made another right angle turn, riding back toward the river, paralleling the trail below.

Tomosito urged his mustang up beside Cole. "Why do you turn back?"

"We'll wait above the ford for Saunders to pass us. Then we'll head downriver in the water. Those Apaches'll have one helluva time figuring which way we went in that river, won't they?"

He halted them in a clearing above the Pecos, screened by juniper and stunted pine, where they could see but could not be seen. Everyone dismounted, easing girths to blow the horses. The sky was turning light with coming day, and Cole became aware that Tomosito had been watching his men with a peculiar intensity. The half-breed spoke, almost to himself.

"I thought one of my *hombres* was shot. That should leave only three. Yet here we have four."

One stood apart from the others, facing away from Cole and Tomosito, face hidden by the huge roll-brim sombrero that was tilted down low in front. Tomosito took three swift steps and jerked that big hat off.

Cole had never seen the half-breed display so much emotion before.

"Por Dios," he gasped. "Carmencita!"

The girl's blue-black hair had been piled into the crown of the sombrero. It fell down about her shoulders as she whirled to face Tomosito, cheeks coloring. She had donned a man's leggings and tight *charro* jacket, and she looked smaller in them, somehow.

"I told you I was coming!" she cried defiantly. "It's too late to send me back now!"

The half-breed recovered his composure. He stepped back, smiling softly.

"Oh, no, *sancha mía,* it isn't too late. Jarales, Rudolfo, take *Señorita* Panuela back to Taos. Avoid Saunders. Use your own judgment if she gives you trouble."

The girl backed up against her skittish pony. Her glance went past Tomosito to Cole, towering there above the others, the ugliness of his face softened a little in the dim light. He had seen the same strange plea in her big dark eyes when Tomosito had asked him about Panuela, back there in the *placita*. This time he didn't try to fathom it. He just answered it, stepping forward and speaking in a quiet way.

"If the *señorita* wants to go that bad, Tomosito, I think we should let her."

Tomosito turned from the girl to Cole, running his hand up and down his serape.

"Since Esperanzado's death, *Señor* Cole, I feel a keen responsibility for his daughter. A responsibility, I may say, in which you have no share. . . ."

His glance moved momentarily toward his three men, and they took on a new significance for Cole. Most of the servants in the *hacienda* served Esperanzado Panuela. But these three *mozos* had always belonged to Tomosito. And manservant was a weak translation of the word *mozo*. A servant does not die for his master, or kill for his master, or belong to his master body and soul.

The degenerate Pueblo Indian, Jarales, stood with his vacant stare fixed on Cole. He wore a pair of silver-plated Remingtons, and the way he caressed their ornate handles reminded Cole of a cat sharpening its claws on a tree.

Rudolfo was from the pueblo of Isleta, a hulking brute with a wit as thick as his solid, square torso. The third *mozo*, Gaspar, Tomosito had brought up with him from Mexico City—a sly little ferret who mimicked his master's way of speaking and smiling and laughing, who seemed to miss nothing with his constantly shifting, beady eyes.

"The girl goes back, *Señor* Cole," purred Tomosito. "I think you understand how unwise it would be for you to force the issue."

The ugly trapper tried to watch them all at once as he let his hand move down toward his Paterson five-shot. The girl was beautiful, and Tomosito's soft smile angered Cole, and unwise or not, he was going to force the issue.

Gaspar snapped the electric tension with his call. "Cimarron Saunders is coming!"

As one, they turned toward the trail below. Tomosito had been right in saying every *maldito* north of Durango would be after Cole. Saunders had gathered a veritable army.

Leading was Tanay, the Mescalero Apache, morning light glinting on the gold watch chains dangling from his ears. With him were the other trackers, lean greyhounds of men on rawhide mustangs. They rode like avaricious hawks, bending low from side to side, scanning the trail. Following the Apaches was Saunders, forking a great raking dun that was harnessed like a Crow bride's horse. The reins and headstall dripped hawk's bells, the saddle was gaudy with red and blue hair tassels, the *tapaderos* plated solid with silver.

The red-haired poacher was drunk as sin, swaying dangerously back and forth. Supporting him on one side was Pablo Rodriguez in his dragoon's coat, and on the other, Enrique Valzabar. As the trio splashed through the ford, Saunders lurched sideways, almost falling from his dun. His violent cursing was quite audible to those on the slope.

"Hold me up, damn you! I'm blind drunk and I know it, but I'm gettin' that devil, Cole, if you have to tie me in a saddle. Hold me up . . . !"

Behind came Claude Tate and his renegade trappers, wild mountain men with smoothbore rifles and wolf-skin hats, who found it easier to poach their pelts than to get them with trap and "beaver medicine". There were *bandidos* from the border, too, in braided *charro* suits and heavily glazed sombreros, and a motley bunch of Indians and half-breeds in dirty buckskins and tattered bayeta blankets. Dangerous men, bandits, killers—the choicest bunch of cut-throats the province could offer.

"And they are all after you, *Señor* Cole," murmured Tomosito as the last rider disappeared down the trail. "Cimarron Saunders who wants you badly enough to ride blind drunk in his saddle, and Tanay who cuts the ears off the men he kills, and Enrique Valzabar who would be ashamed if he had an honest man among his ancestors. They are all after you."

III

Cole turned to the half-breed, expecting to take up where they had left off about Carmencita. But Tomosito stepped calmly to his horse, tightened the cinch, swung aboard. His three *mozos* followed suit.

Apprehensively the trapper mounted his black, looking for an instant to Carmencita. She smiled faintly at him. His twisted, perpetual grin spread a little in return. With a shrug, he led down toward the river. It was probably the oldest way in the world of covering a trail. No horse left tracks in two feet of water. Saunders would either have to split his force, sending some upriver, some down, or he would have to make a guess at which way Cole headed. Either procedure would give Cole a head start.

Late in the afternoon of that first day, the trapper turned west from the Pecos and headed across the Santa Fe plateau, with its detached buttes and lava-capped mesas. The waters of the Río Grande hid their tracks again, as they turned south once more. And after riding up out of the Río Grande and into the great mesa country, they reached Acoma late on the second day.

The cynical Tomosito had doubtlessly seen Acoma—the Sky City—before. Yet he seemed impressed, nevertheless, as the cavalcade topped the cedar-studded rise and suddenly looked westward across the lush strip of pasture land to the dark mesa upon which Acoma was built. The afternoon sun cast the erosion-shaped mesa into red and purple lights that tinted seeming castles with delicate minarets and imposing towers, and shone weirdly on rock formations and twisted abutments.

The Acomans farmed in the valley at the foot of their mesa, and as Cole and the others neared the fields, runners in white cotton trousers could be seen preceding them up an ancient trail.

Tomosito dismounted from his mustang at the foot of that trail. "This is the Horse Trail, *Señor* Cole. But it is hard enough to get a fresh mount up, much less *caballos* as jaded as ours."

A crowd was waiting for them at the top, short, dark-faced men in white cotton trousers of buckskin leggings, jet-black hair done up in the *chongo*—the traditional Oriental queue of the

Pueblo tribes.

Carmencita moved up beside the trapper. "I don't like this. They are all so quiet . . . and where are the women?"

Cole searched the crowd, and couldn't mark one squaw among the men. His big hand grew tighter about his Jake Hawkins rifle. The Pueblos were the most peaceful of all the tribes. Yet the silence of these men held a strangely sullen hostility.

A huge wooden cross was planted to one side of the trail at the very top, and before it stood a man in a rich bayeta blanket that hung to the knees of his white cotton trousers. He had a narrow, finely shaped nose, and his dark, seamed face formed a striking contrast to the pure white of his long hair. There was something about his appearance that tantalized Cole, as if he had known him somewhere before, and couldn't quite remember.

Tomosito spoke swiftly in Keresan, the language of the Acomans. The white-haired old man answered almost angrily, narrow eyes flashing. Tomosito turned to Cole.

"He is Almagre, the chief. We have come at a bad time. One of their young men defiled the old gods and they were preparing the ceremony for his death. But Almagre says he will see us."

The white-haired leader had already turned and the crowd parted for him. Cole followed, looking from one stolid face to another. The Acomans' eyes were veiled, their faces illegible. He felt almost transparent—as if they were looking through him, supremely ignorant of his presence. It was an eerie, disconcerting sensation.

Suddenly someone's soft, small hand was thrust into his. He looked down into Carmencita's pale face, the perfume of her midnight hair coming to him faintly. Something thickened in his throat.

"I'm afraid," she said quietly. "And right now I think I'd rather have you here than all the *caballeros* in Santa Fe."

She had never looked that way at him before, a long, studying look, up from beneath her lashes. It made him feel awkward, and he turned away to look at the buildings.

There were three long blocks of houses, an alleyway separating one from the next. Each house was three stories high, and each story was terraced back from the one below, giving the effect of giant steps. There were no doors in the lowest story. Rickety piñon ladders leaned against the walls; the chief was climbing one, amazingly agile for such an old man.

Cole helped the girl up before him, and Tomosito followed with his three *mozos*. The silence oppressed Cole. He knew there were half a hundred of those sullen-eyed Acomans behind him, yet not one made a sound. Almagre led them up another ladder to the third story, stooping through a low doorway. Tomosito stopped Cole with a hand on his arm.

"You had better leave your rifle outside. Things are touchy enough as it is."

Cole leaned the Jake Hawkins reluctantly against the wall. Feeling as naked without that rifle as without his leggings, he went through the doorway, holding his breath instinctively as he entered the semidark room. It was larger than he had thought, with Hopi-woven blankets and cougar-skin bow cases hanging from pegs in the wall. The chief, or *cacique,* had seated himself on a Navajo rug, drawing his bayeta about him. He turned to Cole, speaking in Spanish.

"We have heard of you, *Señor* Cole, and of your hands. My nephew tells me of an arrowhead you have."

His nephew! Cole's glance swept from Almagre to Tomosito, and he knew why the *cacique's* appearance had so tantalized him. The similarity between uncle and nephew was quite apparent—the same beak-like nose, the strange fire smoldering deep down in narrow, veiled eyes. Yet, in his wanderings, Cole had seen enough fanatical shamans and medicine men among the Sioux and Cheyennes to recognize the subtle difference in the old man and the young one. That deep-seated flame in the *cacique*'s eyes was a consuming fanaticism—the glow in Tomosito's was lit with the greed of his Spanish father.

The trapper tried to remember whether it had been Tomosito or himself who had suggested coming to Acoma. Behind him was a growing undertone, a constant shift and movement that had been going on ever since he entered. Feeling a pressure of bodies, Cole turned. Half the room was filled with young men, eyeing him with that impersonal hostility. They formed a solid wall between him and the door. And there was no other exit. A group of the Pueblos had separated Carmencita from the trapper, forcing her over against the side wall. Cole made a half move toward her, but Tomosito's voice stopped him.

"The arrowhead, *Señor* Cole."

Cole unknotted the whang, held out his hand with the sharp, agatized arrowhead. With an astounded, undrawn breath, Almagre leaped to his feet, throwing his bayeta off, jerking away from Cole's hand.

"The Accursed Lakes!" he screamed. "Abo, Quarai, Ti-Ba-Ra! You have defiled the Forbidden Land . . . !"

Then he broke into a torrent of Keresan, shouting at the Acomans behind Cole. The trapper whirled, with the feel of rough hands on him.

He dived for his Paterson. But an Indian grabbed his arm. Another yanked the gun from its holster. Cole jerked from side to side, biting, kicking, butting. The sheer weight of them drove him down.

On his knees, he got his big trap-scarred hands round one Acoman's neck. He twisted viciously, and something snapped, and the man sagged against him.

That was all, though. The hard floor was against his back now, and the bodies of half a dozen men were struggling all over him. Their shouts were loud in his ears. Their smell was strong—the odor of rich earth from the fields, and of leather, and of sweat. From somewhere, muffled, came Carmencita's terrified scream.

"Cole, Cole!"

He was sorry he couldn't help her. She had counted on him. Her voice was the last thing he heard. Something struck him on the head, and sound and smell and sensation faded into nothingness.

His body held down by the thousand hands of an overpowering lethargy, Cole finally struggled up.

From somewhere in the darkness he heard a groan—and realized it was his own. Then someone beside him spoke.

"Ah, *señor*, you have come to. You were unconscious all night."

He didn't recognize the voice, and because he had always been a simple, straightforward man anyway, he asked: "Where am I?"

"You are in the kiva, *señor*," said the other, "the ceremonial chamber. Only the *caciques*, or those who are to die, ever see this room."

Cole was silent a moment, trying to move his arms, his legs. Rawhide held his hands tightly behind his back, and lashed his feet rigidly. He heard someone breathing on his other side.

"That you, Carmencita?"

"*Sí*," she said in a small voice. "They are going to kill us, Cole. You broke an Acoman's neck up there in that room with those hands of yours. They were going to finish you then, but Tomosito and Almagre persuaded them to wait."

"Is that why you were afraid of Tomosito?" he asked.

"*Dios*, no," she said. "How could I know he was up to this? I don't know exactly why I did fear him. He was always so soft and cultured, so perfect a *caballero*. He never did anything to arouse my suspicions. Yet, there was always something in his eyes, a cruelty. And the way he smiled, as if he were waiting for something, biding his time. Maybe this is what he was waiting for."

She didn't say any more, and the gloom held the three of them for a moment. Finally Cole turned back to the man on his other side.

"Why are you here?"

"I'm Leandro Baca," the man answered. "Almagre had wanted to get rid of me for a long time. Most of the Pueblos, you see, pay homage to two sets of gods . . . Tata *Dios,* the Spaniard's god, and the Trues, our old gods. But Almagre and his followers want to go completely back to the old gods. They would destroy our church and the cross at the head of the Horse Trail. They have gained too much strength here in Acoma. Little by little, those who oppose them have disappeared. Like me . . . when I wandered into the Accursed Lakes country and brought back the things I found in Ti-Ba-Ra, Almagre said I had defiled the old gods and, according to ancient custom, must die."

"Didn't Almagre yell something about the Accursed Lakes when I handed him that arrowhead?" asked Cole.

"*Sí,*" said Carmencita. "He said . . . 'Abo, Quarai, Ti-Ba-Ra.' "

"They are the three dead cities of the Accursed Lakes," said Leandro Baca. "In Ti-Ba-Ra dwells the *brujo* . . . a witch. I heard of him from some wandering Apaches, but I didn't believe them. I was inside the ruins when I heard him laugh. It was terrible. . . ."

Someone fumbled with the trap door in the roof and Leandro stopped, squirmed over to Cole, his voice coming swiftly.

"*Señor,* Almagre took away the stone axe and the knives I

brought back from Ti-Ba-Ra. But he didn't get what I tied into my *chongo*. I've been trying to think of a way to get it for days. If you could reach it, maybe you could saw through your bonds."

He twisted his head down by Cole's hands. Cole shifted his hips until his fingers brushed against the coarse black hair of Leandro's queue. The trap opened, shooting a beam of sunlight into the kiva, blinding Cole. He worked his fingers into the *chongo* as someone's legs appeared on the ladder. Something hard and sharp rasped against Cole's thumb. He closed his hand around it, grunting. Leandro jerked his head away.

And when Tomosito turned on the ladder to look at them, they were lying as before. Only now, some ancient tapering stone implement from Ti-Ba-Ra pressed its sharp edges into the trapper's calloused palm. Almagre came behind Tomosito, followed by a pair of hard-looking Acomans in white cotton pantaloons. The light gave Cole his first real look at Leandro Baca.

He was young-looking, wearing nothing but a faded cloth about his loins. His rangy body with its deep chest and flat belly had the hound-dog look that came to these wanderers who spent most of their life on the trail. His intelligent face was haggard, hollow-cheeked, and there was a tortured look to his dark eyes.

Tomosito smiled at Cole. "I would have done this at Panuela's *hacienda,* but there were too many of his *mozos* around. You must admit I tried to dissuade *Señorita* Panuela . . . she could have stayed in Taos and avoided all this. *Pues,* I suppose one couldn't expect both beauty and brains. As to your story of the arrowhead, *Señor* Cole, even Panuela wouldn't have been fool enough to cache his furs in the Accursed Lakes country. He knows the superstitions of the Pueblos about that place. His servants were Pueblos. I doubt if they would approach within twenty miles of Ti-Ba-Ra. So you are going to let us know what

Panuela really told you before he died."

Cole lurched up against his bonds. "What I told you was the truth, dammit."

He stopped. Tomosito had slipped off a buckskin glove, revealing the ugly bullet-wound in his right hand. He saw the understanding in Cole's eyes, and his smile was no longer soft.

"*Si,*" he said. "It was I you disturbed with Panuela, there on the Pecuris Trail. We were three against your one, Jarales, Rudolfo, and I. Perhaps we could have discouraged you. But, until I found those furs, I wasn't ready to be recognized as anyone but Esperanzado's loyal, honest, soft-spoken partner."

"How could you do that to my father?" cried the girl. "He was your best friend. If it hadn't been for him, you'd still be nothing but a halfway educated peon!"

He turned to her, the fire burning brighter in his eyes, his words sharp, contemptuous. "Do you think I spent all those years working my way into partnership because your father was my friend? *Bah.* He was a way to the top, that's all. I was patient, *señorita.* I waited a long time. But then two hundred thousand dollars' worth of furs is worth waiting for, isn't it? Cimarron Saunders would murder for it. Perhaps I would, too. I was returning from Mexico, and Esperanzado must have been coming back from where he was hiding his furs, when we met there on the Pecos. I suppose he had begun to suspect me . . . he was reluctant about telling where his cache was. When gentler methods failed, Jarales did the honors, as he will do now. . . ."

The renegade had followed Almagre's two young bucks in. All the men in the province carried strips of rawhide around their horse's necks to hobble the animals at night. Jarales had one of those hobbles now, a slit in one end, a wooden button on the other. It was the same device they had used to form the garrote for Esperanzado Panuela.

Jarales slipped it around Cole's head, punching the button

through the slit, drawing the rawhide tight. Then he produced a short length of hickory, slipping it beneath the hobble. Throughout the process he muttered an idiotic little chant.

"*Sí, sí, Señor* Cole, sooner or later they talk for Jarales, sooner or later. If not the garrote, then the bastinado, or the wet rawhide. *Sí, sí, Señor* Cole, sooner or later. . . ."

He had been at the peyote bean. His eyes were glazed, his face set, pale. And he began to twist that length of hickory. With each turn of his hand, the garrote drew tighter. Sweat began to drip into Cole's eyes, salty, blinding. Tomosito bent forward.

"Well, *Señor* Cole, will you tell us now?"

Cole didn't answer. Pain beat through his head in roaring waves. It took a terrible effort of will for him to concentrate on working that sharp piece of rock around in his fingers. Almagre's men stood by, ready to hold him if he struggled. Jarales took another turn.

"*Sí, sí, señor,* sooner or later. . . ."

The white-haired Almagre bent forward. His eyes were filled with a cruel eagerness to see this white man snap beneath the torture. Blood trickled down Cole's chin from where he was biting his lips. But he had that piece of rock against the rawhide on his wrists now. Slowly, patiently he began rubbing its sharp edge across the leather bonds. Jarales twisted once more.

Tomosito began pacing up and down, lips compressed with the effort to control his growing impatience. Cole's body was filled with agony. His head seemed to swell like a balloon. The muscles across his stomach twitched with nervous reaction, and a terrible nausea swept him. Then a strip of his bonds seemed to give beneath his hidden sawing.

The girl's eyes were fixed on Cole, her bosom rising and falling, her cheeks streaked with tears. Tomosito stopped pacing, whirling to the trapper.

"Are you inhuman? *Válgame Dios.* I've seen Apaches break

before this. Tell me, where are the furs?"

Jarales took another turn. The girl could stand it no longer. She struggled to sit up, screaming: "Stop it, you fools! Can't you see he'll never talk. He's no Apache. He's Painter Cole. Haven't you heard of Painter Cole?"

She began to laugh hysterically, then broke into hopeless sobbing, sinking down. And then Cole, too, began laughing, a dry, cracked laugh. The rawhide strands had parted. His hands were free.

It infuriated Tomosito, that laughter. Face twisted with rage, he bent forward, slapping Cole on one side of the face and then the other, back and forth, back and forth, lean torso jerking from side to side with each blow. Cole fought down the desire to reach out and smash the half-breed's avaricious face. He could never hope to overcome them all. It would only be throwing away his chance of escape. So he sat there and took it until Tomosito stopped. The half-breed straightened, finally, trembling with rage.

And through the roaring in his head, Cole heard the small, growing sound in the pueblo outside. Feet pounded by the kiva. A shot rang out. Then an Acoman appeared at the open trap door, shouting in Keresan. Tomosito's voice was harsh, astounded.

"Cimarron Saunders. He is here on the mesa!"

IV

Almagre was the first to break for the ladder, followed by his two men. Tomosito went up last, shouting for Jarales to stay and guard Cole. The renegade still squatted beside the trapper, leering vacantly, mumbling that crazy chant.

"If not the garrote, then most certainly the bastinado. . . ."

He broke off suddenly. Cole had drawn his hands from behind his back.

The trapper lunged up, reaching long arms for Jarales. With a wild scream, the renegade threw himself backward, and Cole's fingers scraped down his buckskins, closing over the hilt of Jarale's big Green River knife. Then Jarales was slamming back against the wall, and Cole was left swaying there on his knees, a handful of buckskin fringe in one hand, the Green River in the other.

Jarales hit the wall, shoved himself away from it, grabbing for his silver-mounted Remingtons. Legs still tied, Cole jerked up off his knees, and before he fell again, launched himself full length at the Pueblo, knife blade gleaming and held out in front of him.

With both guns jerking from their holsters, and thumbs catching at the hammers, Jarales took that knife. It went in hilt deep, Cole crashing in after it. . . .

The trapper picked himself off the dead body, pulling the Green River free. Blood still on its blade, he cut the bonds off his feet. Then he stumbled over to the girl, slashing her free. Leandro Baca's rawhide had dug deeply into his flesh, and Cole took longer with him. When he had finished, the girl worked the garrote off his head, laughing a little, crying.

"I told Tomosito he couldn't break you. . . ."

Fresh pain shot through his head as she loosened the hobble, and his fists tightened spasmodically. Something dug into his palm. He was still holding that piece of rock Leandro had given him. The girl stopped working at the garrote when he opened his hand. There was a catch of excitement to her voice.

"That's the same kind of arrowhead my father gave you."

Yes, it was the same kind—the long tapering point, the singular haft, with its serrated sides. And Leandro said he'd gotten this from Ti-Ba-Ra.

Renewed firing outside raised Cole's head. He tied the arrowhead into a whang, as he had done the other. Then he rose and went to Jarales. He would need those two Remingtons, with Cimarron Saunders out on the mesa. He buckled the belt around his own lean flanks, spinning the cylinder of each gun to check the loads. Then he stooped to lift Leandro Baca.

"No, *señor*," gasped the young Acoman. "I've been tied up so long I can't even walk. You'd never get away if you tried to take me along."

Cole put his big hands under Baca without answering, and swung the youth onto his broad shoulder. Carmencita helping from behind, he finally reached the top of the ladder.

The kiva was really a cellar, its roof only a few feet above the ground level. Its mud sides extended a foot or so higher than the roof, forming a low wall. Cole shoved Leandro out ahead of him, and then climbed through the trap, helping the girl out. Lying on their bellies, hidden from the street by that wall, they could see the whole thing.

Cimarron Saunders would be the one to do it this way—he had always boasted he would poach furs from the devil if he could find hell. The red-headed poacher led his whole cut-throat crew up from the south end of the mesa, shooting, yelling, smashing what little opposition the Acomans put up.

Three of Saunders's men lay in a heap down by the church, arrows protruding from their bodies. Half a dozen Acomans lay sprawled farther on, sun glinting on their white cotton trousers. But the Pueblos had no guns, and Saunders had everything almost his own way.

The walls of the houses were like those of the kiva, extended a foot or so above roof level, forming a low barricade. From behind this rose a desperate Acoman, bowstring making a deadly twang. So swift was he that four arrows had left his bow before the elephantine Pablo Rodriguez turned and shot him from the roof. And down in the dusty street Enrique Valzabar, the man who would be ashamed if he had an honest man among his ancestors, crumpled suddenly, four shafts studding the chest of his fancy *charro* jacket.

Saunders kept right on coming, his pistol in one hairy hand, his *saca tripas* in the other, shouting: "I've come to getcha, Cole! I know you're here. You might as well come out now. I've come to getcha . . . !"

"Wonder where Almagre and Tomosito disappeared to?" muttered Cole.

"Almagre and his fanatics are probably gathering in those ceremonial chambers on the top terrace," said Leandro. "Can't you hear the *tombe?*"

Cole looked up toward the last story of the block of houses. He could see the dim shift of white-clad warriors in the doorways. And he could hear the *tombe* now, the awesome-sounding ceremonial drum of the Acomans, like a monotonous, insistent pulse in his head.

"Saunders is between us and the Horse Trail. Isn't there any other way down from the mesa?" he asked.

"The old North Trail, around behind the houses," said Leandro. "But it is reached from the alley between the middle block and this one. He cuts us off from that trail, too."

"If I showed myself on the roofs," said Cole, "Saunders would come up after me, and that'd put him right in Almagre's hands. While they were cutting each other up, you two could slip around the front of the houses to that alley."

Carmencita grabbed his arm. "Don't be a fool. You would be up there, too, right in the middle of it. And Tomosito is somewhere around. You'd never get out alive."

"For ten years, up in the Big Horns," he said, "I've been playing hide-and-seek with *hombres* who take off your hair when they catch you. And I've still got my hair, haven't I?"

He shoved one of Jarales's silver-mounted Remingtons into the girl's hand. "I'm going now. Don't wait too long for me at the North Trail."

Cole rose to a crouch, slipped over the low wall, and dropped to the ground. Along the front of the pueblo were ladders that led to the second story. He was almost to the first one when Pablo Rodriguez sighted him.

"C-e-e-marron!" shouted the huge, blue-coated renegade. "There ees Cole! C-e-e-marron!"

Cole had the other Remington out then. And Pablo was no fool. He threw his fat body into the street, Cole's slug whining over his floppy-brimmed sombrero. The trapper didn't wait for another shot. The rickety piñon ladder swayed and creaked beneath his weight. Saunders let out an enraged bellow, running forward, shooting.

Slugs pounded adobe around Cole. He threw himself onto the roof, rolling over with his gun ready—the Acomans were looking for him, too. But the only Acomans he saw were the dead ones, forming white blotches on the dark, earthen roof.

Cole crawled across that first terrace and into a dark doorway, gun cocked. It was more sense than sight that told him someone else was in the room. His finger whitened against the trigger— then he expelled his breath in relief.

This, then, was where the Acomans had put their women. Two or three families of them were in the room, and there were probably more in the others. Old women, young women, children, all dressed in the black *manta,* the shawl worn over one shoulder and buttoned down the side with big silver clasps. They cowered against the wall, one or two moaning, frightened to death of that big, ugly man with the long black hair and the greasy clothes.

Outside, Saunders and his men made a raucous racket coming up the ladder and onto the roof. Cole slipped past the terrified women and into the next room.

These adobes had been built before the white man's advent

into the country, before the Spaniard, when the bloody Apaches had held all of the country above Mexico in a century-long grip of terror. The first-story rooms had no doors, their walls presenting a solid front to the street. They were used mainly to store things in, and trap doors led down into them from the floor of the second-story chambers. Cole found the trap, lifted it, and dropped through, allowing the heavy pine door to slam shut above him.

It was a short fall. He landed with bent knees, then straightened, stumbling through piles of rolled bayeta blankets, face brushing against twists of muskmelon and bunches of drying grapes that hung from the *viga* poles. As his eyes grew accustomed to the gloom, he saw trap doors above him, one after the other. When he came to the last one at the other end of the block, he found a ladder and leaned it against the rafters. He climbed up, cautiously shoving open the heavy trap.

Saunders had left his mark—sprawled in the doorway was an Acoman, the white of his cotton shirt reddened by blood. Otherwise the room was empty. Cole cat-footed to the outer door. Saunders's men were spreading across the first terrace, hesitant about entering those dark doors. They respected Painter Cole, and his guns, and his hands.

"I think he went in thees one, Ceemarron," said Rodriguez, waving his .44 at the last door.

"Nah," snarled Claude Tate, hitching at his Yankee galluses. "He went in the next one to it. I saw 'im."

"We'll bottle him up!" called Saunders. "Each one of you take a door. I'll stick my *saca tripas* through any man that lets him get away."

Carmencita and Leandro should have had time to reach the alley by now. Cole was thankful they would escape, anyway. The heavy river boots of Claude Tate thudded on the roof outside. Cole's palm grew moist against the silver-mounted handle of his gun. He cocked the hammer softly.

He had the sudden sense of an insistent pulse beat stopping within him. And standing there with his thumb heavy on the Remington's hammer, it took him a long moment to realize the *tombe* had ceased. . . .

A long, drawn-out, blood-chilling scream sounded from somewhere above Cole, followed by another and another until his ears rang with continuous sound. The roof over his head shook to a hundred bare feet charging across it. Almagre and his fanatics were sweeping down on Saunders, and Cole knew this moment was his chance for escape. He took a long step out the door, whirling to throw down on the first man he sighted.

Claude Tate had jerked his unshaven face toward the second terrace, but he must have caught sight of Cole from the corner of his eye. He turned, Jake Hawkins rifle pulled flat against his belly for a spot shot. Cole's finger tightened on his trigger, the Remington bucked up in his hand, and Tate fell forward on his face.

On past Tate were others of Saunders's crew, the bulk of them gathered at the far end of the terrace. If they saw Cole as he backed swiftly toward the alley, it didn't do them any good. For out of the windowless, third story ceremonial chambers, Almagre's fanatics were dropping like buzzards onto carrion. Half a hundred wild-eyed Acomans in flapping white trousers, armed with deadly short bows. Leading was Almagre, his long white hair flowing out behind him, his dark face contorted. Saunders was caught in a nakedly exposed position there on the open roof of the first terrace. A stringy-haired mountain man collapsed, cursing sickly, one arrow after the other driving deeply into his greasy buckskins. A *charro*-coated Mexican whirled and raced for the ladder leading down into the street. A shaft caught him on the edge of the roof. He was suspended there for a moment, and three others studded his back. Then he toppled from sight, screaming.

Saunders proved his boast about poaching furs from the devil then. Arrows filling the air about him, he stood calmly, emptying his gun into the mass of Indians, bellowing orders at his men. An arrow plunged into his thick leg and he went right on firing. Another caught in his right arm. He tore it out, cocking his gun for another shot at the same time.

And his men gathered around him. Pablo Rodriguez, shouting obscenities, triggering his .44. Tanay, the Mescalero Apache, the watch chains in his ears bobbing back and forth, his face dark with a traditional hatred for the Pueblo Indians. The mountain men, working their deadly smoothbores, along with the *bandidos,* and the half-breeds. Standing together like that, their concentrated fire formed a solid wall of lead that swept away Almagre's first rank of fanatics. White-clad bodies fell over the edge of the second terrace and into Saunders's group. Others hung head down over the low wall. Still firing, the red-haired poacher began his retreat.

Then Cole didn't see any more. He sensed the alley's dark maw behind him, and turned.

Carmencita must have been standing on the top rung of a ladder. Her head and shoulders were above a low wall, and Jarales's other Remington was held grimly in both hands. At the look on Cole's face, she said angrily: "*Pues,* did you think we would leave you alone up here? *Pronto* now, I didn't see Tomosito with Almagre. He's up to something."

Cole followed her down the ladder to where Leandro crouched at its bottom, rubbing his ankles, his wrists. Between them, Carmencita and Cole half carried the Acoman down the narrow alley toward the rear of the houses. They broke into sunlight on the edge of the mesa, and the North Trail dropped down before them, a series of toeholds on either side of a cleft in the precipice. Some circulation had come back into Leandro's legs and arms; he lowered himself hesitantly to the first steps, helped by Carmencita. Cole was about to let himself down when the scuffle of running feet echoed up the alley and three figures were suddenly silhouetted at the other end—Tomosito, Rudolfo, and Gaspar.

Cole's gun glinted a little in the sunlight as he brought it up, and Tomosito and Rudolfo threw themselves aside. Gaspar was behind them, and he hadn't caught that glimpse of shining steel. Cole's shot cracked out, hard and flat, between the mud walls. Gaspar went over backward.

The trapper waited for a moment, half hoping Tomosito would show again. But the half-breed was too cautious. The rock was harsh against Cole's fingers. The cliff fell away below him, reeled dizzily above him. His hands were cut and bleeding by the time he reached the bottom of the first steps.

Carmencita and Leandro waited for him in an enormous amphitheater at the foot of a gigantic Buddha-like rock-formation, carved out by untold centuries of winds and rains. Leandro led them across the bowl, limping, hopping. Then they were climbing into another series of toeholds, moving around a dome of sandstone, through towering abutments. Leandro slipped, cried out. The girl grabbed at him, caught his arm, slipped herself.

Cole flung out a moccasined foot, gasping: "Grab it!"

Her small hand closed around it and the weight of two bodies dragged at him. His bloody fingers began slipping from the handholds. His right hand scraped out. He clawed desperately with his left, conscious of the terrible yawning space below.

Then the hand around his foot relaxed, was supporting him rather than pulling him down, as the girl found a foothold.

They reached a ledge that widened out at the far end, then climbed down a series of notched logs that led to the fields below. Panting, Cole leaned against the cliff, looking back up. It towered somberly above him. Tomosito and Rudolfo were miniature black figures descending the first series of handholds, far beyond the range of Cole's Remington.

"Things seem to point to the fact that Panuela cached his furs at Ti-Ba-Ra," said Cole. "How far is it from here, Leandro?"

"Three or four days' ride over the Manzanos," said the Acoman.

"Will you guide us?"

"*Señor*"— the youth smiled—"if you hadn't taken me out of that kiva, I wouldn't be guiding anybody anywhere. I'll be proud to show you Ti-Ba-Ra, witches and all!"

"Then let's get around to the horses before someone else beats us to it," said Cole.

V

The sun of the third day's ride was low when the three dropped down the last eastern slope of the Manzanos, riding through park-like pineries into a fringe of twisted cedars that bordered the plain. Cole had pushed hard, southeast from Acoma, following the San José to the Río Grande, crossing the mother river and the upland bordering it to the east, gaining the jagged Manzanos the second day.

Saunders's horses had been at the foot of the Horse Trail, as well as the mounts Cole and Tomosito had left. The trapper rounded up a score of them to use as pack animals, stampeding the rest. That would give Cole a few hours' start over Saunders—if he got free of Acoma—and also over Tomosito.

Even Cole's magnificent black was weary now, moving out of the cedars in a dogged fashion, lather caking its flanks. Cole sat easy in the saddle, the lean cast of his long body somehow accentuated by the grueling ride behind them.

"It's just a race now, I guess," he said. "We know Tomosito'll be hot on our tails. And if Almagre doesn't finish Saunders off, that poacher'll be coming, too."

"*Sí*," said Leandro. "And Almagre. He knows we will all be riding for the Accursed Lakes. He isn't one to let his enemies off easily, and he would do anything . . . even the inconceivable . . . to keep us from desecrating the old gods again."

"*Por Dios*," sighed the girl, easing herself forward on her pinto. "I'm sorry I ever got you mixed up in this thing, Cole."

He glanced at her. Dust grimed her face and alkali had dulled the luster of her blue-black hair. Her silk shirt was dirty, her blackened leggings ripped by mesquite and Spanish bayonet. Yet she had lost none of her magic charm.

"Don't apologize," said Cole. "I would've come whether you asked me or not."

The three of them suddenly pulled up short beneath the last twisted cedars, looking out into the valley that stretched eastward. Cole had traveled in wild country most of his life and was used to emptiness and silence. Yet this was like nothing he had ever seen—the hush that hung over this infinite brown plain was morbid with foreboding. A band of antelope drifted across the sere grass like cloud shadows, ghostly, intangible. Leandro pointed to a chain of gleaming lakes some miles off.

"The Accursed Lakes," he said. "Once they were fresh water, and the cities about them were gay and happy. But in Quarai, so the legend goes, lived an unfaithful wife, and because of her sins the lakes were doomed to be salt forever after. Ti-Ba-Ra lies southward."

The boy seemed reluctant to leave the fringe of trees, so Cole urged his black forward into the lead. They toiled down the edge of the ghastly plain into a narrow smooth trough-like valley, skirting a huge, darkly wooded upthrust of rock that Leandro called the Mesa de los Jumanos. Overhead, a buzzard shrieked and wheeled off.

They rode through deep sand that clutched at the horses' hoofs. Leandro's eyes flashed from side to side and he shifted nervously in the saddle.

Cole had lived with Indians enough to know what the Acoman was going through. Leandro was not one of Almagre's fanatics, but as he had said, even the Acomans who worshipped the Spaniard's Tata *Dios,* also worshipped the Trues. An Indian might be utterly courageous in battle, yet cowered like a child in fear of his ancient gods. It took consummate nerve for the Acoman to brave the wrath of the Trues and the *brujo* that dwelt in Ti-Ba-Ra.

It was late afternoon when they sighted a whale-back ridge nosing out into the plain, and, at its tip, an ashen hulk that stood like the ghost of some ancient, irrevocable sentinel set on guarding the sacred soil from infamers. Somber mottes of junipers brooded around it, here and there a lonely cottonwood.

"That is it," said Leandro in a muted voice. "Ti-Ba-Ra."

He fell back until he rode a little behind Cole, hand white-knuckled on the reins, mouth drawn thin. They slowed as they neared the tumbled ruins, and Cole couldn't explain the haunting dread that ran through him. There was something unworldly about this Ti-Ba-Ra

Suddenly, breaking the utter silence, a laugh floated up from the gray walls—a shrill, atonal cackle.

Cole's black shied and the trapper drew tight rein. Leandro's face turned ashen, and he sat his mount with fascinated eyes turned toward the city.

"Did you hear it? That is the *brujo* . . . the witch. He laughed at me when I was here before. He waited until I was in the pueblo, then he laughed like that. . . ."

The three of them quieted their nervous horses, sitting there while the shadows lengthened. Cole's saddle creaked mournfully with the shift of his weight as he finally kneed his black forward, drawing a gun. Warily they approached the huddled ruins.

There were a number of houses, terraced as in Acoma, facing each other across a narrow winding street. At the end of the street was a larger building, high walls, frowning above the other houses. Cole swung down at the first ancient structure, its walls crumbling away from rotting *viga* poles. He had been carrying both guns, and he handed one to Leandro as the Acoman dismounted. They stood there for a long moment, Carmencita's hand tight on Cole's hard arm. Nothing flesh and blood would have ever halted the trapper like that, but the echoes of that laugh still seemed to waft through the city, holding Cole in a strange hypnosis. Finally he took a jerky step forward, then lengthened his strides down that darkening street.

Shadows engulfed him. The intense silence was a malignant, physical thing. The butt of his gun grew sticky with sweat.

A turn in the street brought him within sight of that large building at the other end. There was a gate in its towering wall, topped by a lintel with the minutely carved arabesques of an earlier century still visible. Through the gate, Cole could see a large cuniform room with only a single gigantic rafter to give evidence that it had once borne a roof.

The trapper stopped, then, raising his gun instinctively, he heard Carmencita's muffled gasp behind him. There in that roofless room, sitting on a pile of bricks and rubble, was the *brujo*.

He was as lean and brown as a rawhide whang, his black hair matted and filthy, his face a gaunt bone from which two buttons peered. He wore no shirt and his blackened leggings were frayed, the silver *conchas* long torn off. It took Cole a long moment to recognize Manuel Panuela—Carmencita's brother.

At sight of them he threw back his head and laughed again,

then waved his arms about him, gibbering in Spanish: "It's mine, mine, all mine. My father left me and the others here to guard it, and the others, they went away. Now it's mine, all mine, mine, mine. . . ."

Suddenly he sat down on the rubble and began to cry like a baby. The girl ran to him, kneeling down and pulling his matted head to her breast, sobbing.

Leandro stood gaping at Manuel, trying to reconcile this poor demented creature with his fearful *brujo*. Over against the wall were the bodies of three *mozos,* Apache arrows still sunk to the shaft in their blood-stained buckskins.

"Those Apaches who told me of the *brujo* . . . no wonder they knew," muttered Leandro.

"Ask your brother about the furs, Carmencita," said Cole gently. "I know it isn't fitting to do it now, but we haven't much time."

The girl patted her brother's shoulders, trying to stop his crying. "Manuel, Manuel, where as the pelts?"

"All mine," sobbed the boy. "My father left me and the others here to guard them. All mine."

They tried for some time to question him, but he mumbled incoherently and began to laugh again, and they knew it was useless.

"We'll get him out of here as soon as we find the furs," Cole told the girl. "Leandro, you get up on the wall and watch for Saunders and the others."

Leaving Carmencita with her brother, the trapper walked through the grass-grown tumble of rotting timbers and broken adobe bricks to the entrance of a corridor that led away from the large room. Opening off each side of the hallway were smaller rooms, and from them yet other rooms, turning the place into a veritable catacomb. Cole spent most of his time scanning the ground for footprints or other sign, but the untrammeled dust of centuries shrouded everything. Most of the chambers were one story, roofless, but there were a sparse few two- and three-story houses still standing.

It grew darker as he searched, and finally the moon began to rise, casting back pools of shadows into the roofless hall and sending a bright yellow gleam through the broken doorways and crumbling windows. Cole had climbed to the first terrace of a house when Leandro's frantic shout came to him, muffled and warped by the thick adobe walls between them.

"*Señor* Cole! Here they come. Saunders and his men, and behind him, Almagre!"

Cole scrambled onto a pile of fallen bricks and gained the second terrace. From there he could look west across the plain.

The full moon had cast the whole valley in a golden light. Out past the groves of somber junipers that surrounded Ti-Ba-Ra came the first group of riders.

Cole recognized Saunders, tall and broad in his fancy saddle, and behind him the huge Pablo Rodriguez. There were only three others. Cole didn't see how the red-haired poacher had saved even that many of his cut-throats from Almagre's arrows. But Saunders had always been a rare man, in his way.

The second bunch of horsebackers was just rounding the Mesa de los Jumanos, a mile or so behind Saunders. Cole caught the unmistakable glint of white cotton trousers in the moonlight. Almagre, then, had come, and Cimarron Saunders. The most dangerous man had yet to appear.

With thought of Tomosito, Cole felt a fear grow in him. He shouldn't have left the girl and Manuel alone back there. It wasn't like the clever Tomosito to ride in openly as Saunders was doing. The half-breed might already be inside the walls. Cole had been too intrigued by that treasure of furs and he cursed himself for it, dropping from the last terrace into the velvety shadows of the lower rooms. He stumbled through a doorway, seeking the hall. He barked his shin on a fallen *viga* pole and would have grunted his pain, but—that voice.

"Hurry, Rudolfo, you big *pendejo*. I heard that Acoman call from the big room. Cole must be in there now."

Tomosito. Cole moved more slowly now, making no sound. He came into the hall finally, moving east until he reached the place where the corridor made a last turn before entering the large, cuniform chamber where he had left Carmencita.

The moon had cast the smaller rooms and the narrow corridor into deep shadow, with only vagrant shafts of pale light shining in through infrequent breaks in the wall, or through doorways. But the walls of the larger room had fallen in many places, and those breaches allowed the lunar rays to flood in, revealing everything. From where he hunched at that shadowed turn in the hall, Cole could see Tomosito and Rudolfo, crouching in the entrance to the cuniform room. Rudolfo's voice came thickly.

"*Pues,* Tomosito, it is empty. They are not here."

Not wanting to believe the man's words, Cole searched the brightly lit place with frantic eyes. It was utterly empty. The girl. . . . the girl . . . ?

"*Caracoles,*" hissed Tomosito. "They were here. I saw that Acoman on the wall, heard him call to Cole. . . ."

He didn't finish. Beneath the sound of his voice, the sullen pound of hoofs had been mounting in volume in the street outside. Before either Tomosito or Rudolfo could move, Cimarron Saunders galloped right in through the door, pulling his great raking dun back on lathered haunches. Pablo Rodriguez and Tanay and the others crowded in behind him, guns drawn.

Cole saw Tomosito clutch at Rudolfo. But the big *mozo* had already freed his iron, and it was too late. The shot was a thunderous sound, echoing back from wall to wall. One of Saunders's *charro*-suited *bandidos* pitched from the saddle with a groan. The red-haired poacher was off his dun before that dead man hit the ground, throwing himself behind the pile of bricks and rotting timbers. Tanay and the others followed suit, and Rudolfo's second shot was wasted.

"That you, Cole?" shouted Saunders.

Tomosito had pulled his thick-witted *mozo* back into the shadows, and he didn't answer. Cole couldn't see the half-breed and his man now, but he could sense their soft, barely audible movements, probably shifting into one of the chambers leading off the hall.

Saunders called to his men, not bothering to lower his voice. "Those damn' Acomans are right behind us. We can't stay in here. Head for that hallway, shooting. If Cole's in there, don't let him get those hands on you. You'll die like a beaver in a jump trap, if he does."

The click of cocked guns came to Cole. He moved farther behind the bend in the wall. The corridor would be filled with lead in that next moment, and he knew he would meet Saunders's charge alone. Tomosito wasn't the man to stand before that rush.

But Saunders never got to charge. Through the breaches in those high walls, through the big entrance way, even over the tops of the walls came Almagre's white-pantalooned fanatics.

"C-e-e-marron!" shouted Pablo Rodriguez. "Those *locos* are all around us . . . !"

His voice was cut off by the deadly *thwuck-thwuck* of arrows, and he rose in a jerky, spasmodic fashion from behind the pile of bricks, a dozen shafts feathering his blue dragoon's coat. He tottered backward with a wailing scream. "C-e-e-marron . . . !"

Saunders and the others were already slamming out a thundering volley, drowning all other sounds. One of the white-clad Indian zealots, creeping through a breach in the wall, collapsed suddenly with a sick grunt. Two others, charging through the gate, stumbled over one another, lay writhing on the ground as lead scoured them mercilessly. Up from behind the rubbish pile rose Tanay, the Apache, and Cimarron Saunders, the last diehards of that once roistering cut-throat crew. Their swift, running movement toward the entrance to the corridor was synchronized perfectly. Tanay moved backward fast, facing out toward the room, six-gun roaring. Saunders faced the other way, his gun bellowing death to anyone who might have been crouched there in the hall. One of his slugs nicked adobe into Cole's face, and the trapper drew farther back behind the wall.

Then the two men threw themselves into the safety of the gloomy corridor, panting, cursing. It was silent again, utterly silent. Out in the cuniform room, what was left of Almagre's crowd had taken cover behind that pile of bricks lying beside the dead body of Pablo Rodriguez and the others of Saunders's men who had died there. Saunders and Tanay squatted at the end of the hall, implacable, waiting for someone to make a fatal move or sound. And somewhere in that complex network of rooms was Tomosito and his hulking *mozo*, waiting.

Even taking them on one at a time, Cole knew he couldn't expect to come out alive. He had played Saunders and Almagre off against each other, back there at Acoma—why not here? Everyone was out there, waiting for the other to give himself away. Cole chose a heavy adobe brick lying on the ground, hefted it, tossed it toward the entrance to the big chamber.

It bounced off a wall, thudded against the ground. Tanay's voice was startlingly loud. "*Dios*, what was that?"

Before he had finished, a shower of arrows filled the hall, whirring past Cole there at the turn, caroming off the sides. Saunders triggered out a shot, and somewhere in the large room an Acoman cried in pain.

"I oughta put my *saca tripas* through your gizzard," snarled the redhead to Tanay. "They know where we are now."

"Pues," muttered the Apache. "I didn't. . . ."

"Shut up," said Saunders. "Start moving back. I don't want my hide filled with arrows."

Cole heard them begin to shift toward him. The flash of gunfire would have revealed his own position, so he leathered his Remington. If they feared his hands so much, then he'd use them.

A man's softly expelled breath came to Cole. He reached out around the corner of the hall, feeling for his enemy in that pitch-black corridor. His hands closed around an Indian's smooth jaw. The man tried to pull away.

But Tanay never got his shout out, and he didn't pull away. Cole's long, trap-scarred fingers clamped shut over the Apache's mouth, and his other hand slipped around the muscular neck.

Saunders must have heard the short, sharp struggle, for his voice came through the blackness. "Tanay . . . ?"

VI

This time the Acomans didn't just shoot. At the sound of Saunders's voice, they rose from their cover in the big room and charged across the moonlit space into the black hall, yelling, howling, short bows twanging. They couldn't see Saunders, but he *could* see them, silhouetted there by the moonlight. His gun bucked out one cool shot right after the other, each hitting its target with deadly precision. The first Acoman fell forward and slid on his face. The one behind stumbled over his body, tried to regain his balance, then went down for good with one of Saunders's bullets through him. Another crashed up against the wall and slid to the ground. One last white-clad figure leaped into the doorway, screaming: "Abo, Ti-Ba-Ra, Quarai . . . !"

It was Almagre, and when Saunders shot him, he kept on screaming until his face hit the ground and death cut off his voice. Cole had already let the dead body of Tanay down to the ground. In the silence and the darkness, Saunders began backing up, muttering: "I'm empty, Tanay, give me some of your rimfires."

Cole kept still. The echoes of Saunders's voice died, and the poacher waited for a long, heavy moment. Then he bellowed suddenly, more in anger than fear.

"Tanay, damn you, I said gimme some shells!"

Still only silence. Cole heard the redhead steady himself with a slow, shuddering breath. Then came the sibilant sound of steel against leather. Cimarron Saunders had pulled his *saca tripas* from his belt. When he spoke again, there was no trace of fear in his voice, only a terrible, mounting anger that swept all other emotion from him.

"All right, Cole, so you got the Apache. I know it's you. Nobody else could've finished him off so quiet. But then I warned him. I guess I won't get the furs now, will I? I don't care much. All I want is you, Cole. I'm coming."

He made a solid sound, pacing down toward that turn in the corridor. Cole might have used his gun. But Tomosito was still waiting somewhere, and the flash of Cole's Remington would make too good a target for the half-breed. So the trapper stood there, behind the angle in the crumbling adobe wall, not breathing.

Neither of them actually saw the other. The sound of Saunders's steady footsteps came close to the turn, then around it. He must have sensed Cole as the trapper threw himself forward, hands outstretched, body jerking aside to avoid the knife.

Steel sliced the left side of Cole's buckskin shirt, and Saunders smashed forward against Cole's hurtling body, grunting with having missed his thrust.

They rolled to the ground, slammed against the opposite wall of the corridor, plaster flaking down on them. Saunders stabbed again, viciously. Cole let the knife dig a furrow all the way up

196

his forearm so he could get a grip on Saunders's wrist. Then he shifted his legs and struggled over on top of Saunders.

The poacher heaved his body into an arch, trying to throw Cole off. The trapper still had his grip on Saunders's wrist, and with a terrific jerk he twisted the man's arm beneath his arched body. Then he bellied down hard on Saunders.

The poacher collapsed beneath that driving weight, screaming as his *saca tripas* sunk deeply into his own back.

Evidently Tomosito and Rudolfo had worked through the catacomb of rooms to the other end of the corridor. Before Saunders's dying scream was through, a gun began racketing from the west end of the hall, laying down a methodical barrage about Cole.

The big trapper jerked off Saunders, whirling, drawing his own weapon free. The silver-mounted handle bucked against his palm as he fired at those flashes from the west end. And he must have hit Rudolfo, for the other's shots ceased, and his voice was thick with pain. "*Dios,* Tomosito. . . ."

Tomosito opened fire then. He had used Rudolfo for bait, had kept his own cylinder full, knowing Cole's gun flashes would reveal his exact position. And even as Cole was shifting, cocking his gun for another shot, one of Tomosito's bullets caught him.

He collapsed into a sitting position, back against the wall, long legs across Saunders's corpse. He sat very quietly, numbed. He moved one hand with infinite patience until it was over his belly. The buckskin shirt was sticky with blood.

He cocked his gun slowly, carefully, holding the fleshy part of his thumb over the hammer to muffle the small click. It would have been hard enough waiting in that darkness, that silence. The awful pain made it almost unbearable. It was a game of nerves, now. Whoever could sit utterly still in that terrible place the longest would win. Cole only hoped he could live long enough to get Tomosito.

Then Manuel's laughter broke out, rising from somewhere in that adobe honeycomb, reaching a fearful crescendo, and then falling into nothingness.

It startled Cole at first, sent a chill through him. Then he realized the meaning of that cackle. If the girl's brother were alive, then there was a chance that she, too, lived. His perpetual, twisted grin turned up a little higher. He felt more like playing this game now, in the dead city, with the corpses lying all about him, the black shadows pressing in.

Perhaps Tomosito had only waited to make sure he'd killed Cole. Or maybe Ti-Ba-Ra had penetrated even his cynical armor. He began moving, down there at the other end of the hall.

Cole sat very still, holding his breath.

Slowly, surely the half-breed came forward. Once Cole almost shot, sure that a black shadow halfway down there was Tomosito. But he didn't pull the trigger, waiting to see the shadow move. And finally he realized it was only part of the wall, crumbled in on itself. Then something shifted, something darker than the gloom.

Cole must have made some slight movement, lining up his Remington, because even as the half-breed jerked backward, he began shooting. With lead thudding into adobe beside him, Cole's gun bucked. Tomosito went on backward, staggering, falling flat, his body merging with the blackness. . . .

Cole tried to rise. He got to his hands and knees. Then nausea swept through him. The ground came up to meet his face, and he guessed he was fainting because he couldn't feel the gun butt against his hand, and he couldn't even see the blackness any more, and the taste of dirt in his mouth only lasted a moment, and then that melted away along with everything else.

★ ★ ★ ★ ★

Bright light struck Cole when he came to. He was lying in the big chamber, Carmencita bending over him. Manuel sat abstractedly beside the pile of bricks and timbers, and Leandro stood behind the girl.

"I couldn't wait any longer when I heard those last shots," murmured Carmencita. "It was so dark, so maddening . . . you are bleeding all over."

"Where were you?" croaked Cole.

"Where the furs were," said Leandro calmly.

"You found them, then?"

"*Sí,*" answered the Acoman. "Under this pile of bricks and rubbish is a big chamber, and the furs are stored there. *Señor* Panuela must have dug it and heaped this stuff on top to hide the trap door. Carmencita found the edge of the door beneath a rotting timber. We were inside when everything started. First Tomosito came, and we couldn't get out, then Saunders, and finally Almagre."

The girl was cutting away Cole's buckskins with Jarales's Green River, and the trapper got a look at his wound.

"Isn't as bad as it looks, I guess," he said. "Through my side, somewhere. I was a lot messier than this when the painter finished with me. You just give me the tail end of your silk shirt to tie my belly up real tight, and I'll be able to ride. We've got all the horses we want to pack for us now. Looks like we didn't do such a bad job, after all."

"It was your job," she said.

The catch in her voice made him feel for her hand, closing his big trap-scarred fingers around it. She was suddenly in his arms, crying a little, laughing.

"When I heard the shots and thought maybe they'd killed you, nothing else seemed to matter," she choked.

"Nothing else has mattered with me for a long time," he said.

199

"Ever since I sold my first furs to your father and saw you there in the *hacienda*."

"Why didn't you tell me?" she said.

"I never was much of a hand with women." He grinned. "And I knew how you felt about me. What would you want with an ugly fool of a trapper when you could have any *caballero* in New Mexico."

"You didn't know how I felt about you at all," she said. "And what would I want with any *caballero* in New Mexico? There are hundreds of them, all rich, all handsome, all alike. There is only one Painter Cole, and I love him. . . ."

★ ★ ★ ★ ★

KING OF THE BUCKSKIN
BREED

★ ★ ★ ★ ★

The author's title for this story was "Mountain Man". By May, 1951, when he completed it and knew it was destined for a Popular Publications Western magazine, he knew that inevitably the title would be changed. He was paid $200. Under the title "King of the Buckskin Breed" the story was published in *.44 Western* (11/51), which since the April, 1949 issue was published bi-monthly.

I

In the spring of 1840, Fort Union had stood at the confluence of the Yellowstone and the Missouri Rivers for eleven years. And in that same spring, Victor Garrit came down out of the mountains for the first time in three years. He came down on a Mandan pony, still shedding its winter coat, with his long Jake Hawkins rifle held across the pommel of the buffalo saddle. Those years of running the forest alone had changed his youthful handsomeness, had hollowed his face beneath its prominent cheek bones, had settled his black eyes deep in their sockets. It gave his face the sharp edge of a honed blade, and made a thin slice of his mouth that might have left him without humor but for the quirk that came and went at one tip. He stopped twenty feet out from the huge double-leaved gate in the palisaded wall, calling to the guard.

The small door in one of the leaves opened, and John Farrier stepped through. Chief factor of Fort Union since 1832, his square and beefy figure in its three-point blanket coat and black boots was known from New Orleans to the Canadian Territories. He greeted Garrit with a broad grin. "We saw you coming in, Vic."

"Your Indian runner found me in Jackson Hole last month," Garrit said. "He said you were in trouble, and would give me amnesty if I came in."

"You've got my protection, as long as you're here," Farrier told him. He scratched thoughtfully at his curly red beard. "You know Yellowstone Fur is in a hole, Vic. The Blackfeet trouble has kept my company trappers from working their lines for two years. If we don't get any fur this year, we go under. The free trappers have been operating over beyond the Blackfeet country. They'll have their rendezvous in Pierre's Hole this year. If we can get a train of trade goods through and get their furs, we'll be in business again."

Garrit's eyes had never been still, roving from point to point along the palisaded wall in the suspicious restlessness of some wild thing. "And you want me to take the pack train through?"

"You're the only man can do it, Vic. I can't get any of these mangy lard-eaters around the post to take the chance, not even for double wages and a bonus. The trader's here, but he had to get all of his crew from Saint Looey." The factor put a freckled hand on Garrit's knee. "Yellowstone might forget a lot of what happened in the past, if you saved the day for them, Vic."

Garrit's black eyes never seemed to lose their gleam in their shadowed sockets, and it only added to the wildness of his gaunt face. "You'd go under if the company went under, wouldn't you, John?" he asked.

Defeat pinched at Farrier's eyes, making him look old. "You know I plan on retiring soon. I couldn't do it without Yellowstone's pension."

The quirk at the tip of Garrit's lips became a fleeting grin. "You've been my only friend up here, John. I don't think I'd be alive today without you. Where's the trader?"

A broad smile spread Farrier's beard. He slapped Garrit affectionately on the knee, turned to lead him back inside. There were a dozen company trappers and *engagés* gathered on the inside of the door, gaping at Garrit as he rode through. He followed Farrier past the great fur press in the middle of the compound to the hitch rack before the neat factor's house. He dismounted, still carrying his Jake Hawkins, and followed Far-

rier through the door. Then he halted, shock filling his face with
a bloodless, putty hue.

Enid Nelson sat in a chair by the crude desk, rising slowly to
her feet with sight of Garrit. And beside her, John Bruce took a
sharp step forward, staring at Garrit with red anger filling his
heavy-jawed face.

"Damn you, Farrier!" he half shouted. "You didn't tell me it
would be Garrit. What are you trying to do?"

Farrier dropped his hand on Garrit's tense shoulder. "I gave
him my word he'd have my protection, Bruce."

"Protection, hell!" Bruce stormed. "As an officer of Yellowstone Fur, I order you to put this man under arrest im-
mediately."

"John . . . !" Enid wheeled toward him, her voice sharp. "You
can't ask Farrier to go back on his word."

Bruce glared at Garrit, breathing heavily, held by Enid's angry
eyes for a moment. Three years of soft living had put a little
weight around his belly, but he still bore a heavy-shouldered
handsomeness, in the buffalo coat and cowhide breeches of a
trader. Garrit was not looking at him, however. Since he had
first entered, his eyes had been on Enid. She was a tall girl,
auburn-haired, with a strong beauty to her wide-set eyes, her
full lips. The Palatine cloak with its pointed hood, the tight
bodice holding the swell of her mature figure, the skirt of India
muslin—all brought the past to Garrit with poignant impact.

Bruce finally made a disgusted sound. "I'd rather go alone
than be guided by a wanted man."

"You'd never make it ten miles alone," Farrier said. "The
trader for Hudson's Bay tried it last year. The Blackfeet caught
him. He lost his whole pack train. He was lucky to get his men
back alive."

"Those weren't Blackfeet," Garrit said thinly.

Bruce stared at him blankly a moment, then a derisive smile

curled on his lips. "Don't tell me you're still harping on that Anne Corday fable."

Garrit's head lifted sharply. He turned to pace restlessly across the room, glancing at the walls, like some animal suspicious of a cage. "It's no fable," he said. His voice had lost its accustomed softness. "Anne Corday was with those Indians that got the Hudson's Bay trade goods last year. The same woman that got my pack train down on the Platte."

Farrier stopped John Bruce's angry retort with an upheld hand. "There may be something to it, Bruce. The few trappers of ours that have gotten through haven't been able to keep any pelts on their lines. Their traps have been cleaned out more systematically than any Indians would ever do it."

Enid turned to Bruce, catching his arm. "John, if Garrit's the only one who can get you through, let him do it."

"And let him take another five thousand dollars' worth of trade goods whenever he feels like it?" Bruce said. "I'm not that foolish, Enid. And you have no right to give him amnesty, Farrier. When the company hears about this, there's liable to be a new factor at Fort Union."

He turned and stamped out the other door, leaving an empty silence in the room. But Farrier winked at Garrit.

"They sent Bruce up here to learn the ropes so he could take over when I retire. But he can hardly be factor if there ain't any Yellowstone Fur, can he? And there won't be any Yellowstone Fur if he don't get through to the rendezvous. And he won't get through unless you take him. When he cools off, he'll see how simple it is." With a sly grin he followed Bruce out.

Slowly, reluctantly Garrit looked back to Enid. His weather-darkened face appeared even gaunter. When he finally spoke, his voice had lowered to a husky murmur. "It's funny. I've dreamed of seeing you again, for three years. And when it comes . . . I don't know what to say."

A smile came hesitantly to her soft lips. She moved toward him, reached out a hand shyly, impulsively to touch his mouth. "That quirk's still there, isn't it?"

The touch of her hand was like satin, bringing the past back so painfully that it made him pull away, turn from her, start to pace again.

"It's the only thing that hasn't changed in you," she said. "I don't think I'd have recognized you, at a distance. You must have lost twenty pounds. You're dark as an Indian. And so restless, Vic. Like some animal."

"The woods do that to a man, I guess," he said. "You got to be half animal to stay alive in Blackfeet country." His deep-set eyes filled with that restive gleam as he glanced around the walls. "I never saw such a small room."

She shook her head from side to side, staring at him with hurt, troubled eyes. "Was it worth it?"

He turned sharply to her. "Would you spend five years in jail for something you didn't do?"

"Don't you want to come back, Vic?"

"Come back?" He looked at her an instant, the pain naked in his eyes. Then he turned away stiffly, voice low and tight. "More than anything else in the world, Enid. It's the only thing that keeps me going."

"Things have changed, Vic."

The gaunt hollows beneath his prominent cheek bones deepened, as he realized what she meant. "You . . . and Bruce?"

"I tried to wait, Vic." She turned her face away, as if unable to meet his eyes. "You have no idea how hard it was." Then she wheeled back, catching at his arm, the words tumbling out. "You've got to understand. I did wait . . . you've got to believe me . . . but it was so long, not hearing from you, then someone brought word you were dead. . . ."

"It's all right, Enid. I understand. I had no right to ask that you wait." He paused, then brought the rest out with great effort. "I suppose you and John plan to be married after he makes good on this trip?"

"Oh, Vic. . . ." It was torn from her, and she wheeled around, face in her hands, shoulders shaking with her sobs.

He stared at her helplessly. He wanted to go to her, to take her in his arms, more than anything else he'd wanted in these three years. He started to, then his hands dropped, and he stopped again, as he realized he had no right. She was tortured enough in her dilemma. Even though she knew he was alive, now, it did not change things. He had no more to offer her than he'd had three years ago, when he had fled. Finally, in a barely audible voice, he said: "For your sake, and for Farrier's, I hope Bruce decides to let me take him through. Tell them I'll wait in the hills to the west. These walls are getting too tight."

II

John Bruce's pack train left Fort Union on the 12th of April, following the Yellowstone River south. There were ten men and thirty mules, loaded with the tobacco, Du Pont powder, Missouri lead, knives, traps, flints, vermilion, bridles, spurs, needles and thread for which the free trappers and Indians at Pierre's Hole would trade their furs.

The cavalcade toiled through the rolling grasslands south of the Missouri, forded countless creeks swollen and chocolate with spring. They passed the mouth of the Powder River where the sand lay, black and fine, as Du Pont powder on the sloping banks, and fighting their way through clay flats turned viscid as glue by the rains. It finally gained the mountains.

There had not been too much talk between John Bruce and Garrit during the days in the lowlands. But now, as they pulled to the first ridge ahead of the toiling mules, and halted their horses among the pines, Bruce let out a relieved sigh.

"Thank the Lord we're through that clay. I thought I'd go crazy. I never saw such country."

Garrit sat staring off westward at the undulant sea of hoary ridges and valleys, rolling away as far as he could see. "It's a good country. You've just got to get used to it," he said. His broad chest swelled as he drew a deep breath of air, syrupy with the perfumes of pine and wild roses. "Take a whiff of that. Like wine."

Bruce frowned closely at him. "Don't tell me you actually like it . . . running like an animal all these years in this wilderness."

Garrit tilted his narrow, dark head to one side. "It's funny," he said. "A man doesn't think about liking it, or not liking it. He just lives it. Maybe he should stop to appreciate it more often."

"I used to see those mountain men come into Saint Looey," Bruce said. "I never could understand what made them come back here, year after year, till some blizzard got them, or some Indian."

Garrit glanced at him, the humor leaving his face. "No," he said. "You wouldn't understand."

Surprise widened Bruce's sullen eyes. Then his lips clamped shut, and the antipathy dropped between them again. "You want to be careful, Garrit," he said. "I still think I should turn you in."

A sardonic light gleamed in Garrit's eyes. "But not till I've brought you through safe with the furs that'll make you chief factor of Fort Union."

Bruce's face grew ruddy, and he started to jerk his reins up and pull his horse over against the mountain man's. But a rider came laboring up the slope behind them, stopping Bruce's movement. It was François, a burly man in a cinnamon bear coat and elk-hide leggings, a red scarf tied about his shaggy black hair, immense brass earrings dangling against his cheeks. He drew to a halt beside them, blowing like a horse.

"Now for the climbing, *hein*?" He grinned. "Looks like we go through that pass ahead."

"Not by a long shot," Garrit said. "How long you been in this country?"

"Jus' come north to work at Fort Union this spring," the Frenchman said. "Man don't have to know the country to see that pass is the easiest way through."

"Exactly why we won't take it," Garrit said. "The Blackfeet have caught three pack trains in there the last two years. They don't think there's any other way through Buffalo Ridge. But I know a trail over that hogback to the south."

"These mules are already worn down from that clay," Bruce said angrily. "I'm not taking them ten miles out of our way to climb over a peak when there's a perfect pass through. . . ."

"Farrier sent me along to keep your hair on your head," Garrit said thinly. There was no quirk left at the tip of his lips. "Any time you want to go on alone, just say so."

Bruce grew rigid in the saddle; his eyes drew almost shut. For a moment, there was no sound but the stertorous breathing of the animals, standing in a long line behind them. Finally Bruce settled into the saddle.

"All right," he said, sullenly. "What do we do?"

"It's getting late. I'll scout ahead. I want to be sure what we're going into. If I'm not back by the time you reach that river in the valley below us, make camp there."

Garrit heeled his horse down off the crest and into timber. As the men disappeared behind, the only sound that broke the immense stillness was the sardonic crackle of pine cones underfoot. He could not help his usual grin at the sound. There was something sly and chuckling about it, like the forest having its own private little joke on him. It always brought him close to the mountains, the solitude, and it made him realize what a contrast his present sense of freedom was to the restive confinement he had felt in the fort.

But thought of Fort Union brought the picture of Enid back to him, and his exhilaration faded. Through all these years he had carried with him constantly the painful desire to return to her, to the life they had known. Seeing her at Fort Union had been a knife twisted in the wound. He still felt a great, hollow sickness when he thought of her being promised to Bruce. Could she be mistaken in her feelings? He had seen something in her eyes, something she had been afraid to put into words. If he cleared his name, so he could go back to her, would she realize . . . ?

He shook his head, trying to blot out futile thoughts. He realized he had climbed halfway up to the next ridge without looking for sign. A man was a fool to dream in this country. His head began to move from side to side in the old, wolfish way, eyes picking up every little infraction of the normal rule of things.

It was near dusk when he found the sign. He was five or six miles beyond the pack train, emerging from a fringe of quaking aspen along a stream in the bottom of a cañon, and he caught sight of the early berry bush ahead. A few of the red-black berries were scattered on the ground, and half a dozen of the limbs had been sliced cleanly near the root. As he approached, a magpie began scolding far up the slope. It was another of the forest sounds that invariably turned the quirk at the tip of his lips to a grin. There was something irrepressibly clownish about the raucous chatter.

Just keep talking, you joker, he thought. *Long as you jabber I'm safe.*

He got down to study the moccasin tracks about the early berry bushes. They were only a few hours old, for the grass they had pressed down had not yet risen straight again. As he stood up, the magpie's scolding broke off abruptly. It made his narrow head snap around. The weather seams deepened around his eyes, squinting them almost shut, as he searched the shadowy timber. Then he hitched his horse and headed for the trees. An animal look was in his face now and he ran with a wolfish economy of motion. He reached a dense mat of buckbrush and dropped into it and became completely motionless. He could still see his horse. It had begun to browse peacefully. The timber was utterly still.

After a long space, he began to load his gun. He measured a double load of Du Pont into his charge cup and dumped it down the barrel of his Jake Hawkins. He slid aside the brass plate in the stock, revealing the cavity filled with bear grease. He wiped a linen patch across this, and stuck it to his half-ounce ball of Galena. He rammed the lead home, and then settled down to wait.

For ten minutes he was utterly motionless. His eyes had grown hooded, the quirk had left his lips. The fanwise sinews of his fingers gleamed through the darker flesh of his hands, as they lay so softly, almost caressingly, against the long gun.

Then the man appeared, coming carefully down through the timber. He saw the horse and stopped. The brass pan of his Springfield glittered dully in the twilight. Garrit knew the conflict that was going on within him. But finally, as Garrit knew it would be, the temptation was too great, and the horse decoyed him out. He approached the animal, frowning at it. At last he began to unhitch it.

"Don't do that, François," Garrit said.

The burly Frenchman wheeled toward the sound of his voice. Surprise dug deep lines into his greasy jowls.

"By gar," he whispered, "you *are* an Indian."

Garrit's voice was silken with speculation. "I thought you

were the Indian."

"Ho-ho. I?" The man's laugh boomed through the trees. "That is the joke. He thought I was Indian. And I find his horse and think the Indian take his scalp."

"Shut up," Garrit said sharply. "Don't you know better'n to make that much noise out here? I found sign down by the creek. Some Blackfeet had cut early berry branches for arrows."

François sobered. "We better go then, *hein?* My horse, she's up on the ridge. Bruce, he got worry about you and sent me to look." Garrit unhitched his horse and began the climb beside the man. François sent him an oblique glance. "You really belong to the woods, don't you?"

"How do you mean?"

"I was five feet from you and never see you. Like you was part tree or something."

"A man learns that or doesn't stay alive."

"Is more than that. Some men belong, some don't. Them that do will never be happy any place else."

It touched something in Garrit that he could not define. "Maybe so." He shrugged.

"For w'y you guide Bruce through like this? You hate him."

"It's for Farrier," Garrit said. "He's been my only friend up here. He'll go down with the company if they don't get any pelts this year."

"And for Anne Corday?"

Garrit glanced at him sharply. "What do you know about her?"

François shook his head. "Nothing. Except this is the first trade goods to go through mountains this year. Is like honey to bear. Five thousand dollar' worth of honey. You have been hunting three year for Anne Corday, without the success. Wouldn't it be nice if you were along when she show up to get these pack train?"

Garrit was looking straight ahead, his dark face somber and withdrawn. He would not admit it to François, but the man had struck the truth. Part of his motive in taking the train through had been his debt to Farrier. But another part was his realization of what a strong lure this train would be to the men with Anne Corday. If he could catch them in the act, with John Bruce as witness. . . .

"It's funny you should talk that way," Garrit said. "Most men won't admit Anne Corday exists."

"I only know the stories I hear. You were youngest man ever trusted with Yellowstone Fur's trade goods for the rendezvous. Engaged to Enid Nelson in Saint Looey. Big future ahead with the company." He sent Garrit that oblique look. "How did it really happen? I hear different story every time."

Garrit's eyes lost their focus, looking back through the years. "We had brought the trade goods by boat to the mouth of the Platte. Gervais Corday was camped there. He said he'd been a free trapper till Yellowstone Fur squeezed him out. He'd fought them and some Yellowstone man had shot him. They had to take his arm off. It made him bitter as hell toward the company."

"I would be bitter, too," François said softly.

Garrit hardly heard him. "Anne Corday was his daughter. He'd' married a Blackfoot squaw and kept Anne up there with the Indians. We were the first white men to see her. I guess no white man has ever really seen her since. It was raining. The Cordays invited us into their shelter. There was whiskey. You don't pay attention to how much you're drinking, with a girl like that around. She danced with me, I remember that. She got us so drunk we didn't know what was going on. And her pa and his men got away with our goods."

"But why were you accused of taking the furs?"

"Cheyennes caught us before we got back to Saint Looey. My crew was wiped out. I was the only one left alive. I had to get back the rest of the way on foot. It took me months. Nobody would believe my story. Too many traders had worked that dodge on Yellowstone, and had taken the trade goods themselves. If there had been witnesses, or someone had known of the Cordays, or had seen them, it would have been different. But I was completely without proof."

"And nobody has seen Anne Corday since," François mused. "She mus' have been very beautiful woman."

Garrit nodded slowly. "I can still see her. . . ."

He broke off as he became aware of the expression on François's face. The man tried to hide it. But Garrit had seen the sly curl of the lips. Hot anger wheeled Garrit into François, bunching his hand in the filthy pelt of the cinnamon bear coat and yanking the man off balance.

"Damn you. You don't believe a word I'm saying. You were just leading me on. . . ."

For a moment they stood with their faces not an inch apart. Garrit's lips were drawn thin, his high cheek bones gleaming against the taut flesh. Finally the Frenchman let his weight settle back against Garrit's fist, chuckling deep in his chest.

"Do not be mad with François for making the joke, *m'sieu.*"

Garrit shoved him away with a disgusted sound, trying to read what lay in those sly, pouched eyes. "Don't make another mistake like that," he said thinly. "It's no joke with me."

It was full night when they got back to camp. The mules were out in timber on the picket line, grazing on the buffalo grass and cottonwood bark, indifferently guarded by a pair of buffalo-coated men. The packsaddles were lined up on one side of a roaring fire. Garrit came in at a trot, calling to the trader.

"Bruce, don't you know better'n to build a fire like that in Indian country? Get those mules and saddle up. We can't stay here now."

He broke off as the men about the fire parted. There was a horse near the blaze with two willow poles hooked in a V over its back. From this travois the men had just lifted the woman, putting her on a buffalo pallet by the fire. Before they closed in around her again, Garrit caught a glimpse of the Indian sitting on the ground beside the pallet, head in his arms. Bruce pushed his way free, a flat keg of Monongahela in one hand.

"We can't move now, Garrit. The woman is sick. Our interpreter's been talking with them. Game has been scarce this spring. She's so weak she can hardly talk. The man had tied himself to the horse to stay on."

"That's an old dodge," Garrit sad. "They've probably got a hundred red devils waiting now, out in the trees, to jump you."

"Wouldn't you have run into them on your way back?"

Garrit shook his head darkly. "You just got to learn the hard way, don't you? If she's hungry, that whiskey won't help."

"I was just giving the men a drink. I thought a shot might revive her."

"You were what?"

"Giving the men some," Bruce said irritably. "Now don't tell me I can't do that. Farrier said he gave his men a drink every other night."

"I suppose you had some, too?"

"I did. How else can a man keep his sanity out in this god-forsaken country?"

Garrit shook his head disgustedly, glancing at the laughing, joking, red-faced men. "From the looks of them they've had more than their share. If you want to get anywhere tomorrow, cork that keg up right now."

He turned to walk over to the group and push his way through, to stare down at the woman. She was in an elk-hide dress with openwork sleeves, whitened by bleaching, a stripe of vermilion paint was in the part of her black hair, and more was

216

blotched on her cheeks. She lay with her head thrown back, eyes closed, breathing shallowly.

He felt the blood begin to pound in his temples. He felt shock spread its thin sickness through his belly. Suddenly he found himself on his knees beside her, his hand grasping her arm, jerking at her.

"Open your eyes. You're no more starving than I am. Get up!"

The Indian man raised his head from his arms, calling weakly to Garrit: *"Kola, kola. . . ."*

"Friend, hell," Garrit said savagely. *"Ma yan leci kuwa na. . . ."*

Bruce shoved his way through, grabbing at him. "Garrit, what are you doing?"

"I'm telling him to come over here," Gerrit said hotly. "He isn't weak, and this isn't any Indian. It's Anne Corday."

"Let her go," Bruce said roughly. "You're crazy. You can't treat a sick woman that way."

"She isn't sick, damn you. She's Anne Corday."

Bruce pulled him back so hard he sat down. He jumped to his feet like a cat, whirling on Bruce, so enraged he started to hit him. Then he became aware of the men, sitting down around the campfire. Only one was still standing, and he was rubbing at his eyes, a stupid look on his face. The others were dropping their heads onto their arms, or lying back in their buffalo robes. A couple were beginning to snore stertorously. Even Bruce's eyes had a heavy-lidded look to them.

"What's the matter?" Garrit said.

"Nothing." Bruce shook his head. "Just sleepy."

"How much of that whiskey did you drink?"

Bruce yawned heavily. "Maybe a little more'n I should. But it wouldn't do this. Just been a long day."

"Long day, hell." Garrit spotted the keg of whiskey, walked

savagely over to it. He picked it up, uncorked it, sniffed. "She did this," he said, wheeling on Bruce. "That's laudanum. She's put laudanum in the whiskey."

Then he stopped. Bruce had sat down against one of the saddles, arms supported on his knees, and his heavy head had fallen onto those arms. Garrit's eyes flashed back around the men. François was not among them. He realized he had been too intent on the whiskey. It was too late. Even as he started to wheel, with the heavy grunt in his ears, the blow struck his head.

III

He regained consciousness to the sense of throbbing pain at the base of his skull. Someone was shaking him gently. More pain dug new seams about his eyes as he opened them.

"I thought you'd never come around," John Bruce was telling him. "It's lucky that Frenchman didn't split your head open."

He helped Garrit sit up. It was dawn, with the timber drenched in a pearl-gray mist all about them. The men were gathered around him, grimacing, rubbing their eyes, staring stupidly at each other. One of them was feeding a spitting fire; another was at the edge of camp, retching.

"We came out of it a couple of hours ago," Bruce said. "Been trying ever since to revive you."

Garrit shook his head again, winced at the pain. "How could they have got that laudanum in the whiskey?"

"When I gave her a drink, she tried to hold the keg," Bruce said. "She dropped it, spilled some. The Indian picked it up. There was a little confusion for a minute there, when they could have put it in. I never would have believed laudanum would do that."

"If you drink enough," Garrit muttered. "Farrier used it at Fort Union once. The Indians got so drunk they were going to start a massacre. He spiked their whiskey with laudanum and it knocked them out." He sent a dismal glance to where the packsaddles had stood, beyond the fire. "Did they get everything?"

"Even the animals," Bruce said. "We're stranded."

"Did you send that Frenchman after me?"

"No. He just disappeared."

"I guess he was trying to keep me from coming back," Garrit mused. Then he looked up at Bruce, wide-eyed. "Now will you believe me?"

The man shook his dark head. "I've thought Anne Corday was a myth for so long, it's hard to accept it, even now. I might as well join you in the mountains. This will finish me with Yellowstone Fur."

"It will finish Yellowstone Fur, if we don't get that pack train back."

Bruce's black brows rose in surprise. "What chance have we got? They have a night's start on us, and they're riding. We'll be lucky to get back to Fort Union on foot as it is."

"A crowd like this will never make it back through that Blackfeet country on foot," Garrit told him. "Your best bet is to hole up while I go after our horses. If you can hold these men here till I get back, you still might get a chance to stay with Yellowstone Fur."

Bruce protested, but Garrit finally convinced him it was their only chance. He drew a map in the earth. There was a creek in the next valley that ran ten miles northward into a cañon so narrow and tortuous it could not be reached by horses. Bruce was to do his hunting now, try to get enough meat to last the men several weeks, and then walk in the water of the creek to its head. This would leave ten miles of his back trail covered, and in such an inaccessible place he would be comparatively safe from Indians, if he did not move around.

Bruce finally agreed, and Garrit made up a pack of smoked buffalo meat and dried-corn, rolled it in one three-point blanket, and took up the trail.

They had not bothered to hide their tracks. They led northwest from the Yellowstone, toward the heart of the Blackfeet country. It convinced him more than ever that he had not been mistaken. Only someone with connections in the tribe would have dared head so boldly into their land. And Anne Corday's mother had been a Blackfoot.

He left the mountains for a while, and hit the high plains, rolling endlessly away from him, so devoid of timber in most places that he could not travel much during the day for fear of being seen. On the third day he reached the Little Belts. After the endless plains, it was like coming home. He plunged gratefully into the shadowed timber on the first of the rolling slopes.

Now it was the real running. It brought out all the animal attributes bred in him these last years. There was an intense wolfishness to his unremitting dog-trot, long body slack, head down and turning incessantly from side to side, eyes gleaming balefully from their shadowed sockets, not missing a sign. He ran on their trail till he could run no more, and then crawled into a thicket and lay in stupefied sleep, and then woke and ran again.

He began to see teepee rings, circles of rocks in parks or open meadows that marked the campsite of an Indian band. It made him even more watchful. On the fourth day he sighted the first Indians. He was climbing a slope, with a magpie scolding in the firs. Despite his aching weariness, he could not help his faint grin at the sound. *Just keep talking, you joker.*

His moccasins crushed resiliently into the mat of pine needles, and for another hundred yards he climbed steadily. Then the magpie broke off sharply. He stopped, staring up the slope, and wheeled and darted for a dense clump of chokecherry.

He was on his belly, hidden in the brush, when the Indians appeared. They passed within fifty yards of him and never knew he was there, a party of Blackfeet on the move, with their pack horses, their wives, their children. The scent of their tobacco floated to him, and it was not willow-bark *kinnikinnik*, but the rank plug cut the traders used. There were new axes on their saddles, and new iron bridles on their horses. They had been trading their furs with Anne Corday.

The band of spare horses made his mouth water. But he could not try for one in broad daylight, and since they were heading in the wrong direction, he did not want to lose half a day by following them south to their night camp. So he ran on.

On the fifth day he was out of food and was afraid to shoot game for fear he would be heard. But he knew the Indian tricks. He found *tinipsila* roots and ate them raw, and later on came across some bulrushes by a stream and ate the white part like celery. And farther up the stream were wild strawberries and a few serviceberries. It gave him enough nourishment to keep running.

That night he found three more teepee rings in a shallow valley. The grass had not begun to grow up around the circled rocks, so he knew they had been planted recently. The horse droppings leading north were fresh enough to have been left that morning. It was the way he wanted it.

He followed the trail by moonlight, his lank figure fluttering through the shadow-black timber like a lost animal. He found the new camp near dawn. Three teepees formed pale cones in the center of a clearing, with the horses grazing on picket ropes.

Under ordinary circumstances, he would have moved more slowly, but the squaws would be rising soon, and he wanted to get away before that. So he had to approach the horses directly, not giving them time to get used to him. He picked out a pinto with lots of wind in its heavy throttle. Before he could reach it, however, one of the animals spooked and whinnied.

This brought the dogs from where they had been sleeping near the embers of last night's fire, and their baying raised the camp. They circled him in a pack, snapping at his legs and yapping crazily. Kicking them off, he pulled the pinto's picket pin and ran down the rope to the plunging horse. The first Indian to jump through the door flap had a clumsy London fusil.

He saw that he couldn't get it loaded in time, and started to run for Garrit. The mountain man threw all his weight onto the picket rope, pulling the pinto down so he could throw the loose end around its fluttering snout in a war bridle. He did not have time to unknot the other end from about its neck. He pulled his Green River knife and slashed it.

The Indian reached him then, leaping through the pack of dogs to swing viciously with his clubbed fusil. Garrit ducked and the butt of the gun thumped against the pinto's flank. Holding the plunging horse with one hand, he threw his Green River, blade first, with the other. There was but a foot between them, and he saw it sink to the hilt in the man's shoulder.

The Indian staggered back, face contorted with pain. Garrit scooped up the rifle he had been forced to drop and threw himself aboard the horse, kicking its flanks. He raced out of camp with the dogs yapping at his heels and the other Indians stopping halfway between the teepees and the herd to load their fusils and fire after him. The short-range London guns would not reach him, however, and he plunged unhurt into timber.

He knew they would follow and ran the horse for the first creek. He went south in the water, for they knew all the tricks, too. After two miles of riding the shallows he went out on shore and left sign they would be sure to follow and made them a false trail leading on south till he found a talus bench that led into another creek. The pony was unshod and would not even leave shoe scars on the rocky bench. In the water he turned north again. When he could travel north no longer in the water, he left it once more. He was far enough above the Indian camp to start hunting for Anne Corday and her father's sign now. It took him several hours to pick it up. They were pushing twenty-five pack horses, and he could travel at three times their speed if he drove hard. And he drove hard. All day, with only time out to water the horse and shoot a buck whose haunch he roasted over a fire and ate as he rode. He gave the horse an hour's rest at sundown, and then went on.

By dawn the horse was beaten down but Garrit knew he was near his quarry for all the signs were not many hours old. His belly sucked at him with its hunger and his face, covered with a week's growth of scraggly beard, had the haggard, driven look of some animal. It took all his grim purpose and the bitterness of three years' exile to push him those last miles. Then, in the late afternoon, he topped a ridge and saw the line of pack horses, standing in the park below him.

He left the horse and dropped down through the trees on foot. Closing in on the camp, he became a shadow, flitting from tree to tree. Finally he bellied down and crawled like a snake through buckwheat and chokecherry bushes till he could see the whole camp.

They had evidently just finished trading with more Indians, for there was a pile of unbaled pelts heaped to one side of a campfire, and a packsaddle next to them, with some trade goods still lying on the ground. The Blackfoot who had come to Bruce's camp with the woman was busily loading another packsaddle onto one of the horses lined up near the trees. The other three were at the fire. François was on his hunkers, still wearing his immense cinnamon bear coat, sorting out the pelts they had just gotten. Gervais Corday stood above him, tall, bitter-eyed, one-armed. And Anne Corday was feeding new wood to the fire.

The weather seams deepened about Garrit's eyes, as he stared at her, giving his face an expression close to pain. This was the woman he had hunted for three years. Hers was the face he had seen in a thousand dreams. And now, it was before him. Her blue-black hair no longer had the vermilion in its part. It was blown wild by the wind, and made a tousled frame for the piquant oval of her face, with its black eyes, its ripe lips. She had discarded the Indian dress for a shirt made from a red Hudson's Bay blanket, and a skirt of white doeskin with fringes that softly caressed her coppery calves. Even in his bitter triumph, he could not deny her striking, young beauty.

"Ho-ho," François chortled. "There are over twenty prime beaver here. Another year or so like this and we'll be rich."

Gervais frowned down at him. "You said this would finish Yellowstone Fur."

"Is true." The Frenchman grinned. "They don't turn this pack train into furs, they go under. But why stop? There is still American Fur, Rocky Mountain Fur. Even Hudson's Bay."

"Did they take my arm?" Gervais's voice was acid. He began to pace back and forth, slapping at his elk-hide leggings with his good hand. "Did they ruin me? What do I care about Rocky Mountain or Hudson's Bay? They didn't smash my life. It is Yellowstone Fur that will pay." His voice began to shake. "They can't take a man's life and toss it away like a puff of smoke. Ruin everything he worked for so long. Cast him and his daughter upon the wilderness. . . ."

The girl caught his arm, her voice low and placating. "Father, please, don't get excited again."

"Excited!" He turned on her with blazing eyes. "How can you talk that way? You were ruined, too. All my plans for you. Instead of a great lady you're nothing but a wild animal, running the forest with me."

"One fur company is just as bad as the next," François said.

"You saw how American Fur pushed Lestrade off his rightful lines. If you'd fought them, I'm sure they'd have taken your arm just as quickly."

"François," the girl said sharply. "Don't start him off again. You're just twisting things around. Maybe he had reason to fight Yellowstone, but. . . ."

"I don't know." Gervais pulled away from his daughter, pacing again. "Perhaps François is right."

"Of course I'm right," the big Frenchman said. "What good would it do to stop now? If you take what we've made and try to start again, some other big fur company will only pinch you off again. We've got to ruin them all, Gervais. Only then will it be safe for honest men out here again. They take your arm this time. They're liable to kill you next time."

"They won't get the chance, François," Garrit said, rising from the chokecherry bushes.

The three in the clearing and the Indian by the horses all turned in surprise. Garrit walked toward them, his Jake Hawkins held across one hip. Gervais finally let out a pent-up breath, speaking in a voice thin with shock. "I thought you said you took all the horses."

"I did," François said. "The man's inhuman." Then he let out his bellowing laugh. "*Sacre bleu,* I should have kill you. The only man in the world who could have catch us on foot, and I let him live."

At that moment a quick movement from the Indian spun Garrit toward him. The man had tried to jump behind one of the horses and scoop up a loaded rifle and fire, all at the same time. His gun boomed simultaneously with Garrit's but he had tried to do too much at once. His bullet dug into the ground a foot from Garrit, while Garrit's bullet struck him in the chest, knocking him backward like a heavy blow.

But it gave François his chance. He reached Garrit before the

225

mountain man could wheel back, with Gervais Corday rushing right in behind. Garrit was off balance when the Frenchman grabbed his rifle. It was his first true sense of the man's bearlike strength. He felt as though his hands had been torn off with the rifle when François wrenched it free.

The big Frenchman swung it wide, clubbed, and brought it back in a vicious circle. It would have broken Garrit's head open. All he could do was drop to his knees. The heavy gun whistled over his head and smashed Gervais right in the face as he came rushing in on François's flank.

The one-armed man made a choked sound and dropped like a poled ox. Garrit came up off his knees into François, locking the rifle between them. It knocked the Frenchman back off his feet, and he rolled to the ground with Garrit on top, fighting like a cat.

The quarters were too close for the rifle and the Frenchman let it go to pull his knife. Garrit tried to grasp the wrist but the Frenchman straddled out for leverage and rolled atop Garrit.

The mountain man saw the flash of a blade and jerked his whole body aside. The knife drove into the ground. François yanked it out, but Garrit got hold of the knife wrist with both hands and twisted it inward as he lunged upward with his whole body.

It drove the knife hilt deep into the Frenchman. He let out a great shout of pain and flopped off Garrit. As the mountain man rolled over and came to his feet, he saw Anne Corday on her knees beside her father, fumbling the pistol from his belt. Garrit ran at her, reaching her just as she raised the weapon. He kicked it out of her hand.

She threw herself up at him, clawing like an enraged cat. He caught both hands, spun aside, used her own momentum to throw her. She hit on her back so hard it stunned her, and she made no attempt to roll over or rise.

Garrit wheeled back in time to see François staggering into the trees, one hand gripped over his bloody side. Garrit got the loaded pistol and ran after the man. But by the time he reached the timber, François was out of sight. Garrit heard Anne Corday groan and roll over. He didn't know how much time it would take him to find François. He couldn't risk it. He couldn't take that chance of losing the pack train again, with the girl and her father still in the clearing.

Reluctantly he turned back to Anne Corday. The anger was gone from her face. Grief and shock rendered it blank. She was staring at her father, as if just realizing how crazily his head was twisted. Garrit knew, then, what she must have known. The blow of the rifle butt had broken Gervais Corday's neck.

IV

It was two days before the girl would talk to Garrit. He buried her father and the Indian up there in the Little Belts, and took the pack train and started back to Bruce.

The second night he made camp on the white beach of a creek in a narrow gorge that rose a hundred feet above them and would hide the light of their fire. The girl sat on a heap of buffalo robes, watching him draw a spark with his flint and steel. When he had the blaze started, her voice came softly out of the night.

"You love this country, don't you?"

He was silent a while, staring into the flames. "I guess you're right. The country gets into a man without him even knowing it." He paused, then slowly turned to look at her. "You don't hate me?"

"I've been mixed up these last two days." She spoke in a low, strained voice. "For a while I thought you were to blame for my father's death. But the Frenchman killed my father." She shook her head slowly. "Something like this was bound to happen sooner or later. Father was changing so. I thought he was bitter enough, at first. But he was getting even worse. He was becoming a fanatic. Actually you have as much reason to hate me. We ruined you, didn't we?"

He turned and walked to where she sat, towering above her, his face narrow and dark with thought as he gazed down at her. "I should hate you. I've tried to. But what I saw in that clearing

228

changed a lot of things. Don't you realize how François was using your father?"

She stared at the sand, her lips still pinched and white with grief. "I realize now. François didn't show his true colors till that afternoon. We thought he was a friend, another man who had been ruined by Yellowstone Fur. But he was nothing more than a thief, using my father's bitterness against Yellowstone to further his own ends."

"And your bitterness?"

Her face turned up to him defiantly. "Were we wrong? Wouldn't you despise the people who ruined your father?"

He dropped beside her, caught her hands. "It wasn't Yellowstone Fur itself, Anne. Has your father so filled you with his bitterness that you can't see that? There are decent men in Yellowstone. There's a man named Farrier down at Fort Union who could have turned me in, but he gave me a break."

"They sent a man out to kill my father. . . ."

"Did your father really convince you of that? I saw a copy of the Yellowstone man's orders. He was sent to try and negotiate a new deal with your father for his territory. It was your father who started the fight. The Yellowstone man was only defending himself."

She jumped to her feet, eyes flashing. "Now you're trying to twist it up. I forgave you my father's death. Isn't that enough?" She wheeled away from him, walking to the end of the sand spit. She locked her hands, staring out into the night for a long time. Finally she said, thinly: "You think you'll take me in. You think you'll show me to all those men who don't believe Anne Corday exists, and it will clear your name."

"It's what I've been working toward for three years," he said in a low voice.

"You'll never even get me back to Bruce," she said.

"Where would you go, if you escaped?" he said gently.

"My mother is still with the tribe, up near Flathead Lake," Anne said. "I would be safe with any band of Blackfeet I met. But I don't need that. Don't you know who is following us?"

He felt his head lift in surprise as he realized what she meant. "How could he, with a wound like that?"

"I know him," she said. "When he sets out to do something, nothing can stop him. You could stab him a dozen times and he could still walk a hundred miles. François is following us, Garrit, and he will catch us. You will never take me in."

Garrit did not sleep much that night. He tied Anne Corday's hands and spent most of the time scouting the gorge. It rained the next day, a spring thunderstorm that made the creeks overflow their banks and wiped out the trail of the pack train. Garrit pushed hard, knowing there was little chance of meeting Indians in the storm. But thought of the Frenchman hung more heavily upon him than any danger of Indians. If Anne Corday was right, the man would be a constant threat, hanging over them till they reached Bruce. It made Garrit jumpy, imbuing him with more than his normal restlessness.

They made a miserable camp in a cave, both of them soaking wet, and he hung a three-point for Anne to undress behind, and then she wrapped the blanket around her and huddled over the fire.

"Do you remember how it was raining the first night we met, down on the Platte?" she said.

"And you took us into your shelter and let us dry our clothes and drink your whiskey and we got drunk as Indians on ration day. I had been drunk before. It was more than that. It's bothered me ever since."

"It has bothered me, too," she said softly.

He stared down at her, trying to fathom the strange look in her eyes, to untangle the mixed emotions in himself. Her lips, so red, so ripe, seemed to rise toward him, until they were touching his, with her body in his arms.

After a long while, he backed away, staring down at her. There was a twisted look to her face, a shining confusion in her eyes. Then, for an instant, the expression in her face changed. Her eyes seemed to focus on something behind him. When they swung back to his face, she reached up to pull his lips down to hers once more.

Only senses developed through three years of living like an animal would have detected it. Some sound, unidentifiable in that instant, reached him. He tried to tear himself loose and twist around. He shifted far enough aside, so that the knife went into his arm instead of his back.

The girl scrambled away from him, lunging for the rifle he had kept loaded at all times these last days. Sick with pain, he tried to wheel on around and rise. He had a dim view of the Frenchman above him, the pelt of his coat matted with dried blood, a murderous light in his eyes.

Then his fist smashed Garrit across the face, knocking him back against the wall of the cave, and his other hand pulled the knife free of Garrit's upper arm. Garrit rolled over, dazed by the blow. His eyes were open, but he could barely see the Frenchman, lunging up above him, raising the knife for the kill. He tried to rise, but his stunned nerves would not answer his will. Anne Corday stood on the other side of the cave, the loaded Jake Hawkins in her hands. There was a wide-eyed vindication on her face.

The Frenchman straddled Garrit with a triumphant bellow, and the uplifted knife flashed in the firelight as it started to come down.

Then the shot boomed out, rocking the cave with its thunder. As if from a heavy blow, the Frenchman was slammed off Garrit and carried clear up against the wall of the cave. He hung there a moment, and then toppled back, to sprawl limply on the ground. Garrit stared blankly at him, until he finally realized what had happened. A Jake Hawkins packed that much punch, close up.

Slowly he turned his head, to see the girl, still holding the gun, smoke curling from its muzzle. Her face was blank, as if she was surprised at what she had done. Then that same confusion widened her eyes. With a small cry, she dropped the rifle, wheeled, and ran out of the cave. He got to his feet and tried to follow, but almost fell again at the mouth and had to stop there. He heard a whinny, then the drumming of hoofs. He stared out into the dripping timber, knowing he was too weak to follow her. The knowledge turned his face bleak and empty.

John Bruce's pack train returned to Fort Union on the first day of September. The trade goods were gone from the packs now. They were bulging with dark brown beaver pelts and buffalo robes. The saddle-galled horses filed soddenly in through the great double-leaved gates, met by cheers and greetings of the *engagés* and hunters and trappers of the post.

Farrier took Bruce and Garrit to his office. Enid was there, in a wine dress, a pale expectancy in her face. Bruce grasped her arms, a boyish eagerness lighting his heavy features momentarily. Garrit thought the presence of himself and Farrier must have restrained them from an expression of their true feelings, for, after looking into her eyes a long moment, Bruce turned to Farrier, telling him of Anne Corday. When he was finished, Farrier turned in amazement to Garrit.

"And what happened to the girl?"

Garrit stared around at the walls, feeling that constriction again. He rubbed at his arm, still sore from the knife wound François had given him. "She got away," he said curtly. "I couldn't help it."

"Your name will be cleared anyway," Farrier said. "Bruce's

whole crew is witness to what happened. You've saved Yellow-stone Fur, Garrit, and they'll certainly reinstate you with honors." He scratched his beard, studying Bruce and Enid with a knowing grin. "Maybe we better go out and talk it over, while these two reunite."

Bruce had been watching Enid, whose eyes had never left Garrit. "Perhaps it is I who had better go out with you, Farrier," he said.

Enid turned sharply to him. "Bruce, I. . . ."

"Never mind, Enid." His voice had a dead sound. "I guess I should have known how you felt, ever since you saw Garrit here last April."

He turned, shoulders dragging, and went out with a perplexed Farrier. Garrit felt sorry for the man. He knew he should have felt elation for himself, as he turned back to Enid, but it did not come.

"I have always wondered, Vic, why you let her make such a fool of you, that first time, on the Platte," Enid said.

He stopped, frowning deeply. "I've wondered that myself."

"Perhaps, Vic, it was because she is really the woman, and I never was," she said.

He turned to her, tried to say something. She shook her head.

"You'll never be happy with the old life. I can see that now. If you want to go to her, Vic, you're free."

He stared at her a long time, realizing she had touched the truth. And he knew now why Anne Corday's face had been with him in so many dreams. It hadn't been there as a symbol of his revenge, or vindication.

"Thank you, Enid," he said softly.

He left the fort with but one pack horse and enough supplies to take him as far as Flathead Lake. He rode across the flats and into the timber where a magpie's scolding drew a fleeting grin to his lips. He stopped, to take one look backward, and then he turned his face toward the mountains, and rode.

ABOUT THE AUTHOR

Les Savage, Jr. was born in Alhambra, California and grew up in Los Angeles. His first published story was "Bullets and Bull-whips" accepted by the prestigious magazine, Street & Smith's *Western Story*. Almost ninety more magazine stories followed, all set on the American frontier, many of them published in Fiction House magazines such as *Frontier Stories* and *Lariat Story Magazine* where Savage became a superstar with his name on many covers. His first novel, *Treasure of the Brasada,* appeared from Simon & Schuster in 1947. Due to his preference for historical accuracy, Savage often ran into problems with book editors in the 1950s who were concerned about marriages between his protagonists and women of different races—a commonplace on the real frontier but not in much Western fiction in that decade. Savage died young, at thirty-five, from complications arising out of hereditary diabetes and elevated cholesterol. However, as a result of the censorship imposed on many of his works, only now are they being fully restored by returning to the author's original manuscripts. Among Savage's finest Western stories are *Fire Dance at Spider Rock* (Five Star Westerns, 1995), *Medicine Wheel* (Five Star Westerns, 1996), *Coffin Gap* (Five Star Westerns, 1997), *Phantoms in the Night* (Five Star Westerns, 1998), *The Bloody Quarter* (Five Star Westerns, 1999), *In The Land of Little Sticks* (Five Star Westerns, 2000), *The Cavan Breed* (Five Star Westerns, 2001), *Danger Rides the River* (Five Star Westerns, 2002), and *Black Rock Cañon*

(Five Star Westerns, 2006). Much as Stephen Crane before him, while he wrote, the shadow of his imminent death grew longer and longer across his young life, and he knew that, if he was going to do it at all, he would have to do it quickly. He did it well, and, now that his novels and stories are being restored to what he had intended them to be, his achievement irradiated by his powerful and profoundly sensitive imagination will be with us always, as he had wanted it to be, as he had so rushed against time and mortality that it might be. *The Joker's Den* will be his next Five Star Western.